HER DANGEROUS BEAST

ROGUE'S GUILD

BOOK TWO

SCARLETT SCOTT

Her Dangerous Beast

Rogue's Guild Book Two

Published by Happily Ever After Books, LLC

Edited by Grace Bradley

Cover Design by EDH Professionals

For more information, contact author Scarlett Scott.

https://scarlettscottauthor.com

For my sister, with love

CHAPTER 1

Through the crack in the partially ajar door, Theo saw toes.

Bare, without the veil of stockings or slippers, illuminated by the fading glow of afternoon light and a brace of candles. Against his will, the lack of decorum intrigued him. He took a silent step closer and was rewarded by the sight of trim, well-turned ankles, crossed and peeping from beneath the hem of a pink-and-white gown. Reminding him he was a man for the first time in…

As long as he could recall.

He should turn around. Leave those beautiful ankles and toes to their solitude. Hunt House was vast, and he'd spent the last few hours acquainting himself with every corner, from top to bottom. And yet, he still had chambers to inspect.

But instead of leaving, Theo hovered at the threshold of the Duke of Ridgely's salon, as if his boots were cemented to the hallway Axminster at his feet. If he didn't know better, he would have sworn he'd conjured this unexpected vision. But then he heard her talking to herself, mumbling something unintelligible, and he knew she was real.

Who was she?

Who would dare to wander about in her bare feet, inhabiting the duke's divan, lighting his candles? She was not dressed in the familiar garb of a servant. There were only two other females in residence aside from the domestics. One was the duke's ward, and the other his sister. Neither were women Theo ought to linger about, admiring. He was being paid handsomely to guard the duke's London town house. Not to dally with his women.

Theo cleared his throat, making his presence known.

A feminine gasp sounded from within, and the toes and ankles disappeared.

Pity.

He'd rather been enjoying the view.

"Who is there?" demanded the owner of the ankles and toes.

The sharp, crisp, perfect elocution, even tinged with an edge of trepidation, was as pleasant as a warm caress. He had spent most of the years since his exile in London, and he had come to appreciate the English language in all its peculiar accents, so different from his native tongue. There was something about this voice, however, the odd mix of starch and huskiness it possessed, which settled over him. That voice was like sinking into a hot bath after a punishing day on horseback.

"One of the guards, madam," he said cooly, tamping down his unwanted reaction.

Theo flattened his palm on the paneled door and pushed, allowing himself one step over the threshold. He was accustomed to London's rules of polite society. It was unseemly for a man to linger alone with a lady to whom he hadn't been introduced, but at the moment, he didn't give a damn about convention. He was ever mindful of the reason for his presence here at Hunt House.

An assassin had attempted to murder the duke in his sleep in the early hours of the morning.

But the moment he saw her fully, his mind became empty as a night sky without stars. His reason for being here—hell, even his name—left him. For she was unspeakably lovely.

Standing by the divan she had so recently been occupying, she held a leather-bound folio before her as if it were a shield. She possessed a classical beauty reminiscent of the ancient goddesses captured in the marble sculptures of his homeland. Her golden hair was bright, the same color as the rolling wheatfields he remembered from his youth in Boritania.

"A guard?" the lady repeated, eyes wide, tone wary as her gaze darted about.

With some amusement, he wondered if she was searching for an object which might be used as a weapon against him. Some candlestick with which to bludgeon him.

"One of the guards hired by His Grace," he added, for he did not know how much the duke had revealed to his womenfolk of the danger surrounding him.

Apparently not the necessity for hired protection, judging from her confusion.

Belatedly, Theo offered as elegant a bow as he could muster, given that he was carrying a small pistol, two knives, and ligatures. Reminders this was no social call; his days as a courtier had long since ended. He was a mercenary now, happy to live unfettered by the twin crushing weights of duty and obligation.

His own man. Free from the past in body, if not in mind.

"Why should Ridgely have hired guards?" she asked. "Does this have something to do with the housebreaker who fell down the stairs last night? And why would I not have been informed? I was told of no such amendment to the household, and I am His Grace's sister."

Ah, he had his answer about the mystery goddess's identity. Not the duke's ward, then. But the widowed marchioness, Lady Deering.

"I'm given to understand it's a precaution," Theo said. "As for the rest, I couldn't say, my lady."

Her eyes narrowed on him, and he felt the intensity of her stare to his marrow. They were blue, he realized. The deep, dark blue of the moonlit sea.

"What is your name, sir?" she asked next.

He remained as he was, grave and unsmiling. "They call me Beast."

It was a name he'd earned, unlike Theodoric Augustus St. George, the hated appellation of his birth.

"Beast," she repeated, her tone steeped in disbelief.

He inclined his head. "Yes, my lady. Beast."

"I cannot fathom what Ridgely could have been thinking, inviting such a rogue into Hunt House." Her voice possessed the chill of winter ice.

And she wasn't wrong. He *was* a rogue.

"It would not be for me to guess at His Grace's thoughts," he said simply, humbly, mindful of the man he was now.

Even if there was something about Lady Deering's hauteur that made him wish, for the briefest of fleeting moments, that he could tell her who he truly was. Or rather, who he had been, what seemed as far away as a lifetime ago now. But then he recalled all the reasons why he had left that world behind him, the dangers that were never far, and the instinct faded quickly.

"Why are you wandering about and entering rooms unannounced?" Lady Deering demanded to know.

Her suspicions almost amused him. But neither Beast nor Theo had ever had much use for levity.

"I was tasked with protecting Hunt House and its occupants," he answered simply. "I cannot do so if I am not inspecting the chambers and familiarizing myself with the house's plan."

She was frowning, brow furrowed. "Where are you from, sir?"

He kept his expression carefully blank. "London."

Her chin went up. "Before London. Your accent is unfamiliar to me."

No one had remarked upon his accent in years. He'd thought he had lost all traces of his native language, for he had been raised to speak both English and Boritanian. That this woman detected suggestions of his past gave him pause.

"London," he repeated anyway, undeterred.

She tilted her head, considering him in a way he did not like, a way that made him feel as if she saw *into* him, plumbing his very soul for his many dark secrets. "Why do you lie?"

Because he had to. Because lying about who he was had become as instinctive as breathing. But he wouldn't—couldn't—tell her any of that.

Theo bowed again instead of answering her question. "I dare not linger any longer. If you will excuse me, my lady, I must continue with my task. I bid you good day."

"You haven't answered me," she pointed out.

He had already pivoted and was making his retreat, holding his tongue. The truth would serve neither of them.

"Wait," she called after him. "Don't go just yet."

And, fool that he was, he paused, casting a glance at her over his shoulder. The sunlight caught in her hair, granting her an ethereal glow, and he had never seen a woman more lovely or tempting than the Marchioness of Deering, barefoot at half past three in the afternoon. Theo had a sinking feeling within that of all the perils he would face in his role as Hunt House bodyguard, none would compare to the maddening heat unfurling within him now, the undeniable danger of desiring a woman who was forbidden to him.

He clenched his jaw against a rush of longing he had no right to entertain. "What is it, madam? I've a duty to attend."

He'd had far more duties once. Vast duties to his kingdom, to his family, to his people. Enough to last an eternity. And he had shed them all when he had been banished from Boritanian soil. Despite the viciousness of that farewell and all that had come before it, he found himself thinking about it now, standing before a beautiful stranger. Hellfire, what was it about the woman before him that so stripped him of defense that she had his mind traveling back to those lost years? Had it been nothing more than the wheat-gold of her hair, reminding him of the rolling fields he had once known?

"What manner of name is Beast?" she asked, tilting her head, curiosity flickering in her glistening eyes.

She was bold, Lady Deering. He liked it. Something about her felt familiar. Called to him. Not just lust, but a need far stronger. Deeper. One a man felt to his marrow. There was a name for such a connection in his native tongue. He didn't know an English equivalent. Perhaps there wasn't one. It hardly mattered.

"It's the name of a man who hasn't much left to lose," he answered honestly.

Anything of value he'd once possessed had been taken from him. He had coin now, earned rather than inherited.

Her brow was furrowed, her expression softening, a hint of shadows and sadness in her moonlit-sea eyes. "I understand what it is like to lose everything."

What had the lovely goddess ensconced in this Mayfair manse lost?

He found himself wanting to know. Theo was strangely

moved by her statement. By the melancholy she exuded. Part of him wanted to linger. To dare.

To touch.

He bowed instead. "I am sorry, my lady."

And then, he took his leave, continuing on as he knew he must, belonging nowhere and to no one.

Heart pounding, Pamela watched the mysterious man called Beast disappear into the hall as soundlessly as he had first arrived. He had caught her in a state of dishabille, her feet bereft of slippers and stockings. It was an old habit, eschewing the trappings of full dress unless she left the house. One she should have stopped. It embarrassed her to have been caught thus, so devoid of her customary polish. But it gave her pause in a different way as well. She was gripping her sketching folio so tightly that her knuckles ached. And she was shaken by the unexpected intrusion. Shaken by the violent upheaval of the previous night.

But she was also shaken by the intruder himself.

Who was he?

Was he truly a guard as he had claimed?

What if he was another housebreaker? In the early hours of the morning, a man had slipped inside Hunt House with the intent to pilfer whilst the household had been asleep. Instead, he had met a grim end on the cantilevered stone staircase when her brother, the Duke of Ridgely, had given chase. The man had broken his neck.

A shiver passed down her spine, dread unfurling low in her belly. If this Beast were a miscreant come to prey upon the undeniable wealth Ridgely possessed, surely he would not have politely conducted conversation with her just now. Surely he would not have appeared by the light of day, as bold as any man who belonged within Hunt House's immense walls.

She frowned. Unless he was posing as a guard so he might better familiarize himself with the house and avoid the unfortunate fate of the last housebreaker? If so, lulling her into a false sense of comfort would certainly behoove the man. Should she have screamed, the whole house would have come down upon them.

Misgiving blossomed, along with something else she didn't like. Something she hated, in fact. Awareness of this stranger, this Beast, as a man. Pamela made haste to extinguish the candelabra before hurrying from the salon.

As she rushed back to her chamber and donned stockings and slippers, more questions arose. Would not Ridgely have informed her of such an addition as a guard? For the last four years, since her husband's death had left her once more at the mercy of her family's charity, Pamela had been overseeing the household at Hunt House. First for her father, and then, after his death and the deaths of her two older brothers Bartholomew and Matthew, for her brother Trevor, now Duke of Ridgely. Their mother preferred the country seat at Ridgely Hall, which was far from the gilded London monstrosity in which their father had often installed his mistresses. Surely someone—the housekeeper Mrs. Bell, the butler Ames, Ridgely himself—might have mentioned the presence of a man named Beast?

By the time Pamela finished dressing and left her chamber, she was determined that she must find Ridgely to confirm her suspicions. She felt sure she would have been told of this. She and her brother were close. They spoke daily. Ridgely was...vexing. But he didn't keep secrets. Not like this one, a strange man prowling about.

No, the wickedly handsome intruder with the magnificent eyes and commanding air had been lying. There had been a few tense moments between them during which she had found herself beneath his thrall. Struck by his features, which seemed so very different than the gentlemen of her acquaintance. By the mysteries in his husky, slightly accented voice.

But now she had broken free of the spell. She was not a fool, and nor would she allow this Beast fellow to make her one. She reached her brother's study and knocked at the door. No answer came from within, and a peek inside revealed it empty and cast in late-afternoon shadows. She was striding past the library when suspicious cries from within caught her attention and sent more worry crashing through her. They were feminine cries. Cries which sounded alarmingly like that of Ridgely's ward, Lady Virtue Walcot.

If that miscreant Beast was within, harming Lady Virtue, Pamela would never forgive herself for tarrying long enough to don stockings and slippers. In a rush, she threw open the door, only to discover the man lying atop a familiar feminine form on the library's Grecian couch was not Beast at all.

Rather, it was her own brother.

And he was…oh good heavens. A gasp tore from her. There was no reason for Ridgely to be so intimately entwined with his ward save one. Shock and outrage rose to prominence. Pamela crossed the threshold, feeling every bit the mother hen who had just caught a fox about to devour one of her innocent chicks.

"Ridgely, what have you *done*?" she demanded.

She had the presence of mind to discreetly close the library door to fend off prying ears and the wandering eyes of servants. Lady Virtue was attempting to find a husband, and any hint of scandal would prove ruinous for her. Ridgely knew this, and yet he had dared to conduct himself in such egregious fashion. Oh, she could box his ears for this.

"Christ, Pamela," her brother muttered. "What are you doing in here?"

"Looking for you," she snapped, furious with him for this outrageous display of lechery. "And not a moment too soon, judging from the look of it."

Ridgely was rumpled and rakish, his cheekbones tinged red. Lady Virtue was flushed, her gown lifted to her waist, and Pamela hastily averted her eyes before she saw something she didn't want to see.

"Hell," her brother said, which was most certainly not an explanation or a defense of himself.

But then, how could he defend being atop his innocent ward with her skirts raised and his face buried in her bodice?

"Your language is as deplorable as your ability to control yourself, Ridgely," she told him, hoping she had interrupted them before every boundary had been crossed.

If Ridgely had gone too far with Virtue, he would have to marry her himself. And Pamela knew her rakish brother had no intention of marrying anyone, let alone his ward.

Still holding her hand to the side of her face as if it were a blinder and averting her gaze, Pamela added, "Virtue, compose yourself, if you please, and then I'll take you to your room. Ridgely and I need to have a discussion."

"We do?" Ridgely asked, sounding wry.

For him, Pamela had no compassion. She'd been concerned about the man named Beast roaming the halls, but now she had far greater troubles than another potential housebreaker facing her. And she wasn't in the mood to find mirth in any of it.

"Yes," she said. "We do."

The rustling of fabric told her Virtue had risen from the Grecian couch and was approaching her at last. Pamela fixed the girl with a pointed look of disapproval. "Come with me, my lady." With a glare in her brother's direction, she said, "I'll return for a word with you."

In grim silence, she led Lady Virtue from the library. They didn't speak until they were in the sanctity of Virtue's chamber, where no one could overhear them. Pamela simply couldn't afford to allow the winds of scandal to blow in her charge's direction. Were any hint of Ridgely's conduct today to become known to others, she shuddered to think about the consequences for them all.

"Would you care to explain what happened in the library?" she asked softly, knowing she must not allow her fury for Ridgely, who knew better, to taint her voice.

"I…" Virtue bit her lip, her lovely countenance a combination of uncertainty and embarrassment.

Her dark hair looked as if it had been pulled free of her chignon by experienced hands. Thank heavens they hadn't passed anyone in the halls, for she looked thoroughly ruined. Anyone would have taken a look at her and known what had occurred when she had been alone with Ridgely in the library.

"You needn't say anything," Pamela added with a heavy sigh. "I can see for myself what happened. Ridgely is a rake, my dear. You must never again find yourself alone with him. If you do, the consequences may be far greater than you can possibly imagine."

Oh yes, when she had her brother alone, she was most definitely going to box his ears.

Lady Virtue nodded, pressing her lips together. "It won't happen again, Lady Deering. I promise."

"I don't blame you for what happened," Pamela felt the need to explain, for she genuinely cared for her. Lady Virtue was twenty, and she'd been abandoned by her father, who had died and left her in the care of Ridgely. And her brother most definitely hadn't wanted the responsibility. "Ridgely should have known better. I'll go and speak with him now."

As furious as she was with her brother, Pamela wasn't certain just how much calm, polite speaking would happen. Likely not any.

CHAPTER 2

She found her brother in his study, still looking guilty as sin and holding an empty glass of brandy, as if spirits could serve as penance for what he had done.

He offered her an exaggerated bow. "Pamela."

She didn't curtsy in response, but crossed her arms over her chest, pinning him with a fresh glare as she watched him refill his glass. "Will you tell me what happened, or am I to guess?"

Ridgely lifted his glass to her in a mocking toast. "Need I elaborate?"

Pamela was decidedly not amused by his attempt at humor. "*Ridgely.*"

Her brother took a sip of his brandy and then sighed, looking suddenly weary beyond his one-and-thirty years. "After the guards were in place, I wandered to the library and fell asleep."

Guards.

The word instantly brought to mind compelling hazel eyes and a sinfully sculpted mouth and a deep voice with the slightest hint of an accent that she couldn't help but to find intriguing. But no, she had a far-more-important matter to discuss before she asked her brother about *him*. About Beast.

"That doesn't explain how you came to be atop Lady Virtue on the divan," she said, struggling to keep her voice *sotto voce*.

She waited for her brother to enlighten her as to why he would have taken such liberties with his ward. Why he would have been foolish enough to do so at all, let alone on a Grecian couch in the afternoon, where anyone could have walked in upon them. But Ridgely appeared lost in his thoughts, sipping at his brandy with a contemplative air. Objectively, she could well see why someone as naïve as Lady Virtue had been tempted by a man of her brother's experience. Every lady in London swooned over his dark-haired handsomeness, and he'd likely won half of them into his bed.

Which only served to render his conduct all the more egregious.

"Have you nothing to say?" she demanded of him, frustrated and furious beyond measure.

"I've quite forgotten your question."

A few more steps, and he would be within reach of a sound boxing of the ears.

"My question," she repeated, sharply, "was what happened between you and Lady Virtue in the library?"

"She's still a virgin, if that's what you're asking," he said with an indolent air, as if he hadn't a care.

And perhaps he hadn't. He was a man, after all.

She felt her face going hot, anger crackling up and down her spine. "That is *not* what I was asking, though I am gratified to hear it. Good sweet heavens, Ridgely. This is beyond the pale, even for you."

"Well." He waved a careless hand before him, flashing her a self-deprecating smile. "Allow me to alleviate you of any concern in that regard, nonetheless."

"How long has this been happening?" she gritted from between clenched teeth. "Have you been debauching her for the entirety of her stay at Hunt House, beneath my very nose?"

"Such matters tend to be delicate and require privacy," her brother drawled. "I'd never dream of debauching my ward whilst you watched, Pamela. What manner of scoundrel do you take me for?"

Oh, the rogue! That was it.

"Cease jesting!" she hollered, losing her temper entirely, her control and composure going with it. "How can you dare laugh about this, Ridgely? Are you completely callous and cold, utterly without conscience? Do you not feel badly about what you've done to Lady Virtue?"

Ridgely sobered. "I'm not laughing, sister dearest. I'm being perfectly calm. You, on the other hand, are rather making a spectacle."

How dare he accuse her of making a spectacle after what he had just done? The sheer arrogance. How she longed to toss something, anything, at his head.

Pamela stormed forward, ready to wage war. "How long, curse you? How many times have you trifled with her? I warned her against the dangers suitors might bring to her reputation, but I never dreamed the greatest danger would be here in her very home."

"It was a mistake," he told her coolly. "One that won't happen again. That is all you need concern yourself with."

"I am her chaperone," she reminded him tartly. "Only think of the damage it will do, not just to Lady Virtue, but to me, were it to become common fodder for the gossips that her own guardian had ruined her beneath my nose."

She threw her hands up in despair, and then looked about, seeking an object. Any object. The inkwell on his writing desk would do, she decided, before picking it up and hurling it into the fireplace. It shattered within, sending ink splattering all over the interior brick. The violence of the action ameliorated some of her frustration, but then it reminded her of the last time she had lost her temper and what it had cost her, and the sadness that was never far crowded her mind with renewed vengeance.

"I am exceedingly fortunate you have excellent aim," her brother said. "I should hate to think of how all that ink would look on the wall coverings."

No, she wouldn't think of the past. Not now, when she was faced with Ridgely's problems. Far better to concern herself with his woes than her own.

She raised a scolding finger and wagged it at him as if he were a petulant child, because at the moment, she felt very much as if he were one. "If you touch her again, next time, I shall aim for your head. Sow your rakish oats anywhere else in London. Go to your sordid little house of ill repute. Take a mistress if you haven't one. But leave Lady Virtue *alone*."

Ridgely nodded, surprising her. "I intend to do precisely that. As I said, what happened was an unfortunate lapse in judgment. It won't occur again."

"If it does, you'll have no choice but to marry her yourself," she felt compelled to warn him. "There won't be any other way to protect her from the damage."

Ridgely's expression turned properly horrified at the prospect.

"Rest assured that I have no intention of marrying Lady Virtue or anyone else," he said smoothly, his rakish, devil-may-care façade firmly back in place. "I promise I shall keep my distance. You, meanwhile, will encourage her to marry. Quickly." He paused, wincing. "But *not* to Lord Mowbray."

"What is your objection to the viscount?" Pamela asked, indignant, for his lordship had only just begun paying attention to Lady Virtue recently, and her charge seemed to welcome his suit.

"I don't like him," said Ridgely in a dismissive tone. "He isn't good enough for her."

For the first time, it occurred to her that there was something about her brother that seemed different when he spoke of Virtue's suitor. He was almost...defensive. As if he didn't like the notion of her being courted by anyone else. Which made no sense, for her brother was a wicked rake who had no intention of marrying.

Unless...

"Hmm." Pamela narrowed her eyes, studying Ridgely. "They seemed taken with each other last night at the Montrose ball when they shared a dance."

"I said no," he said curtly. "Now, is there anything else you wish to take me to task for, or are we done?"

Now that the fires of her ire had been dampened by the violence she had visited upon the inkwell and her brother's fireplace, her original reason for seeking out Ridgely returned to her. Beast.

It was his eyes. She told herself that was the reason she had found him so unusually compelling. They had been hazel —not quite brown, and neither green nor blue. Its own unique, mysteriously complex shade. Beautiful, just like the rest of him. She ought not to have noticed how handsome he was. And that she had still nettled her.

"Will you tell me why there are suddenly ruffians sauntering about Hunt House?" she asked crisply, doing her best to conceal the ill-advised effect the stranger had upon her. "There is a man called *Beast* roaming about as if he were an honored guest. It is all quite scandalous, even for you."

"They're trusted men here to ensure the safety of the household," Ridgely explained, frowning. "You needn't concern yourself with them."

Not a housebreaker, then. It would have been so much easier for her if he were. But no, he was here, beneath the same roof. Beast was a guard, just as he had claimed. He hadn't been lying.

She forced her mind to the reason for his presence, concern churning in her belly and tightening into a knot. "This is because of the dead man, then? I thought he was a common housebreaker."

Her brother sighed, and the weariness of that sound didn't escape her.

"There is a possibility he was not," Ridgely allowed. "The guards will remain until I deem them no longer necessary, for the safety of everyone within Hunt House."

Good God.

She felt all the anger drain away.

"I don't like the sound of this, Ridgely. What are you not telling me?"

Her brother smiled, but she couldn't help but think it false. She knew him too well to believe it.

"Nothing, my dear," he said. "I am merely being excessively cautious. Now, will that be all?"

He was dismissing her.

"I do hope they will be sleeping in the stables," she added, thinking again of Beast wandering the halls beyond her chamber door. Laying his head upon a pillow in a guest room.

Ridgely sighed again. "Thank you for your concern, sister. I'll take it into consideration."

Pamela supposed she had pushed him far enough for now.

Reluctantly, she dipped into a curtsy. "Thank you. But be warned, brother. I meant what I said about Lady Virtue. If you compromise her any further, you'll have to marry her."

She took her leave, unable to banish thoughts of the man

who had come upon her in the salon from her mind. Hopefully, this dreadful business would be over quickly, and Beast would be nothing more than a forgotten memory all too soon.

As usual, Pamela couldn't sleep.

Only, this time as she lay in bed, staring into the murky shadows playing across the plasterwork above her, it wasn't loneliness plaguing her or the dreams and regrets that haunted her sleep. It wasn't sorrow or bittersweet remembrances.

No, much to her shame, it was thoughts of the guard her brother had hired.

"Beast," she whispered the name aloud, still thinking it an unlikely appellation for a man. Surely not his Christian name.

Who was he? Where had Ridgely found him? And why had he invaded her mind, inhabiting it as if he belonged there, leaving his indelible mark upon her as surely as a touch? What was it about him that had filled her with an inexplicable yearning?

He was handsome, yes. Dark-haired, mysterious-eyed. He was tall and lean, and yet he had exuded an aura of strength and power. He had prowled like his namesake, a beast of prey.

And she hadn't been able to keep her thoughts from straying, wondering what it would be like to be possessed by such a man. By a man who was all complexity and sharp angles, coldness and violence encased in the trappings of a gentleman.

By *him*.

Her body stirred, a restless ache blossoming between her

thighs as she lay alone, fingers clenched on the counterpane, desperate to lull herself to sleep. How very wrong it was. And although she was alone, the darkness pressing around her like heavy weights threatening to drown, no one else aware of her wanton yearnings, her cheeks went hot.

What was wrong with her?

How could she tarnish Bertie's memory and the love they had shared by feeling such base lust for someone else? And worse, for someone to whom she hadn't even been properly introduced. A man of questionable origin and family, one who called himself Beast and regarded her so boldly that she had felt, for a fleeting moment, as if she hadn't been wearing an afternoon gown at all when that hazel stare had swept over her.

With a sigh, she rolled to her belly, struggling to find a comfortable position. Perhaps she should have taken a posset as her lady's maid had kindly suggested, noting her state of unease earlier. But she hadn't, for she had forced herself to rely less and less upon such measures, fearing herself too dependent upon them. No, instead, she must lay here in misery, thinking of—

A scrape sounded in the hall beyond her chamber, cutting through the chatter of her own roiling musings. She lifted her head, listening, holding her breath. Perhaps she had imagined the sound.

Creak.

No, there it was again, only louder this time. It was the sort of sound a hushed footfall might make.

Her heart pounded as she thought of Ridgely's admission earlier in his study, that there was a possibility the dead man on the stairs hadn't been a housebreaker after all. But what he hadn't said was far more telling than what he had. Although her brother had claimed he wasn't keeping anything from her, she would wager her meager widow's portion that he was. Which meant that the dead man on the stairs had intended to do Ridgely harm. The presence of the guards alone was all the evidence she required of that.

Creak.

There it was again. Pamela was not mistaken, and she very much feared that another miscreant was beyond her door, creeping through Hunt House in the bowels of the night, plotting to do further harm. If there was indeed a housebreaker in the hall, she had to do something.

Her mind whirled frantically, searching for a solution.

There was a possibility that it was one of the guards her brother had hired, but it was also entirely likely that something more nefarious was happening just beyond her door. She could scream and bring all the servants raining down upon her, but that would risk the man's escape. She could run to Ridgely's chamber, but doing so possessed inherent risk. If whoever was lingering in the hall suspected she was going to inform her brother he was being robbed, he might cause Pamela harm.

The most expedient method would be to dispatch the villain herself.

Swallowing hard against a sudden rush of fear, Pamela slid from her bed, her bare feet carrying her across the chamber to where a banked fire still provided warmth from the grate. The fire iron in its place called to her. The slim, steel tool would have to do as a weapon, for it seemed most likely to cause damage.

Licking lips gone dry, she reached for the fire iron. Her fingers closed over the cool, twisted metal. She could hit the villain over the head with it, if necessary.

Pamela knew a moment of regret, a visceral twinge inside, at the notion of harming someone. But then she reminded herself that the someone in question was possibly a housebreaker intending to steal from Ridgely and cause heaven knew what other manner of mischief. Summoning her courage, she slowly opened her door, holding her breath as it inched wider, revealing the inky shadows of the hall.

There, she paused for a moment, waiting for the sound. For something to alert her to the presence of another. The house was eerily quiet. No sign of the source of the creaking floorboards. Nary a footfall. She had to release the breath she was holding and move forward, into the abyss. Had she been imagining the sound, then? Had she been mistaken?

Hesitantly, she ventured deeper into the hall, clutching the fire poker tightly. There was no sound to be heard but the whisper of her own labored breaths as she moved. But then she heard it suddenly. The soft sweep of footfalls over carpet, warning her she wasn't alone. Someone was approaching her through the shadows. Striding toward her with sleek haste. She raised the fire iron, preparing to strike, but before she could land a blow, warm fingers caught her wrist in an almost punishing grip, staying forward motion. Another hand clamped on her waist, and then she was being propelled as if she weighed nothing more than a feather.

Forced back across the threshold of her bedchamber and whirled about, the motions so quick and skillful that she almost felt as if she were being guided on the dance floor. But this was no ballroom, and the man in whose clutches she had found herself was no fawning suitor. He held her in a skillful grip, propelling her to where he wanted her. The door of her room closed with a soft *snick*, confining them together. It happened so fast, she hadn't had a chance to even scream. Another dizzying spin, and her back was suddenly pinned to the wall, a hard, masculine body pressed firmly against hers from hip to chest, keeping her from moving. Crowding her.

Trapping her.

Hot breath fanned over her lips when her captor spoke. "Exceedingly poor choice of weapon, my lady."

Pamela recognized that low, faintly accented voice.

It was him. *Beast.* And he'd caught her. Had forced her into her chamber. Was holding her in place. They were alone. No one but the two of them in the night. Their bodies were scandalously aligned. And she could feel him. *All* of him. Part of her liked it. But part of her knew she must not. Didn't dare trust him. What manner of man, what manner of guard, would treat her thus?

A scream rose in her throat, but it scarcely had a chance to emerge before a mouth settled over hers, muffling her cry. Shocking her. His *lips* were on hers. And they were hot and firm, pressing with the intent, she thought, of silencing her. And something was wrong with her. So very wrong. Because she savored those lips. She *enjoyed* the way they felt against hers.

Pamela forgot to struggle. In the darkness, she was surrounded by him. His scent, citrus and the sharp cleanness of soap, mingling with a hint of leather. His strength. His height. He was taller, looming over her. Keeping her where he wanted as he gentled the kiss, his lips coasting over hers with hunger instead of brutish force. Teasing a whimper from her.

It wasn't fear, that sound.

But desire, rising from a part of herself she had banished years ago. How? For this stranger, this man who had dared to push her against a wall and put his mouth on hers?

He lifted his head, ending the kiss.

"Don't scream."

He spoke with such authority, this trespasser in her own home. This man who did not belong here. This man who was dangerous to her welfare. To the rest of her as well.

She shouldn't listen to him. He was a villain. It didn't

matter if Ridgely had hired him, if he was a guard. He had caught her and kissed her and intended to do only heaven knew what with her. Her lips tingled, and her body was humming with awareness she remembered but had done her utmost to forget in her widowhood.

"Unhand me," she demanded, coming to her senses.

He chuckled, the sound low and somehow pleasing despite the circumstances. "Not until I'm certain you won't do something both of us will regret."

Was he threatening her?

It occurred to her then, a place where men were so very vulnerable. She brought her knee up, intending to strike him between the legs, but he was too quick, anticipating her movements and neutralizing her effort by sliding his own knee between hers instead.

Through the thin linen of her night rail, she felt every inch of his muscled thigh, pressing intimately into her. And heaven help her, but a twinge of raw pleasure arced through her at the contact.

"Like that," he muttered, then rubbed his cheek along hers. There was the slightest abrasion of his neatly shorn whiskers over her skin. His lips were on her ear then, grazing the shell as he spoke. "It wasn't wise to attempt to unman me, Lady Deering."

His warning words should have incited more fear within her, and yet, all she felt was his mouth on her ear, his breath falling like hot silk on her suddenly sensitized flesh. All she knew was an ache deep in her core. But that was wrong, so wrong. Her mind spun with questions as her body grappled with all the sensations filling her head with fire.

"What are you about, sir, taking such liberties?" she asked, struggling to free herself of his hold.

But it was fruitless, for Beast was incredibly strong. The fingers on her wrist remained tight, keeping her arm restrained to the wall at her side. And when she used the palm of her free hand to push at his shoulder, attempting to shove him away, he caught that wrist as well. All that her movements had succeeded in doing was dragging the hem of her night rail higher. Cool air kissed her bare feet, her calves, and even her knees.

"What do you think I'm about?" His voice was deep and mesmerizing. A taunt in the darkness.

Oh, she reckoned it didn't matter *what* he was about. All that did matter was freeing herself.

Pamela shifted again but his thigh remained wedged between her legs, the warmth of him searing her through their meager combined layers. Her breath hitched, her nipples going hard and tight. The part of her which had long lain dormant had burst forth to vibrant life.

But how could it be so? How could she know such all-consuming desire for a stranger, for a man who had captured her and then stolen her lips as if they belonged to him? Shame burned through her, mingling hot and dangerous with vexing yearning. She had to put a stop to this.

"If you don't let me go, I'll scream again," she warned him, breathless from her exertion and her reaction to him both. "I'll set the entire household upon you. But if you release me, I promise I'll not utter a word to my brother about your transgressions."

Or her own.

"How do I know I can trust you?" he asked. "How can I be sure you'll not try something foolish again?"

His wicked lips suddenly found a place she had not previously known to be so very sensitive. A place just behind her ear. He kissed her there. Such a strangely intimate spot, and its effect upon her was molten.

Another noise fled her lips before she could stop it.

"What...what are you doing?" she managed weakly.

Whatever it was, the wickedest part of her didn't want him to cease. She never wanted it to end.

"Trying to calm you." He kissed her neck next. "Showing you that you needn't attempt to murder me with that fire iron."

Oh, he had an interesting notion indeed of producing a calming effect upon a woman. Her heart was positively galloping. Quite the opposite of what he claimed was his intent.

"Or trying to trick me." She had to keep her wits about her, which was growing increasingly impossible with this man touching her, his lips on her.

She should scream again, she thought frantically. He was trying to seduce her into releasing her weapon. Trying to render her mindless with his knowing mouth and manly heat. She couldn't allow it.

"Does it feel like I'm trying to trick you, my lady?" His thumb rubbed over her inner wrist, taking some of the sting from his tight grip. "Now hush, and give me the poker, and I'll release you."

She didn't believe him.

Pamela opened her mouth and began to scream.

With a guttural curse, his mouth returned to hers.

CHAPTER 3

He was kissing her.

Again.

But this time with more masterful insistence. Using those lips of his against her, opening her to him so that his tongue could slide sinuously into her mouth. And then she tasted him. He tasted sweet, like tea. And like sin. Danger, too.

And something else she hadn't tasted in so very long: man. Man and desire and blatant, erotic, carnal yearning.

The things it did to her. His tongue, the way he tasted, the way he kissed. Every part of her was suddenly, exquisitely alive and so very aware. Desires she'd believed long dead throbbed to life, slid through her veins. Danced hot up and down her spine.

The carefully constructed walls she had built around herself in the years following her husband's death collapsed. Her defenses, which she had prided herself on being impenetrable, were gone. She made a helpless sound of longing, the whimper hatched from her throat and unable to be quelled by reason or pride. And then her tongue was writhing against his, licking at him, devouring him as he consumed her. They were feasting on each other, their kisses turning ravenous. Battling each other for control.

A thump and clang interrupted the stillness of the night, and she realized it was the fire poker, fallen from her limp fingers to bump into the wall and land on the carpets. His grip on her wrist eased until he released her altogether, and his hand went instead to her waist, holding her in a firm, intimate grasp that made her feel like someone's lover. Made her long for midnight kisses and caresses sweeping over her bare skin, for whispers in the darkness and long, languorous kisses, and a man who wanted her desperately.

Curse her body's traitorous response.

Pamela pressed her palm against his shoulder, but the instinct to shove evaporated as surely as her resolve. Because her fingers curled into the cool softness of his waistcoat, burrowing into the powerful muscle bunched beneath, and there she stopped. Not pushing him away from her, but grasping a handful of fabric instead to pull him nearer.

He made a low sound in his throat. Approval? Desire? Victory?

She didn't know. All she did know was that he was kissing her as she hadn't been kissed in years. Making her feel things she had no right to feel as a proper, respectable widow alone in the darkness with a man she'd only just met in passing earlier that afternoon. A man filled with secrets and mysteries, with cold hazel eyes and an impassive countenance that was as stark as it was handsome.

He deepened the kiss, his lips moving with skillful seduction over hers, and suddenly her other wrist was free as well. But this one, too, rebelled against her conscience's firm determination to do what was right. Her hand rose, tentative, to rest on his cheek. The prickle of his whiskers delighted her as he cupped her nape, long fingers cradling the base of her skull, keeping her from the hardness of the wall at her back. Almost gently, tenderly, as if he wished to protect her even as he consumed her. The gesture was at odds with the arrogant man who had whirled her into her room and entrapped her. Who kissed her and made himself so familiar with her person.

She was shocked and a little horrified at her response to him, and yet she could not seem to stop now that she had begun. She was starving for his touch, for his kisses, for that old remembered sensation of being the object of a man's desire. How had she convinced herself, for all this time, that she had no needs? That she could be content alone and untouched?

For years, she had been so careful, so guarded. Her sole indulgence had been shopping. But fans and gowns and haberdashery had not filled the aching void inside her the way this scoundrel did. The way she knew, instinctively, he could.

What would it be like to be this man's lover? To take his hand in hers and lead him to her bed, to seduce him under the forgiving moon? To forget past and future in favor of one night? She'd never believed she'd had it in her. But he had brought something to life, and the resurgence demanded to be answered. As they traded kisses and touches against the wall of her chamber, everything seemed possible.

She could remember what it was like to be desired.

To lie beneath a man, his big body hovering over hers, the thickness of him gliding inside her, filling her. And it wasn't Bertie at all whom she was picturing in her mind, atop her in bed. It wasn't Bertie she was longing for. Rather, it was this stranger whose kisses were turning her to flame and making her knees melt, inducing her to want things that must remain well beyond her reach.

She was wicked.

On a cry, Pamela turned her head, breaking the kiss, for

she had gone too far. Beyond the pale. She mustn't allow a moment more of this man, this *Beast's,* mouth on hers.

Her heart was beating fast. So fast. It was almost as loud in her ears as her ragged breaths, rising like a chorus of disapproval. Taunting her.

"What is it, Marchioness?" The hand at her nape moved slowly, almost affectionately, until he caressed her cheek.

She felt the metallic slide of a ring against her, warmed by his skin. Somehow, the lack of light made every intimacy they shared seem so much more heightened. How softly, how gently he touched her. It was the caress of a skilled seducer, she thought. Not the rough, bruising force of a villain who intended her harm.

"Who are you?" she asked again, because she couldn't believe he was the man he had presented to her. There was nothing simple about him. He was more than a mere guard. He was intelligent and seductive, quick-witted, and thoroughly dangerous to her restraint.

"I've already told you. Beast, my lady." His thumb—callused and rough—traced her cheekbone.

"No one is named Beast." She wetted her lips and tasted him on her tongue, and it was like kissing him anew.

What had she done?

"*I* am."

She still didn't believe him. "Why are you roaming about in the halls?"

"How else am I to guard the house and its occupants, keeping them safe?" Amusement laced his tone. "Do you suppose villains wishing to do harm respect the sanctity of sleep?"

The hand at her waist shifted, creeping to her ribcage. He caressed her there slowly, as if he had every right to do so. And worse, she allowed it.

Because she liked the way it felt.

"Of course not," she said reluctantly, heart still beating hard and fast. Body still helplessly under his spell.

Slowly, his thumb traveled in maddening motions. After the frenzy of his kisses, such a simplistic touch should have been a disappointment, and yet it secretly thrilled her.

"You can trust me," he added softly. "I'm here to keep you safe, Marchioness."

But she didn't feel safe, pressed against his warm, muscled body. She felt quite definitely in danger. In danger of losing her ability to resist him. In danger of losing her sanity. Her morals. Her self-respect.

"Why should I believe you?" she asked, keeping her voice to a hushed whisper. "No gentleman would dare to treat me as you have done. You claim to be safeguarding this house, and yet you have forced me into my chamber and are holding me captive."

He found a tendril of hair and tucked it behind her ear, stealing her ability to think. The gesture was so unexpected. His fingers grazed the place behind her ear where his mouth had been. They lingered there, his fingertips brushing her skin.

"Is that what you believe, my lady?"

The deepness of his voice made more unwanted feelings rise.

"Of course I do," she managed. "You've accosted me in the darkest depths of the night."

"I was keeping you from folly, not accosting you," he countered, using the backs of his fingers to slowly travel over her throat. His knuckles left a trail of fire. "Keeping you from bringing the household down upon us with your screams or from committing murder."

"Murder?"

"Murder, my lady. Mine. Unless I am mistaken about your plans for the fire iron?"

He wasn't. She would have hit him as hard as she could, believing him another housebreaker, or worse. But the sins he had committed against her were of a different, most unexpected sort. Never mind that she had thrilled at every one of them.

"And you...what you...*this*," she hissed meaningfully, unable to utter the word *kiss*, for fear it would make her long for his lips on hers again more than she already did. "How do you explain your actions, sirrah?"

"What is *this*, as you say?" he asked.

He was goading her.

Enjoying the sparks between them.

And so was she. Her own actions had been equally shameful, and she knew it. She had *participated*. She was lingering now when so easily she could escape. She was savoring the sensation of his muscled thigh between hers, parting them. Delighting in the illusion of him holding her captive. As if he sensed the direction of her thoughts, he shifted, his knee going higher. An answering burst of pleasure radiated from her core.

And that was when she became painfully aware of her reaction to him. Her most intimate flesh was wet. Scandalously, embarrassingly so. She didn't recall ever having a response like this, so sudden and wanton.

"You didn't answer me," Beast pressed.

Pamela swallowed hard against a fresh rush of desire, telling herself she was stronger than this. She had been a faithful widow for years. She had avoided temptation and sin. She had held the memory of her husband in her heart, firm and strong, and she had never, not once, wavered in her devotion to him. There was a reason she was known as the Ice Widow in polite society behind her back. How had Beast turned her so quickly and relentlessly into flame?

"Kissing me," she elaborated, furious with herself and

overwhelmed with yearning for a man she couldn't even see properly in the lack of light. A man with one name. "Touching me. Making yourself so familiar with my person. How do you describe that if not accosting? I will tell you plainly, sir, that after I tell my brother of what has passed between us, you will be gone by morning light."

"Tell him, then, Marchioness. And while you do so, tell him how you responded to me. Tell him how you kissed me back. Tell him how you put your tongue in my mouth."

Oh, sweet heavens above.

Those low, gruff words coiled around her like a serpent. Made all the molten heat coursing through her veins burn hotter still. She had done those things, had she not? But how ungentlemanly of him to taunt her so, to give voice to the unspeakable.

Her cheeks went hot again, and between her legs, she was even hotter. "You accosted me."

Perhaps if she repeated the words enough, her protests would render them true.

"I defended myself." His hand had curled around her throat now in a light hold that shouldn't have felt erotic and yet somehow did. "You intended to do me harm with that fire iron, did you not?"

Her every sense was heightened. From the coast of her own breath over her kiss-bruised lips to every place they touched. They were yet entwined most intimately, like a pair of lovers who'd met under the cover of darkness for fear they would be discovered. And it shocked her to realize they could have been, so very easily. He could unbutton his falls and drive inside her in one hard thrust. Her inner muscles clenched in delicious anticipation at the thought. How appalling to think she would welcome his possession.

No, Pamela. You mustn't allow yourself to go down this disastrous path. A path which leads only to ruin and scandal.

But was that her voice inside her mind, or the judgmental voice of her mother? Sometimes the two were difficult to differentiate between. Mother had raised her to be a paragon, and Pamela had fallen desperately short of the mark.

"I heard creaking in the hall and thought it another housebreaker," she admitted.

"And you thought it prudent to confront a dangerous man yourself, alone?" he demanded, his voice harsh. "Promise me you won't do something so imprudent again, my lady."

He dared to call her imprudent, when *he* had swept her into her chamber as boldly as a lover and then had kissed her breathless? When he remained so close that his scent was wrapped around her like an embrace and the slightest shift of his body against hers incited her rebellion against the chaste life she had been living as a proper widow.

Four long and lonely years.

"I owe you no such promise," she told him. "I'm not beholden to you. I don't even know you."

"You know me well enough, Marchioness."

His tone was arrogant. Taunting. And he was not wrong. She did know him. She knew his thigh thrusting against her aching flesh. Knew the way he tasted, the way he kissed. Knew his touch, the hardness of his body melding with the softness of hers. But Pamela couldn't shake the feeling that acknowledging any of that aloud would render her even guiltier. It felt like a forbidden secret that should never be uttered.

"You are a stranger to me," she countered defiantly, refusing to allow him to make the connection between them that filled her with such undying shame. "How am I to know that you aren't every bit as dangerous as the men you presume to guard this household against?"

The hand on her ribs had moved slowly, until his thumb brushed against the tender underside of one of her breasts. Oh, how she wanted that touch higher. Wanted his hand on her, coaxing a response she shouldn't have.

Mustn't have. Not tonight. Not ever.

"Because you have my vow, and I'm a man of my word," he said smoothly in his voice of velvet and sin. "You're safe with me." His face lowered to hers, and she knew the warmth of his kiss on her cheek. Soft, so soft. Almost reverent. "As safe as you wish to be."

Her body was awash with disgraceful desire. The way he'd said the last, *as safe as you wish to be,* made his words sound like a challenge. She had been safe for years. First her marriage to Bertie—a love match. And then a safe, untouched widow for four years following the shock of his untimely death. Safety was a cold bedfellow these days.

"Do you dare to proposition the sister of the duke who has given you this post?" she asked, trying to keep her voice chilled and unaffected.

Failing.

There was a husk in her tone that she couldn't hide, founded in the desire that was burning her from the inside out.

Another scrape of his whiskers against her cheek. His lips grazed her ear as he spoke so quietly she almost didn't hear.

"Trust me, Marchioness. If I had propositioned you, you'd be in that bed behind us, naked, and I'd be deep inside you, and you'd be begging me for more." He kissed her ear, then straightened abruptly. "But I didn't, so I'm afraid this must be good night."

His words—his wicked, wonderful, terrible words—made her ache to be touched. Ache for more than this brief, delicious, ill-advised encounter in the night. Ache for everything he had said. To be in her bed with him, Beast atop her, no barrier of cloth keeping her skin from his. To know his hardness, touch and kiss and caress every inch of him. To take him inside her. Would he be thick and long and hard? How would it feel to have a lover again? To wake her body from its self-imposed sleep?

It was confusing and horrid, and later she would drown in her shame. But there was no one else awake, no one about, to know what wicked deeds they might engage in for just a few, fleeting moments. Temptation had never been stronger.

But then, he was shifting. Lowering his thigh. Freeing her entirely, the decadent weight of his muscled form against hers lifting. And desperation seized her. Pamela's hand shot out of its own volition, burying in his cravat, fingers grasping starched linen, holding him to her.

"No," she said, the word torn from her. "Don't."

Not yet, she added silently. *Just a few moments more of this madness first.*

And then she pressed her lips to his.

~

SHE HADN'T EVEN BEEN polite.

She'd demanded.

No, that wasn't right. She had *commanded* him.

Lady Deering had caught his neckcloth and pulled him to her, those soft, luscious lips taking his with a fierce hunger that had his prick straining against his falls, begging to be let free. And although he knew better, he was kissing her in return. Allowing her to seduce him with her oddly enthralling combination of ice and fire. Surrendering to the need for her that had begun when their paths had first crossed earlier in the salon. The same need that had him making certain he was watching the halls on the floor with the bedchambers rather than one of the other guards.

Because the thought of one of the men near her as she slept had somehow felt wrong. It made no sense, this surge of possessiveness he felt for the woman he was kissing. But he was a Boritanian by birth, and he hadn't forgotten the old ways of his homeland, the old ways that still ran in his blood. His maternal grandmother had believed firmly in fate, and she had instilled that same sense of acceptance in him. He felt a deeper connection with Lady Deering. Acknowledged it despite the inherent wrongness.

The wrongness of being paid handsomely to watch over a household and its occupants and yet pinning one of its ladies to a wall and ravishing her mouth with his. He'd told himself the earlier kisses had been to muffle her screams and keep the rest of the household abed. He'd told himself he was saving his own hide from a thorough braining with a fire poker at the dainty hands of a golden-haired goddess.

But he didn't have an excuse for lingering here and returning her kisses now. For allowing his hand to slide from the delicate framework of her ribcage until he was cupping the voluptuous fullness of her soft breast in his palm. No excuse at all. Nothing he could say would make what he was doing right.

And he fully intended to keep doing it just the same.

Because her nipple was hard, and when he teased it with his thumb, she gasped into his mouth and wrapped her leg around his hip. The movement made the hem of her thin night rail ride up. He caught her thigh in his other hand and knew the glory of soft, lush skin. So smooth and firm and yet with decadent curves that made all his resolve melt like ice beneath a blistering sun. Awareness shot up his arm, past his elbow. He raked his nails lightly over her and wished he could see the faint white traces his fingertips would momentarily leave behind. He licked into her mouth, tasting her again.

Mint, perhaps from her tooth powder. Fresh and crisp and everything he wanted more of. Her tongue teased his and her kisses grew into a frenzy. He was aching, desperate for her touch, for any part of her curves to align with his cockstand. Needing friction, if not release. In the darkness, her scent surrounded him, floral and exotic. Jasmine, he thought, with a hint of hyacinth.

Intoxicating, just as she was.

He should know better. He should *be* better. And yet, how could he tear his lips from hers? How could he deny himself her mouth, her tongue, her enticing curves wrapped around him? *Just once,* whispered a voice inside himself he'd thought he had silenced years ago. It was the voice of the self-indulgent prince, the man he had once been.

The careless man.

The one who hadn't given a damn about anything of import until it had been too late.

These old reminders, remnants of the life he'd left behind, should have been pinpricks to his conscience. Should have stayed him or at least doused some of his ardor. But he couldn't seem to get enough of her hungry kisses, the throaty sounds she made when he lingered over her nipple, the breathy sigh she gave into his mouth as his hand slid higher until he palmed a handful of her bare flesh.

Her bottom was as finely shaped as the rest of her. He ground his cock against the apex of her thighs, wishing he were inside her instead of separated by unwanted layers of clothing. So much heat radiated from her that he swore she'd scorch him like flame. And he'd happily burn in her fire, even if he wasn't meant to.

Blinding need forced logic and reason from his mind. It didn't matter that she'd been determined to brain him with a fire poker. That she had looked at him with icy disdain earlier in the salon. That she spoke to him with such cool hauteur, the likes of which he once would have visited upon others, a lifetime ago. She had come to life in his arms, like a carved marble statue of a deity suddenly turned into flesh and bone.

They engaged in a battle of supremacy, fighting over dominance in their kisses. She caught his lower lip in her teeth and bit, and he did the same. Their teeth clacked together, their tongues twined sinuously, demanding more. His cock was pulsing in his trousers, and he couldn't recall ever being this hard, this desperate. Almost dizzied by his reaction to her, Theo tore his mouth from hers. Their breathing was well matched, equally ragged and rough, the only sounds in the stillness of the night.

Her head fell back against the wall with a thump, and he took it as an invitation, burying his face in her throat as he kneaded the soft flesh of her rump and teased her breast. He inhaled deeply, mystified by his body's response, of having lost all control. His restraint had disappeared into the inky night just as the fire iron had. He found the place where her pulse galloped fast and kissed her there, in the hollow at the base of her neck.

Another sound emerged from her, part whimper, part plea. He raked his teeth along her throat, found his way to her ear and licked the hollow until she moaned softly. She had released her grip on his cravat, leaving her hands free to caress his chest and shoulders. He longed to tear away his coat and waistcoat, to strip off his shirt so that he could feel her smooth fingertips on his bare skin.

The urge was foreign, the suddenness of it alarming, for he hadn't allowed anyone to see him thus, to witness the hideous scars that marred him. The inclination shocked Theo, reminded him of the reason for the marks covering his body beneath the trappings of gentility.

Memories returned with visceral vengeance. For a

moment, the sweet floral scent of Lady Deering was replaced by the tang of sweat and blood. The husk of her dulcet voice was drowned out by the cruel lash of a whip and his own screams.

And that swiftly, Theo remembered who he was, why he was here. His cockstand withered and he jerked his lips from the silken benediction of the marchioness's skin. He released her, disentangling himself so quickly that she made a sound of protest and stumbled to the side, sliding along the wall.

He wanted to catch her, to protect her, to keep her from falling, but the demons had rendered him immobile. Incapable of doing anything other than staying stoic and still and trying to drown them out with calm, measured breaths.

"Beast?"

Her hesitant voice cut through the night and his memories.

He swallowed hard against a rush of bile threatening to climb up his throat. Yes, Beast. That was who he was, who his past had made him. Not the soft-palmed prince, not the rake who had won over court and had his choice of any woman in the kingdom as his bedmate. Not the unscarred, undamaged, perfectly spoiled scion of the Boritanian king.

Just Beast. A mercenary. A scarred recluse. A dangerous man. One who couldn't afford to allow himself to become distracted by the supple curves of a beautiful widow or the promise of burying himself inside her and forgetting all the ugliness which had blemished his once-promising life. A woman like her deserved so much better than the shell of a man he'd become.

What had he been thinking?

"Remain in your chamber where you belong, my lady," he forced out, the words emerging as a growled warning, harsh and biting. "Fair warning: if I catch you wandering the halls with a fire iron again, I won't be nearly as forgiving next time."

With that, he hastened from her chamber, blotting out the temptation of her and returning himself to the darkness where he belonged.

CHAPTER 4

Pamela did what she always did when she was overset.

She went shopping.

Ordinarily, a lengthy visit to Bellingham and Co. provided a temporary cure for what ailed her. But she'd purchased two lovely fans, an assortment of lace, and five pairs of kidskin gloves, and she still felt despicably overwrought.

Overwrought and overheated, her body awash with sensations that were a betrayal in every sense of the word. A betrayal to Bertie's memory, a betrayal to herself, to her brother's household. Heavens, even to Lady Virtue, who had accompanied her on this outing, and whom she was regularly offering stern advice on the necessity of firmly adhering to propriety, avoiding rakes, and never allowing herself to grow weak for the lures of a handsome, unscrupulous gentleman.

"Do you think we might return to Hunt House now?" Lady Virtue was grumbling at her side as Pamela examined a selection of furs she absolutely did not need.

Returning to Hunt House seemed most unwise at the moment. Because there was a man roaming about who had been in her chamber last night. A man she had kissed. A man who had cupped her bare derriere in his big, callused hand without a scrap of anything between them. A man whose anatomy had been thoroughly pressed against hers, informing her without words that he was large *everywhere*.

Pamela cleared her throat. "Not yet, my dear."

Not ever if she could help it.

She didn't think she could bear crossing paths with Beast again. Not by the light of day. Catching his cool hazel stare, knowing what his lips felt like on hers, all the desperate hunger he had sparked within her, would fill her with shame.

"My feet are beginning to hurt," Lady Virtue complained.

Pamela had no doubt they were. They had been shopping all afternoon in a desperate bid to keep herself from being beneath the same roof as the man she would have allowed far greater liberties than those he had taken. She loathed herself for what she had done. She'd been despicable. It was a miracle she had been able to face her brother at the breakfast table after she had so upbraided him for his conduct with Lady Virtue.

What a hypocrite she was.

"Just a few minutes more," she consoled her charge, thinking that she would have left Lady Virtue at home if she hadn't feared Ridgely would somehow find an opportunity to ruin her further.

She didn't trust her brother.

But then, she also didn't trust herself.

It would seem they were two sinners cut from the same wicked cloth.

"You said that an hour ago," Lady Virtue pointed out, sounding grim.

"I was just thinking that perhaps I ought to have a look at

the bonnets," Pamela said brightly, ignoring the younger woman's complaint.

At the moment, Pamela was inclined to shop for the rest of her life as long as it meant she could avoid the wickedly handsome, utterly despicable guard haunting the halls of Hunt House. Why had his kisses been so exquisitely skilled? Why could he not have been a dreadful kisser as some of the gentlemen who had courted her before her marriage had been? She would never forget Lord Garson's wet-lipped attempts, his kiss in the moonlit gardens which had tasted not of illicit romance but of onions instead.

No, Beast's kisses had been demanding and hungry. He had dismantled every stone in the wall she'd crafted around herself after Bertie's death, and she hated him for that. Hated herself for it even more. Which was why she had to continue avoiding Hunt House—and Beast—altogether.

She led the way to the department where bonnets in a wide array of fashions were on display. Lady Virtue trailed in her wake after heaving a frustrated sigh. Pamela knew her brother's ward didn't particularly enjoy shopping unless they were at a book shop. Then, her charge's eagerness for more reading fodder kept her locked within the shelves for hours. Unfortunately, Bellingham and Co. did not possess a book department in which Virtue could lose herself.

Pamela stopped before a muslin morning bonnet which had been trimmed with lace and white ribbon. It was lovely, although she already possessed three quite similar in appearance, none of which she had yet worn. Ridgely was more than generous in allowing her to charge whatever she wished to his accounts. Unfortunately, Bertie had left her with a minuscule widow's portion along with her broken heart. Pamela repaid her brother however she could, most recently by taking his ward under her wing.

Ridgely wanted Lady Virtue married off with all haste.

And Virtue very much wished to remain unwed and return to her home in Nottinghamshire. Both, coupled with the unexpected debacle in the library the day before, rendered Pamela's attempts at achieving a beneficial outcome tangled indeed.

"What do you think of this bonnet, my dear?" she asked Lady Virtue of the morning bonnet she'd already decided she wasn't purchasing.

Perhaps her charge could be distracted, and their shopping expedition thus prolonged. More time away, less time in alarming proximity to a man Pamela never should have been alone with, let alone kissed or touched. And yes, touched him she had. He was well-muscled and lean, and the leashed strength beneath his clothes haunted her fingertips even now as she pretended to examine the white bonnet.

"It's rather plain," Lady Virtue said, making no effort to disguise her ennui.

"It could use a bit more color," she agreed, struggling to ignore the maddening feelings that had been threatening to overwhelm her ever since the night before.

How long had she lingered against the wall after he had left, leaning into the plaster on the shaky knees of a newborn foal, trying to calm her racing heart? Trying to forget the lush heat of his sensual lips on hers, the brazen way he'd kneaded her bottom and worked his thumb over her aching nipple?

No, no, no. She had to cease thinking of Beast altogether.

She wished she had one of the fans she had purchased at hand so that she could use it to cool her flaming cheeks. But instead, she had instructed the shopkeeper assisting them to see the fans sent to Hunt House later, along with her other purchases as was her custom.

"Are you feeling well, my lady?" Lady Virtue asked, her voice considerate, her gaze astute.

And assessing.

"I'm feeling perfectly lovely," she lied with a false smile.

The girl was far too intelligent, Pamela thought. Likely all those books she forever had her nose buried in. Oh, she supposed Lady Virtue wasn't a girl any longer at twenty years old, but Pamela felt every last one of her eight-and-twenty years. When she had been Virtue's age, she had been married to Bertie, naively believing in a future of endless happiness surrounded by at least half a dozen children and the undying love of her husband. The love, she'd had. Until Bertie had unexpectedly grown ill, leaving her alone.

"Are you certain?" Lady Virtue persisted, intruding upon Pamela's tortured memories of what might have been. "Are you overheated? It is a trifle warm in here, is it not?"

"Quite warm," she agreed with studied nonchalance before turning her attention to another selection of millinery.

To her everlasting shame, she had been overheated since last night. Nothing chased the fires of desperate yearning that terrible man had lit within her. What was it about him? He was not the polished, poised gentleman Bertie had been.

Her husband had been incredibly charming, always ready with an infectious smile that had encouraged everyone to laugh along with him at whatever scrape he'd managed to find himself in. And, being Bertie, there had been a great many scrapes indeed. Her heart gave a pang at the memory of his crooked, rapscallion's grin, forever lost to her now. Regardless of how much time passed, she would never cease missing him.

No, the stranger who had made her so weak with wanting had been nothing at all like Bertie. The two men could not have been more different. He was cold and aloof, menacing and strong, all sharp angles and rugged planes, his sensual lips perpetually unsmiling. He exuded danger.

Stop thinking of him, Pamela, she warned herself inwardly.

"Are you very angry with me over…what happened yesterday?" Lady Virtue asked.

And for a moment, Pamela's heart threatened to leap from her chest. Until she realized Virtue wasn't speaking of what had happened with Pamela and Beast yesterday, but of what had happened between herself and Ridgely. What a hen-wit she was. Of course, no one else would know. They had been alone in the depths of the night. In her chamber.

"My dear, we shan't speak of that again," she told her charge sternly, giving her a meaningful look. "Particularly not in such a place as Bellingham and Co."

Sometimes, the girl's country naivete shone through the town bronze Pamela had been struggling to instill in her. It was a wonder the wolves of the *ton* had not torn her little sheep apart. Fortunately, she had Pamela to protect her. And protect her she would, however she must. Especially by not allowing herself to engage in any conduct as scandalous as she had last night.

No, that must never, ever be repeated.

"Of course," Lady Virtue said. "It is only that you have been rather unusually quiet today, and I wished to know the reason for it. I know you are displeased with me, and I understand. I acted foolishly, and I'm sorry for it."

Displeased with her? Good heavens, if Pamela was displeased with anyone, it was herself, and for her own transgressions last night with Beast. And Ridgely, too, for he was one-and-thirty years old, a seasoned rakehell, and the girl's guardian. He knew better than to dally with innocents.

"I'm not displeased with you, my dear," she denied quietly. "I am merely pensive today."

Pensive indeed. Plagued by thoughts of a certain rogue. And his wicked kisses. And his hands. Oh, how she had liked those hands of his on her. How she longed for them to return, only this time without the encumbrance of her night rail.

Lady Virtue was frowning at her. "If you insist, Lady Deering."

Was she so transparent to a neophyte like Virtue? Pamela shuddered to think what would happen if Ridgely were to learn of what she had done. Beast's taunts from the night before returned to her, scalding her cheeks and the place between her legs with equal heat.

Tell him how you responded to me. Tell him how you kissed me back. Tell him how you put your tongue in my mouth.

"This is a lovely hat, do you not think?" she choked out with forced cheer, politely gesturing to a straw bonnet ornamented with a silk ribbon and fetching sprigs of lilac and roses.

"It is quite handsome," Lady Virtue agreed, sounding distinctly unimpressed. "Perhaps you should buy that one as well, and then we might return to Hunt House for a respite."

Return to Hunt House? No, she could not. She didn't dare. Far too much temptation awaited her within those familiar walls. Temptation where, just days before, there had been none.

"Not just yet, my dear," she said merrily. "Perhaps a visit to Bond Street before we go back."

At her side, Virtue sighed heavily, her displeasure obvious. "Must we?"

"Oh yes," Pamela said grimly, determined to force all inconvenient longing for the man named Beast from her before she returned to Hunt House. "We must."

~

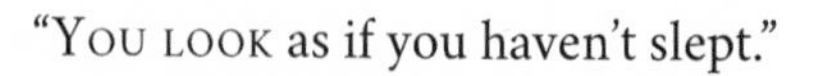

"YOU LOOK as if you haven't slept."

The unkind observation was issued by Archer Tierney as Theo settled into a chair in the other man's study.

He met the green-eyed stare that never failed to see too much without flinching. "That's because I haven't."

He and Tierney had known each other for several years. It hadn't been long after Theo's arrival in London, broken and exiled and angry at the world, that he had crossed paths with the then-moneylender. Tierney's ruthless reputation had preceded him. Theo had proven his mettle by *encouraging* those who owed him money to repay their debts. One fist at a time. Their association had been informal and forged in steel ever since.

Tierney raised a brow, taking a long pull from a cheroot. "More mysterious housebreakers with broken necks at Hunt House?"

"None," he reported.

More like one luscious goddess of a woman who had all but brought him to his knees with her kisses. But he wasn't about to admit to his shocking lack of discipline where Lady Deering had been concerned. If there was anything he'd learned from his uncle's torture, it was to hold his damned tongue.

"Did you see anything suspicious last night?" Tierney asked, eyes narrowing as he studied Theo.

He hesitated a moment longer than he should have in answering the question, his thoughts drawn as ever to the woman who had been haunting his every second since they had parted in the night. Hunger for her, a need to possess, to protect, surged. He should have known better than to think fate could be ignored. His first warning had been in the afternoon when he'd spied her sketching in the salon, barefoot and beautiful.

"You did see something," Tierney guessed shrewdly. "What was it?"

"Only someone who mistook me for another housebreaker," he said swiftly, keeping his expression guarded, his tone even.

"Surely not Ridgely?"

"No." Theo shook his head, not elaborating.

He didn't want to think about Lady Deering. Didn't want to linger over that fateful meeting. He'd do best to forget it had ever happened.

"One of the servants, then?" Tierney guessed next, apparently unwilling to allow the matter to go undissected.

Damn it, Tierney could go on guessing all afternoon. And that would only serve to prolong his suffering.

"His Grace's sister," Theo allowed, his voice curt.

He was being careful, so very careful, to keep any evidence of what had passed between them from his expression. Tierney wasn't a man who was easily fooled, and he understood far more than most. He was inherently intelligent for someone who had lived much of his life in the brutish stews of the rookeries. But then, he would have had to be, to have risen as he had from the depths.

"Ah, the widowed Lady Deering," Tierney said slowly, his look turning assessing.

It occurred to him that Tierney was on friendly terms with the Duke of Ridgely. There was every possibility that Tierney knew Lady Deering. Perhaps more than knew her.

A sudden possessive burst overwhelmed him.

"Are you acquainted with the marchioness?" he asked, far more sharply than he had intended.

Another raised brow, another contemplative puff on his cheroot. "No." He flashed Theo the devil's own grin. "But perhaps I ought to be."

Theo's fingers bit into the arms of the chair until his knuckles went white, and he clenched his jaw tight to stave off words he shouldn't say. Words that laid claim to her when he had neither the right nor the true intention of doing either.

He inhaled slowly, thinking of how perfectly her lips had molded to his, as if they had been meant for him, and forced out different words instead. "As it pleases you."

"Hmm." Tierney stroked his jaw idly.

Theo held his gaze, refusing to give any more of himself away than he already had. Of all the men he'd come to know since finding his home in the bowels of London and being, effectively, born again, Theo trusted Tierney best. But there was nothing to tell.

He'd kissed a beautiful woman last night. Had allowed himself to become distracted by the long-dead memory of what it felt like to desire a woman when he'd been a whole man, a prince instead of a monster. It wouldn't happen again.

"The rest of the men," Tierney said at length. "Have they reported anything amiss?"

Of the half dozen men they had assigned to guard Hunt House, not one had reported even a hint of danger. But they would be prepared for it when, or if, it happened.

"Nothing," he confirmed. "What of the investigation? Have you learned who the dead man is?"

In a rather unusual development, the would-be assassin who had attempted to attack the Duke of Ridgely in his sleep had been unknown to the duke. Which meant the man had been hired by someone.

"Not yet," Tierney said enigmatically. "I'll expect another report at the same time tomorrow. If anyone sees anything untoward, if there's a bloody sneeze in the night, send word to me."

Theo inclined his head, for he was being paid handsomely to do whatever Tierney asked of him. "If that is all, I should return."

Although returning was the last thing he wanted to do.

What he wanted—*needed*—was to be as far away from Lady Deering as possible.

"Just a moment, if you please," Tierney said, granting him a momentary reprieve. "There's someone who's been making inquiries about you."

"I'm afraid my services aren't available at the moment," he said wryly, for he had no notion of how long he would be needed at Hunt House, and he intended to fulfill his contract, even if it damn well killed him.

He had survived his uncle's dungeon. He could survive a few more days or weeks without succumbing to the temptation to touch one widowed marchioness.

"It's not your services that have been asked after," Tierney said.

Someone from Boritania, then? It seemed unlikely after the intervening years, and yet the past was never far from his thoughts. Damned difficult to forget when every day, he had to see the tracery of scars covering his body.

Theo went cold, that old, familiar knot of dread tightening in his gut. "Who was asking?"

Tierney watched him with a curious expression, rather akin to a cat studying a mouse, awaiting the moment when he might pounce. "A lady."

Not his uncle. Thank Christ. Theo had vowed that if he ever looked upon his uncle again, it would be with his dagger sunk deep between the bastard's ribs, watching his lifeblood spew from his mouth as he choked on it.

But a woman? That hardly made sense.

"What is her name?" he asked, struggling to keep the intensity of his reaction from showing on his countenance.

"She claims to be Her Royal Highness, Princess Anastasia Augustina St. George."

"Stasia?" His pet name for her fled him before he could help it, so great was his shock.

He could scarcely credit it. His sister was in London? How and when had she escaped their uncle's tyrannical rule?

Tierney calmly exhaled a cloud of smoke. "A mercenary who knows a Boritanian princess. Rather an intriguing development if you ask me."

"When did she come to you?" Theo asked, ignoring the pointed question in the other man's words.

Tierney was no fool, but Theo wasn't in the mood to discuss the particulars of his violent past as a former prince. Not now, not ever. He'd buried that part of himself long ago.

"Yesterday," Tierney said mildly, inhaling from his cheroot.

His gut churned. He'd never thought their uncle would allow any of his sisters to leave Boritania alive. They were far too useful as pawns, just like his brother Reinald. And Gustavson would be able to marry them off to other rulers and increase his own power and position. Had Stasia somehow fled?

"Why should you think she was looking for me?" he demanded.

"Because she said she was searching for her brother." Tierney tossed his cheroot into the grate of the fireplace as calmly as if they were discussing what he'd eaten for lunch. "The exiled Prince Theodoric Augustus St. George, a man she had reason to believe has been living in London and calling himself Beast."

Damn it.

He struggled to maintain his composure, to show not a hint of his rising inner turmoil. "I've never heard of him."

"Indeed," Tierney drawled. "And what am I to tell the princess, should she lower herself to pay me another call?"

Theo rose, needing to leave. Needing air and space and freedom. Needing to get the hell away from the demons he'd thought he had outrun. The demons that had suddenly reappeared, threatening to drag him back down to the bowels of hell.

Not this time, he vowed inwardly. Theo had fought too hard, had survived too much, to surrender without a fight.

He held the other man's feral green gaze. "Tell her that her brother is dead. I killed him myself."

With that, he took his leave.

CHAPTER 5

Pamela returned from her shopping expedition exhausted, irritable, and in a grim mood. But despite her lack of sleep the night before, she knew there was no solace to be found in a nap. Instead, she delivered a much-wearied Lady Virtue to the safety of her bedchamber. After making certain that Ridgely was not at home and there was no danger of him skulking about Hunt House, ready to practice more of his rakish wiles upon his innocent ward, she ventured to her own rooms to retrieve her folio and porte-crayon.

On days such as this, when she felt as prickly as an embroidery needle, she often found solace in her drawings. Despite the chill of the late-afternoon air, she gathered a wrap and slipped outside into the calming quiet of the Hunt House gardens. Its unique position on a sprawling parcel set back from the streets afforded room aplenty. Her father had spared no expense on the spectacle of Hunt House, from its massive carved staircase, to its painted ceilings within. But it was out of doors, in the garden, that Pamela had always found herself most at home.

Gravel paths led gracefully through intricately planned plantings of hollyhocks, roses, and columbines. Although the flowers had lost their blooms, some of their greenery remained. As always, she wound her way to the farthest corner of the gardens, to where a small stone bench was situated along a neatly trimmed boxwood hedge and a triple-tiered fountain whose cheerful gurgling sounds provided soothing accompaniment.

She settled herself on the bench, opened her folio, and chose the black chalk end of her porte-crayon to begin. In her solitude, Pamela found her mind wandering back to the source of her distress.

Beast.

She hadn't seen him since he'd slipped through the night and left her chamber. Not that she had been looking for him. Indeed, she had spent the entirety of her day ensuring she would *not* see him, until she had finally acknowledged there was only so much shopping even she could indulge in during the course of one afternoon.

She wasn't going to draw him.

She needed no reminders of what had passed between them, and when he was gone from Hunt House and nothing more than a regret looming in the darkest corners of her mind, she hardly would wish to page through her folio and see his face.

And yet, her crayon moved over the paper, seemingly with a will of its own. Despite her best intentions, there was soon the roughly outlined figure of a man looming on the salon's threshold. Perhaps if she committed him to the page, she could expunge him from her mind, she reasoned, adding the broad lines of his shoulders, the long sweep of his legs.

She was so consumed by her task that she failed to hear the crunching of soles on gravel above the din of the splashing fountain until a long shadow fell across her folio.

Pamela glanced up, expecting to see her brother, for Ridgely often joined her in the garden when she was drawing.

A cool, hauntingly familiar stare met hers, sending shock and awareness coursing through her.

He stopped, his angular countenance an impassive mask, and offered her a bow that would have put any lord to shame. "Lady Deering."

She snapped her folio closed and rose from the bench, clutching it to her bodice, hoping he hadn't taken note of the subject she had been sketching. "Sir. What are you doing in the gardens?"

He was the last person she had expected to intrude upon her solitude. And now that he was here, a queer sensation had begun, low in her belly. One she recognized as the prelude to desire. Curse him for the most unwanted effect he had upon her. If only he were not as handsome by the afternoon light as she had recalled. But he was only more compelling than she had remembered, exuding a magnetism that forced her to recall every second of last night, his body pinning hers to the wall, his mouth feeding her kisses until she had turned into a wanton she scarcely recognized.

"I'm searching them," he said simply.

Pamela blinked, trying to call to her mind what they had been speaking of, and realizing belatedly that she had asked him why he was in the gardens.

"For me?" she asked, so startled by the notion that her voice emerged higher than was natural.

Good heavens, she sounded like a giddy girl, when she was a matronly widow. What was wrong with her?

That hazel gaze slid to her lips before flicking back to hers. "For intruders, my lady."

How mortifying. Her cheeks went hot, and she was grateful she was wearing a bonnet to cover the evidence of her humiliation. All this silliness, over a trifling kiss or two.

She was no inexperienced virgin. She had kissed before. Had been more than familiar with the marriage bed. What had happened between the two of them last night had been scarcely anything at all.

"Of course," she murmured, doing her utmost to keep her embarrassment from showing. "I will leave you to your task."

When she moved to skirt around him, however, he stepped before her, blocking her escape. "You needn't go on my account. I'll be gone soon enough, leaving you to your drawing."

He had seen her sketching, then. She hoped he hadn't looked closely at the page. That he hadn't realized she had been drawing him. That she had been thinking of him or chasing thoughts of him from her mind almost every waking second since their encounter. And every sleeping one, too.

She tilted up her chin, pinning him with the cold look she gave to anyone who dared to overstep. "Were you spying on me?"

His lips—so full and perfectly formed, sinfully so—twitched, as if he suppressed a smile. "Why should I wish to do that, Marchioness?"

She wished he would call her something else. No one referred to her as *Marchioness*. It felt wrong, particularly after the intimacies they had shared. But she could hardly ask him to be familiar, to use her Christian name.

She stifled the impulse.

"I cannot say, sir." She tilted her head, considering him. "Perhaps you ought to tell me. It seems rather as if you have been following me since your arrival. I can only suppose why."

Another quirk of his mouth. Just the corners. She wondered if he ever *truly* smiled. There was something harsh about his face, as if mirth would break him. He was like a forbidding statue, hewn from cold, impenetrable marble. Only, she knew how very hot he was to the touch.

"Following you, my lady?"

It was a ridiculous accusation, and she had known it when her pride had forced it from her tongue. How much easier it would be to pretend their every interaction had been spurred by him. To feign icy disinterest. To act as if she were entirely unaffected by his presence when secretly, her heart was pounding hard and fast, and desire had begun slithering through her, as insidious as any serpent.

"Yes," she responded crisply. "How else do you explain your continued presence when it is least wanted?"

What a liar she was. Already, she could feel awareness settling over her like a mantle. Gliding down her spine like warm honey. Her mouth tingled with remembrance of his possessive, masterful kisses, and every part of her longed for his touch.

"As I recall it, last night, you were the one following me," he pointed out, cocking his head so that the faint strains of sun filtering through the gray skies overhead caught in his hair, bringing out strands of gold that were mixed with the rich brown. "And brandishing a fire iron with the intent to maim me."

Why wasn't he wearing a hat as an ordinary gentleman would do? She had no wish to take note of such intricacies of detail. She had no use for them.

"As you may also recall, I had no notion who was prowling about in the night beyond my chamber door. I was only seeking to protect myself and my home."

"You truly want to revisit what happened, Marchioness?"

His question had her in such a state that Pamela dropped her porte-crayon. It landed in the gravel at her feet with a metallic clink, and when she bent to retrieve it, her folio fell as well, the leather-bound volume cracking open to the page she had been working upon when he had appeared.

Cheeks stinging, she made to snatch it up, but Beast had knelt as well. The realization had her jerking her eyes to his. At this proximity, both of them lowered to their haunches, they were at the same height. A breeze kicked up, bringing his scent to tease her senses.

He had not shaved again this morning, the evidence of the omission shading his strong jaw. The absurd urge rose to run her fingers over it, to test the prickle of his whiskers against her fingertips. Bertie had always been cleanly shaven by his valet each morning. She'd never felt even the hint of stubble. That she should be so close to another man, thinking of such intimacies, should be shocking. Her mind had not caught upon the complexities of another man's morning ablutions until this very moment.

"You, sir, are a scoundrel," she told him with not nearly enough bite.

Her words sounded hushed. Almost breathless. She hated herself. Hated him. Hated the way he made her feel.

"I'm a great many things, Lady Deering," he told her, taking up her folio with a show of care that took her by surprise.

How gently he touched it, as if it were fashioned of spun gold rather than leather and paper. Her hasty sketch work taunted her from the opened page, the lines of his form, the doorway surrounding him. She saw it so clearly when she looked upon it, the black marks of her chalk mocking her. Bringing more heat to flood her cheeks.

"My sketchbook, if you please," she said, extending her hand to receive it, palm up.

But he didn't return it to her as she had demanded.

Instead, he lingered, perusing her with a thoughtful sweep of his cool eyes that made her feel as if he had run his hands over her body. “I’m surprised you’re wearing slippers today. I thought you preferred to draw in bare feet.”

A surge of indignation rushed through her. How dare he refer to her feet? To her lack of stockings and shoes yesterday?

But just as quickly as her outrage peaked, it faltered. For she realized how silly it was, to fret over her toes when she had kissed him as boldly as any strumpet. When she had, as he had so boldly phrased it, had her tongue in his mouth.

“A lack of footwear is inadvisable out of doors,” she told him, grateful to have found her wits.

For the composure she somehow managed to cling to in the face of his stunning magnetism. He was so potently, powerfully male. And his features, his mannerisms, were quite different from the gentlemen of her acquaintance. She was accustomed to preening fops with starched shirt points and staid widowers who rambled on about the need for a second wife whenever they tried to lure her to their beds. She had withstood them all. Every invitation, every lewd look, each intimation. No one had turned her head.

“I can imagine how it would sting, the sharp points of these stones against your soft skin,” he commented, snapping her folio closed.

She would have demanded how he knew whether or not her skin was soft, but that would be reckless. He knew because he had touched her. The sensation of his hand wrapped around her bare thigh was emblazoned upon her flesh. Her gaze slipped to his long fingers, to the ring on his forefinger that she had felt intimately gliding over her, and yearned to have those hands on her body again.

“Of course it would,” she snapped, shaking herself from the reverie but not able to banish the desire. She moved her fingers in an impatient gesture. “My folio, if you please.”

But he didn’t relinquish it as she had expected he would.

Instead, he trailed his fingertips over the leather cover, the gesture somehow idle and yet sensual all at once. "Do you draw often, Marchioness?"

She plucked the folio from his grasp quite rudely, grappling for the self-preservation and sangfroid that had both fled her the moment he had arrived on the path. "It's no concern of yours what I do."

"Hmm." His noncommittal hum nettled her, but he seemed remarkably unaffected by both her proximity and her ire as he reached for her fallen porte-crayon, retrieved it, and offered it to her as well. "What bothers you more, the fact that you kissed me back last night, or the fact that you enjoyed it?"

His question, issued so calmly, took her aback.

Made heat flood between her legs.

"I didn't," she lied as she snatched the porte-crayon from his grasp, once more unable to utter the word *kiss* in his presence.

To give voice to what had passed between them in the darkness.

"You didn't kiss me back, or you didn't enjoy it?"

Heat crept up her throat, and she was sure she was red as the roses that had withered on the bushes behind her when they were in full bloom. "Neither." Her distress was so great that she didn't even know what she was saying. "Both," she corrected.

Why was she lingering here, crouched in this position, continuing to engage with a lowly guard who called himself Beast? Surely he had a given name. He didn't look like a beast at all to her just now. In fact, he looked quite appallingly gorgeous. He was even dressed as a gentleman, in black trousers and a crisp white shirt beneath his coat and waistcoat that only served to enhance the mysterious color of his eyes.

He smiled then, robbing her mind of all capacity for reason. The smile was slow and bold and knowing. Good heavens. She felt the full effect of it in her belly, between her legs, down to her toes.

Everywhere.

If Beast had been handsome before when he was cold and menacing, he was beautiful when his sinfully formed lips curved upward.

"Which is it, Marchioness?"

His tone was not light, and yet, she imagined that it was the way he might speak to a lady he was courting. A voice he would use in the ballroom beneath the glitter of blazing chandeliers. She swallowed hard against a powerful flood of attraction and pure, unadulterated lust.

Lust? How mortifying. How shameful. She had to gather what remained of her dignity and flee.

"You are insolent, sir," she told him, summoning all the cutting coldness that had served her well these last few years as she had resumed her role in society.

Pamela rose then to her full height, so quickly that she was almost lightheaded. Or perhaps that was merely the effect of this seductive man's nearness. His words. His smile. She shook her head as he rose to his feet as well, towering over her with ease.

"And you like it," he told her boldly, his gaze sweeping over her form and making fire lick through her veins. "Good day, Lady Deering."

Another bow, and then he was gone, leaving her standing alone on the path, more shaken than she'd ever been.

Because he was not wrong. She did like his brazenness, his touch, his kiss. She liked everything about him far too much. He tempted her. Melted her. And she could never allow whatever this nonsense was between them to progress any farther than it already had.

~

"HAVE you anything new to report, Beast?" the Duke of Ridgely asked with a calm Theo wouldn't have expected from a man who had nearly been attacked in his bed two nights before.

Dressed in evening finery, he was, from head to well-polished toe, the consummate English gentleman. He possessed a congenial air of perpetual amusement, as if he were so jaded with the world that he had decided to regard the entire affair as one big joke solely for his entertainment. Theo had liked him from the moment they had met, even when the other man had been clearly shaken by the events that had led to Theo and his men being hired.

He knew a stab of guilt that he had kissed the duke's sister. Repeatedly. That he had been alone with her in her chamber the night before. That he knew the sounds of surrender she made, the soft, breathy sighs. What she tasted like, the sweet, seductive weight of her breast in his palm.

He cleared his throat, struggling to maintain his composure for the third time that day, which was precisely three times too damned many. "Nothing new as of yet, Your Grace. I have thoroughly inspected the perimeter of Hunt House, and I've stationed my men at all areas I've deemed most vulnerable."

Ridgely gave him a wry look. "We've vulnerabilities? I confess, I rather thought my sire had commissioned a fortress. An homage to his colossal sense of self-importance, as it were."

It wasn't for Theo to investigate Ridgely's relationship with the previous duke, but he could relate to the apathy he heard in the other man's voice, tinged with a hint of all-too-human bitterness. One undeniable truth was that, regardless of anyone's station in life, every man, woman, and child was every bit as capable of feeling the same emotions that plagued the classes above and below them. He had learned that lesson in most brutal fashion.

"The garden presents an opportunity, particularly for someone with nefarious purposes to hide and then gain entry through another means under the cover of darkness," he said instead of offering solace or commiseration, as he might have done a lifetime ago when he would have outranked the Duke of Ridgely. "The entrance from the mews is quite vulnerable as well, as there are many who come and go from it, and the stables are not as secure as they ought to be. Then, there are the doors beneath the terrace on the western façade. I've seen to it that guards have been posted at each of these locations."

"Hell." The duke's devil-may-care mask slipped, and he appeared, for the first time, incredibly weary as he raked a hand through his hair. "I hadn't thought of any of those places. Little wonder someone nearly killed me in my bed. Too much time as a duke makes a man mutton-headed. I must present a fine, fat goose for the plucking."

"Perhaps not a fat goose, Your Grace," he allowed, unsmiling. "But a goose, nonetheless."

The duke's gaze narrowed. "You're an odd one, aren't you? Not one to mince words. I rather like that. Sincerity is a rarity in society these days."

He inclined his head. "I wouldn't know."

"Of course you wouldn't. Not the sort of chap to gad about at balls, are you?" Ridgely gave him an appraising look. "You seem as if you'd be more at home with a dagger in your hand than a walking stick."

"I'll not deny it." Theo felt a small smile tug at his lips that the duke had taken his measure so easily. He prided himself on his ability to remain mysterious and impenetrable. The less anyone knew or thought about him, the better. Which was why his preoccupation with the widowed Marchioness of Deering was fast becoming a problem.

Not the only reason, however. The list, it seemed, could carry on for miles, wrapping itself about all the thoroughfares of London before turning north.

"Tierney says you're the best, and I've never known him to be wrong," Ridgely said. "Would you care for a brandy? God knows I need one after the last two days, and I hate to drink alone unless I haven't a choice."

"No brandy, thank you, Your Grace," he denied, for he scarcely ever imbibed now.

There had been a time when he had drowned himself in liquor and indolence. When he had allowed his guard to fall because he had been too deep in his cups to know the difference between a snake and a blade of grass. But he knew the difference now, and he wasn't going to repeat the mistake. Once had almost been deadly.

"Blast," Ridgely muttered. "Good fellow. I suppose you've more important matters to attend to this evening. Do you sleep, Beast? I swear I've seen you prowling the halls at all hours of the day and night."

"Very little when I'm at a post."

And when he wasn't as well, but that was none of Ridgely's concern either. His kindness was misplaced; Theo didn't deserve it. Indeed, if the duke had any notion of the thoughts which had been passing through Theo concerning his sister ever since last night, he would have challenged him to a duel instead of offering him a brandy.

He shouldn't have lingered in the garden with her earlier. The moment he had spied her on that bench, chewing on her full, sweet lower lip as her chalk had flown over the folio in her lap, he should have left. Instead, he had gone closer, drawn to her as ever, telling himself it was all in the name of the duty he performed when the truth was far less selfless.

He had gone to her because he had been hungry for the sultry lilt of her voice. For the scent of her perfume on the breeze. Because he was so taken with her that he would seize upon any excuse for the chance to clash with her.

"Your dedication is commendable," Ridgely said, intruding on Theo's thoughts and filling him with a fresh wave of guilt that threatened to drown him.

"If you don't require anything else of me this evening, Your Grace, I should return to my post," he managed.

"Of course," Ridgely said easily, "you are a free man, sir. I'll not force you to tarry any longer."

"Thank you," Theo said, rising and offering a bow.

The duke was wrong, however. He wasn't a free man. He hadn't been since the day he'd been born the heir to the king of Boritania. He wasn't now. As he took his leave of the duke's study, his mind drifted again to thoughts of his sister. Stasia was in London. Close. Close enough to find him if she truly wished it. But he didn't know what her sudden arrival or her questions about him truly meant. It had been over ten years since he had last spoken with his sister, since well before he had been taken to their uncle's dungeon. Although they had been close once, it was entirely likely that she had become one of their uncle's minions, if for no reason other than self-preservation.

No, he hadn't been wrong in telling Tierney that Stasia's brother was dead. Because the Theo she had known was gone forever. He had died somewhere on the floor of that cold, stone dungeon beneath the August Palace, died as his lifeblood had seeped from the lashes and cuts and burns on his body and the infection had taken hold.

He was far better in the present, even if there was a maddening widow tempting him beyond measure beneath this same roof. Theo chastised himself for his stupidity again and again as he threw himself into the task of making certain

Hunt House was secure. Even if the widowed Lady Deering was amenable to an illicit tumble or two, he couldn't truly be intimate with a woman.

Not with his hideously scarred hide.

She deserved better, were she inclined to lower herself to bedding a nameless bodyguard who had been tasked with keeping her brother's home free of assassins. Better than a broken man haunted by the evils that had been visited upon him. She deserved a soft-palmed lord who could whisper sonnets in her ear and spoil her with gifts and jewels and whatever else it was that made a woman like her smile.

He hadn't seen her smile yet.

It shocked him to realize how much he wanted to watch those pretty pink lips turn up, to watch the ice in her eyes melt into brilliant heat.

What a damned fool he was.

The hour grew later, and Theo told himself he would stay away from the private hall where Lady Deering's chamber was situated. Told himself no good could come from another meeting between the two of them in the night.

He stopped to speak with the two men he had stationed in the halls belowstairs where the entrances from the gardens were scarcely used and ripe for invasion. Thomas and Richard reassured him that nothing untoward had occurred. The night had been quiet, nothing but the occasional scuffle of a mouse skittering along the cold cellar floors.

He left the capable men behind and ventured to the mews, where something of a commotion was unfolding despite the lateness of the hour. His booted footsteps carried him nearer as he heard one of the grooms speaking to the stablemaster, and *her* name reached him on the cool night air.

"...Lady Deering's carriage...damaged badly..."

His strides increased in speed.

"How is her ladyship faring?" the stablemaster was asking the groom.

"Well enough," the groom said. "None too pleased about being left on the street, I expect. I told her I'd fetch some help and return."

"Mark Coachman is waiting with her?"

By Deus. The marchioness had been stranded somewhere in a damaged carriage at this late hour? Fear crept up his throat, along with a surge of protectiveness.

He approached the groom and coachman. "What has happened?"

The groom gave him a look tinged with suspicion. "And who are you, wanting to know?"

"I'm the guard assigned to watch over this house and everyone in it, including Lady Deering," he bit out. "Now tell me what's happened."

The groom looked to the stablemaster, who nodded, for they were already on familiar terms after Theo's extensive exploration of the mews. "He's called Beast, and he's trustworthy. Tell him what's happened to Lady Deering's carriage."

"There's a problem with the rear wheel," the groom reported. "A large hole in the road couldn't be avoided on account of the street traffic, and the coachman hit it. He doesn't dare travel farther until the wheel is repaired, for her ladyship's safety."

It occurred to Theo that there was a possibility the duke's carriage had been tampered with, causing damage to the wheels on an uneven surface of road. Perhaps the person who wanted Ridgely dead had grown more creative after their previous attempts—which had begun before the death of the man on the staircase, with Ridgely being set upon in the street.

And if so, that could mean Lady Deering was in danger.

His gut clenched. "Who is there to offer her ladyship protection?"

"There is Mark Coachman," the groom said, not allaying Theo's fears.

For he had met the coachman, and the fellow was thin as a whip and white-haired and didn't appear as if he could harm anything of greater substance than a fly. "Take me to her."

CHAPTER 6

Waiting in a cold carriage with a damaged wheel was decidedly not the way Pamela had hoped to end her evening. Lady Virtue had pleaded exhaustion following their lengthy shopping expedition, and after her unexpected clash with Beast in the gardens, she had decided to venture to an intimate supper being held by her friend Lady Penwicke. Selina was a devoted patroness of the arts, and as usual, she had peopled her dinner party with a host of intriguing poets and artists.

It had been an excellent distraction and just the cure for the restlessness ailing her. Pamela had imbibed a trifle too much wine, lost too much money at whist, stayed later than was polite chatting into the evening, and laughed louder than was ladylike on more than one occasion. Dear Selina was forever courting the razor's edge of scandal, and although Pamela could never imagine allowing herself to be so daring, she secretly admired her friend's fast ways. Even if the rest of their set didn't approve of Selina's increasing boldness.

However, all her delight in the evening and her ability to banish thoughts from a maddening, mysterious-eyed stranger had been dashed the moment the carriage had struck that dreadful hole in the street. The carriage had thudded mightily, shaking her from the silk tabberett squabs and sending her crashing to the floor. She'd landed on her rump, which still ached dreadfully from the sudden impact.

And now she was waiting.

Peering out into the night through the Venetian blinds covering the carriage window, hoping no enterprising cutpurse would come along and run off with her reticule. Or worse.

She shivered at the chill in the air, which would not have been nearly so cold had she arrived at Hunt House in the time her trip should have taken. Would have taken, had not the Hole of Doom interfered in an otherwise thoroughly lovely evening. Mark Coachman had been very apologetic for not being able to maneuver the carriage out of the way in time. A groom had been dispatched to Hunt House. And Pamela was waiting, toes growing ever colder in her slippers.

The din of masculine voices reached her then, piercing her thoughts and sending hope to chase the knot of dread residing in her belly. She had supposed she would be made to linger in the carriage for longer yet, waiting for the groom to carry out his task.

But just as quickly as her hope had risen, the opening of the carriage door sent it fleeing. For there, framed in the flickering glow of the carriage lamps, was a man she recognized all too well. Not the fresh-faced groom who had leapt from the box with the promise to return in all haste. Rather, a ridiculously handsome man whose countenance looked as if it had been chiseled in marble.

The man she had been doing her utmost to avoid, both in thought and presence.

"Beast," she said, dismayed.

"My lady," he returned, looking and sounding characteristically grim. "Are you well?"

Well? How could she be when he was here? Warmth suffused her as his cool stare passed over her form as if he were searching for any hint of injury. What was he doing at her carriage at this hour of the night, appearing as if he were some knight of old riding to her rescue? Why would Ridgely have sent him? Did he not know the inherent danger of leaving a woman alone with a man as deviously alluring as Beast?

When she didn't answer with sufficient haste, he leveraged himself into the carriage with graceful ease, quite crowding her as he seated himself at her side. "Lady Deering? Is aught amiss?"

Yes, everything was amiss.

Because she was a trifle in her cups just now from all the wine she had imbibed at Selina's supper, and because his thigh was pressing against hers in intimate fashion. And because she could not bring herself to slide away from him on the squabs and create a proper distance.

She found her voice at last. "I'm well enough for a lady who has been left in her broken carriage at midnight."

Particularly after the man who had arrived to offer her assistance was the last man she would have chosen for the job.

"You're uninjured?" he demanded, his voice low and soft.

For her ears alone. Although he was brusque, his countenance every bit as bereft of any hint of cheer as always, there was an underlying tone in his voice that was new. Dare she think it was concern? For her?

She sniffed, telling herself she was a ninny. "I'm tired, sir. Tell me why you've come."

"To take you home." He offered her his hand, ungloved, palm up. "I'll help you alight."

Pamela didn't want to touch him, because even with the barrier of her own kid gloves, she feared the effect it would have upon her. She kept her hands in her lap.

"I don't require your help."

"Didn't say you did, but I'm offering it just the same."

He stared at her, unsmiling, a lone brow raised, and it occurred to her that he wasn't dressed for the out-of-doors. He hadn't a greatcoat or even a hat, quite as if he had dashed away from Hunt House to find her the moment he'd heard of her plight.

Despite her every intention to guard herself against him, something softened inside her. She found herself relenting. If she refused him now, she would only seem a churl.

Reluctantly, she settled her hand in his, unprepared for the sensation that overcame her when he laced his fingers through hers, the indisputable rightness of it.

"Very well," she allowed, her voice a husky rasp that she couldn't hide.

"Come. I'll drive you home, and the grooms and coachman will see to the carriage."

She obeyed, allowing him to gently guide her from the carriage, out into the street where Ridgely's prized new cabriolet awaited. The conveyance was small, suitable for only two—one driver and a passenger—and pulled by a lone horse. It was the sort of vehicle she had imagined her brother might use for courting, or perhaps even to squire about a mistress. Not a means of transportation for a proper widow in the night, alone with a man who was far too enticing.

But Beast didn't seem inclined to allow her time to contemplate the wisdom of taking such a route home. He began pulling her toward the cabriolet. He was still holding her hand, and they were in the midst of town, where any passing carriage might see the Marchioness of Deering being led away by a disreputable rogue.

"You cannot think to drive me home," she protested. "Anyone will be able to see I'm riding alone with a strange gentleman at midnight."

"Let them see." He continued on without hesitation, pulling her with him.

She tugged her hand free, stopping. "I have no wish for scandal."

"Do you wish to remain on the street all night long instead?" he asked, a gust of wind ruffling his hair, the carriage lamplight making his eyes glisten.

Surely he was cold, and yet he had ventured out to find her. What a strange man he was, so aloof and yet capable of such passion, seemingly unconcerned and yet protective.

"I hardly think it will take all night to repair the wheel," she protested.

He stepped nearer to her suddenly, lowering his head so their faces were close. "Madam, your brother is in danger, and it's possible that you are as well. I'll not be leaving you here to the mercy of cutthroats and villains."

The stark reminder was akin to a fist closing on her heart. She couldn't forget the true reason for this man's intrusion into her life. Someone wanted to harm her brother. The danger was very real. And even so, Beast wasn't giving her a choice. Another breeze whipped her wrap around her, cold air licking at her ankles and calves beneath her petticoats and gown.

"My reputation," she said, still feeling as if she couldn't simply give in, knowing how unwise it would be. "No doubt you haven't a concern for yours, but a widow's place in society is never certain."

A stray curl blew free from her chignon, flying from beneath her bonnet to catch on her cheek. Before she could tuck it away, Beast's fingers were there, grazing her cheek, callused and cool, touching her with a tenderness she wouldn't have expected. He slid the tendril behind her ear.

"It's cold and growing colder," he said quietly. "You'll take a chill if you linger any longer."

The change in him was having an odd effect upon her. She hadn't expected his worry, his gentleness. It was almost as if he had a care for her, which was silly, because they scarcely knew each other. They'd shared nothing more than a few ill-advised kisses.

"Why did Ridgely send you to me?" Pamela asked, frustrated with herself for her vulnerability where this man was concerned. Frustrated, too, with her brother for leaving her with no choice but to accompany Beast back to Hunt House.

Surely, he must have known how wrong it would be for her to have to ride in proximity to the guard. To be seen escorted through the night with him. If anyone with a wagging tongue passed them, she would be instantly pitched headlong into scandal. And as for her ability to continue chaperoning Lady Virtue... Well, it would be equally destroyed.

"Ridgely didn't send me to you," Beast said quietly, sullenly.

She frowned, shivering as another ripple of wind tore past them. Although Mark Coachman and the grooms were already at work behind them on the coach wheel, and carriages rumbled past on the street, she couldn't shake the sense that they were the only two people in the moment.

"Then who did?"

"I sent myself, Marchioness." He took her hand in his, not even asking permission this time, linking their fingers together. "Now come before you take ill in this cold. I'll see you home."

Bemused, Pamela followed him to the cabriolet, allowing him to lead her to the waiting conveyance. His revelation was heightening her confusion, multiplying the feelings deep inside her that she was so struggling to ignore. He had come to her of his own accord.

Why? Because he had wanted to help her? Because he had feared for her safety? Or had he only done so out of a sense of obligation? Oh, why should she even care about the reason? It mattered not. She had no intention of acting upon this inconvenient attraction she felt for him. Not on the ride back to Hunt House, and not ever.

Beast helped Pamela up, and she perched on the seat, watching as he swiftly climbed into the cabriolet and settled at her side. Yet again, his lean thigh pressed against hers through the civilized layers of fabric separating them, and just as before, she was not nearly as unaffected as she would have wished.

Not unaffected at all.

The cabriolet rocked into motion, taking them down the street. She noted he held the reins with an eased, experienced grip, deftly guiding them along the narrow street. The roof of the cabriolet surrounded them, making the ride feel far more intimate than it truly was, for the front half was left open, the cold wind of the night painting her cheeks as they traveled. The carriage lamp shone, highlighting all the sharp angles of his face and glinting off the ring he wore on his forefinger.

He kept his gaze trained upon the road, his lips compressed in a grim line as silence stretched, punctuated only by the clop of the horse's hooves and the jangling of tack. Pamela didn't know if it was the wine she'd consumed, bubbling up inside her and filling her with recklessness, or if it was merely the man at her side who had such an effect upon her, but she was suddenly rather nettled that he had come to her rescue, only to ignore her.

"Are you not going to speak to me, now that you've had

your way?" she asked curtly, clutching her reticule and her wrap in a white-knuckled grasp.

He didn't speak for the span of a few hoof clops.

"I haven't had my way, Marchioness," Beast said at last, not even deigning to glance in her direction.

Her gaze dipped and caught again on his hands, so large and capable, holding the reins. The urge to feel them on her was a visceral ache she couldn't control. She wanted them on her, skin to skin.

No, Pamela, she cautioned herself inwardly. *You must not allow yourself to succumb to temptation.*

"It seems to me as if you have," she couldn't resist adding, careful to keep her voice cool. And above all, to cease looking at his hands and thinking about how they would feel, learning her body. "You have coerced me into being paraded about London in the midst of the night with you instead of waiting in the private comfort of my carriage."

"Hmm," was all he said, a noncommittal sound that bordered on a grunt.

More quiet ensued, during which time Pamela became acutely aware of his thigh brushing against hers with each rattle of the cabriolet over the roads. She pressed her knees together in an attempt to keep from touching him, but that only served to heighten the need pulsing between her thighs.

"Why did you come for me?" she blurted, unable to keep from asking the question that continued to prod at her. "If Ridgely didn't send you, and if the groom was already returning with help to repair the coach, why would you seek me out and demand I accompany you to Hunt House?"

Still, he refused to look at her. "Your welfare is my responsibility."

She knew a sharp stab of disappointment at his response, but then she realized it didn't quite pass muster.

Pamela pursed her lips and watched him before adding, "I thought my brother's welfare was your responsibility."

"The safety of everyone in his household is my duty," Beast replied.

His response didn't appease her. If anything, it only increased her frustration and irritation. But then, what had she supposed it meant, him seeking her out? Did her foolishness know no bounds?

"I suppose I must thank you, then," she said acidly. "For doing your duty."

"You needn't." He cast her a quick glance that she couldn't read before returning his eyes to the road. "I'm being paid handsomely by His Grace."

That quite set her teeth on edge. "Of course."

Her voice was tight, even to her own ears. All the warmth that had flooded her at his sudden appearance had fled. He had made it clear that he hadn't been playing the gallant knight riding to her rescue. And that was just as well, for if he had, then what would she do? What could she do?

Nothing. Pamela turned her attention to the darkened street, trying to ignore the possibility that the other carriages passing them could contain someone who would recognize her and carry the tale of this midnight drive to others. She could simply ignore his presence at her side. Keep her gaze averted, her head down. In the shadows, in an unmarked cabriolet, it was likely that no one would know her.

"All the same, I'm happy no harm came to you this evening, Marchioness," he said suddenly, so softly that she almost thought she'd misheard him.

She blinked, her head jerking toward him. But he simply sat there, holding the reins in his grasp as easily as before, gaze straight ahead. There was nothing for her to look at but his handsome profile, which she cursed for being so dratted perfect.

"Undoubtedly, I ought to say something polite in return, but I don't think I like you very much," she told him. "You're likely only pleased nothing ill befell me because it would keep you from your precious coin."

"Hmm," he said again.

And then, he uttered not a word more as the cabriolet rattled through the streets, taking her to Hunt House. Pamela told herself it was just as well. But every jostle of the conveyance that brought their bodies into contact made a liar of her.

CHAPTER 7

Theo told himself he should wander to the chamber he'd been given for the night—one of the less-formal guest bedchambers a floor below Lady Deering's, a nod not to his formerly royal roots but to the fact that the Duke of Ridgely wanted him to be nearer to the sleeping quarters during the night hours. He hadn't slept the night before, and although he had intended to garner a few hours of slumber during the daylight, he hadn't managed it either. Between reporting to Tierney and the duke and taking another assessment of Hunt House, there simply hadn't been the opportunity.

He was weary, and he trusted the men on duty tonight with his life. He knew that no intruder would find his way within the newly fortified walls of the duke's massive town house. And yet, here he was, navigating slowly through the darkened hall on the floor above. Because apparently, having her deliciously curved body rub against him the entire ride in the cabriolet hadn't caused him sufficient anguish.

Every part of him had been yearning to take her in his arms and kiss her as he so longed. To kiss her before every passing carriage and show the damned world that she was his, that he'd laid his claim upon her, as impossible and ridiculous as that foolish notion was.

The Marchioness of Deering would never be his. Could never be his. And anyway, she didn't like him. She'd proclaimed so with cutting certainty on their ride back to Hunt House. He had been sitting at her side, calling upon all the restraint and control he possessed to keep from touching her, looking at her, or worse, hauling her into his lap. All the while, she had been stewing that he had dared to endanger her reputation by driving her home at midnight instead of leaving her to her fate.

There had been a few, brief moments when that same awareness which had struck him at their first meeting had flared between them, the fiery acknowledgment that there was a powerful attraction burning hot and bright. But then she had vanquished it with her ice, and he had held his tongue and bit his cheek to keep from saying anything he'd later regret.

He passed by the chamber he knew was hers, noting the lack of light beneath the door. At least one of them was finding solace in slumber this evening. But he didn't begrudge her the rest. Even when he wasn't at a post, Theo slept as little as possible. The dreams couldn't haunt him when he was awake.

After another pass of the hall, he had satisfied himself that there was no movement, no sounds, and no intruder. Nor was there a golden-haired goddess wielding a fire iron and intending to do him mortal harm.

Pity, that.

He found his way to the cantilevered stone staircase at the heart of Hunt House and descended to the next floor, where lesser guest chambers were mixed with various antechambers. A music room, a salon, a second drawing room which was less grand than the first a floor below it. When he neared the opposite end of the hall, a flickering glow beneath one of the doors captured his attention.

It was damned unlikely that an intruder would have stopped to light spills and illuminate a brace of candles, but one could never entirely be certain when it came to criminals. With a hand on the hilt of the dagger he kept concealed in his waistcoat, Theo stealthily crept down the hall, stopping just short of the closed door. Holding his breath and taking care to move as soundlessly as possible, he reached for the latch and slowly, so slowly, opened the door.

As the portal inched wider, a familiar scene within was revealed to him.

He exhaled and released the cool metal of his dagger, pulling the door open to announce his presence. Lady Deering was draped over a chaise longue, clad in a frothy confection he supposed was meant to be a dressing gown, but which only served to heighten her alluring femininity. She was all sweet, womanly curves and cascading golden locks, bare toes peeping from the hem of her garment, ankles crossed in an indolent pose he'd never seen a lady affect before.

In her lap was the same leather folio he had seen her drawing so furiously in earlier in the garden. She held the porte-crayon in her elegant fingers, her face drawn into an expression of deep concentration. It was in that moment Theo realized that, despite his having opened the door, in spite of his presence on the threshold to the chamber, the marchioness had no inkling that she was no longer alone.

By Deus, she was like a newly hatched duckling ready to fall prey to the gnashing teeth of a vicious, hungry fox. First, she had been abandoned on the street with no protection save an aging coachman. And now, she had failed to notice she was not alone. Unlike the night before when she had set about to brain him, this evening, it seemed as if all her defenses had been toppled to the ground.

Perhaps it had been the wine he'd noticed on her breath earlier. He still could not keep himself from wondering where she had been this evening, and whom she had been with. But that curiosity was every bit as blockheaded as the rest of the nonsense flitting about in his mind, so he ruthlessly forced it away.

Theo cleared his throat quietly, announcing his presence.

With a startled jolt that sent her porte-crayon flying to the Axminster, her gaze flew to his, a gasp falling from her parted lips. Her hand splayed over her heart, drawing his attention to the fullness of her breasts beneath her dressing gown. His cock twitched.

"Sir," she hissed, making no attempt to hide her displeasure at discovering him there, intruding upon her solitude in the private drawing room. "What are you doing here? Do you never sleep?"

He didn't answer her questions, merely strode deeper into the room, allowing the door to fall closed behind him "If I were a villain intent upon doing you harm, I could very easily have done so, given how distracted you were by your sketch. You need to take better care with yourself, Marchioness."

She rose to her feet in a swirl of pale linen. "Who is to say you *aren't* a villain?"

She had a point there. "But not a villain who intends to harm you, my lady."

No, indeed. Harming her was the furthest intention from his mind. Everything he wished to do to her involved a great deal of pleasure. Unfortunately, those things were all doomed to remain lodged inside his head rather than ever coming to fruition.

She bent down to retrieve the implement she had

dropped before straightening and flashing him a cool smile. "As you can see, I am not an intruder, and nor is one skulking about in the corners. The only intruder is standing before me. Shall I fetch a fire iron?"

Was she taunting him? He could scarcely credit it.

Theo drew so near that the faintest hint of her scent teased him. "Not unless you wish to repeat what happened the last time you attempted to brain me, Marchioness."

Her nostrils flared, her chin going up to a defiant angle that made him long to kiss her until all that ice melted to molten flame. "You wouldn't dare."

"Perhaps you'd be surprised by what I'd dare," he told her, stopping before her, holding her stare.

Blue, lush blue. He could lose himself in those eyes with perilous ease. But he was no longer the careless young prince who had flirted and seduced so many eager ladies at court. He hadn't had a lover since coming to England, and he had no intention of taking one now. Not that the icy widow before him would deign to welcome him into her bed.

"I suspect you're a man of many hidden surprises," she said softly, some of the chill in her voice unexpectedly thawing.

More than she could ever imagine, he thought wryly.

But aloud, he offered simply, "Not more than any other man."

Her lips pursed, her eyes narrowing as she considered him with an intensity that made him instinctively want to look away. "I think you are bamming me, sir."

Bamming her? His English was very good, but that was an unfamiliar term, one that evoked incredibly wicked thoughts. He didn't reckon it meant what a certain part of his anatomy hoped it did.

He suppressed the desire threatening to rise. "You seem

the sort of lady who believes whatever she wishes, regardless of what she is told. Believe as you like, Marchioness."

"I shall, and I don't require your approval to do so," she said tartly.

Unbidden, a memory rose of how she had felt in his arms, lush form pressed against him, the wet heat of her on his thigh, the taut bud of her very responsive nipple. Oh, to surrender to needs he'd thought long dead, like the man he'd once been. Her coldness made him yearn to prove just how affected she truly was beneath the frigid pretense of her impassive exterior. He admired her tenacity. Her sharp-wittedness. The way she carried herself, as boldly as any princess.

These were all stupid, fruitless thoughts. Theo chased them from his mind, weariness suddenly weighing upon him and reminding him that he hadn't slept in over a day.

He inclined his head, intending to leave and sever this damned unwanted connection between them. Fate could go to the devil to dance as far as he was concerned.

"I will leave you to your solitude, my lady. I beg your pardon for the interruption." He sketched a half bow.

"You may as well sit," she shocked him by saying.

Theo straightened, wondering if he had misheard her. "Sit?"

"The act of folding one's body and gently lowering it into an accommodating piece of furniture," she said, raising a wheat-colored brow. "Although I've yet to witness you doing so indoors, I trust you are familiar with the practice."

By Deus. She was making a joke. Or making a joke of him. Theo wasn't quite certain which it was, but he wasn't sure it mattered. Lady Deering had invited him to sit with her, and it was well after two o'clock in the morning, and she was wearing only an ethereal dressing gown. His gaze slipped to her bare, pretty toes and he swallowed hard. He should politely refuse and find his bed for a few hours of much-needed slumber.

"I am indeed familiar with the process," he said instead, playing her little game, uncertain what it meant. Loving every moment.

"Then do so, Mr. Beast." Airily, she waved a hand toward a nearby armchair. "Seat yourself, if you please. I'm in need of a subject, and since everyone else is abed, I suppose you shall have to do."

Theo frowned at her. "Not Mr. Beast. Just Beast."

"Is Beast your Christian name, or your surname?" she asked, tilting her head in the manner of a curious bird.

She was stubborn, Lady Deering. He had been living in the shadows for years, and no one had ever questioned him the way she did. No one had ever looked at him as if she were seeing inside him, straight to the ugliness he kept hidden from the world.

"Both," he said, because no one had called him Theo in years, and he didn't think he could bear to hear it on the marchioness's delectable lips.

She huffed a sigh of displeasure and gestured to the chair. "Keep your secrets if you must, but do take a seat. I cannot draw you if you are hovering over me."

Draw him? Ah, yes. She had said she was in need of a subject. His overly stimulated mind hadn't understood the full implications of that. The very thought of remaining seated in her presence for any length of time while she studied him made his cravat and his trousers feel suddenly tight. It was an absurd request, and one he should absolutely ignore. He was already exhausted, likely to the point that he preferred, where he could fall into a bed and sleep the rest of the dreamless dead for the span of a few precious hours.

But his feet were moving, taking him across the carpet, skirting her so narrowly that jasmine and hyacinth filled his head with fire. He stopped before the chair she had requested him to occupy and turned back to find her watching him. She was still standing, and he wondered if she hadn't believed he would obey her edict.

Hell, he hadn't intended to. But here he was.

A small smile curved her full lips, and something deep inside him clenched at the sight. "Just as I said, a man of many surprises." With that pronouncement, she gracefully resumed her seat on the chaise longue, this time with rather less abandon than when he had initially come upon her, carefully tucking her bare feet to the side and making certain they were fully hidden by the hem of her dressing gown.

Even seated as she was, she still looked regal. But somehow less cold and aloof. There was a softness about her he had never seen before, and it struck him that he was seeing her without her shield and coat of armor. That this was how she must look when no one else was about.

"Do sit, Beast."

Feeling stunned, he did as she commanded, resting stiffly on the edge of the cushion, spine straight as a ramrod. He hadn't been seated in an intimate setting with a woman in what felt like a lifetime, and he was suddenly, horribly aware of that fact. Of just how uncivilized he'd become, just how far he had fallen from the prince who had flirted and seduced with an innate ease that was forever lost to him now.

"You look positively ferocious," Lady Deering observed, her brow furrowed.

He felt ferocious. And he felt other things, too. Too many things. Unwanted things.

Forbidden things.

"I am only sitting here at your demand, madam," he reminded her.

She opened her folio, holding the porte-crayon in her slender fingers. "Try to relax, if you please."

Indolence was for men who didn't fear for their lives. It was for the weak and vulnerable. For the man he'd once been.

He placed his forearms on the stuffed rests in an effort to comply with her request. For some reason, the notion of pleasing her filled him with warmth. He wanted to, he realized, the thought itself astonishing.

"How is this, my lady?"

She shook her head. "I'm afraid you still look as if you are about to tear someone in two."

He felt as if he could, just to keep her safe. To keep her here with him in the sanctity of this moment, no one to interrupt.

"How am I meant to look, then?" he asked gruffly, trying his best to banish these inconvenient longings.

Lady Deering sighed. "You're still scowling, you aren't properly sitting in the chair, and your spine is stiffer than a staff."

He glowered at her some more. This was the height of lunacy. It was the bowels of the night, she had told him she didn't like him, and now she was directing him about as if he were a recalcitrant child in her charge.

"What would you have me doing, Marchioness?" he growled. "Dance a cotillion whilst grinning like a Bedlamite?"

Remaining here in the salon with her and indulging her whims had been a mistake. He ought to go at once.

But Lady Deering was huffing out a little sigh of irritation that somehow landed directly in his cock, and then she rose to her feet, padding across the Axminster until she hovered over him with her maddening scent and equally maddening curves. His fingers itched to touch, so he burrowed them into the plush arms of his chair instead.

She had abandoned her folio and porte-crayon on the chaise longue, and he liked to think if he'd have known her intention when she'd risen, he too would have shot up from his chair and made haste in quitting the chamber. Because her small, elegant, ladylike hands were now upon his, as soft as they looked.

"Let go of the chair, if you please," she grumbled, sounding thoroughly put out with him.

And all Theo could think about was that touch, the wonder of her skin against his. Her hands on him. His breath froze in his lungs. She had touched him in the darkness the night before, but he had been so overwhelmed by her kisses that he hadn't felt the full effect sink into his bones. A woman touching him of her own volition—how long had it been? Ages. A lifetime. And not just the touch, but the manner in which she did it, bare fingers plucking nimbly at his as if she truly believed she possessed superior strength, enough to force his hands from the chair if she wished.

He gave in, not because he had to, but because he could. And he wished to please her, to soothe the furrow from her brow. For a moment, she held his hands in hers, her success giving her pause.

"There we are," she said triumphantly. "You were holding on to that chair as if it were your enemy. Isn't this so much..." Her head came up, her gaze colliding with his, and her words trailed off for a moment before she finished them. "Isn't this so much more pleasant?"

"Yes," he agreed. "It is."

But he wasn't talking about releasing the damned chair and relaxing his grip upon it. He was talking about her hands in his. Her proximity. He was talking about the ability to pull her into his lap and take her lips with his.

Which he shouldn't do.

He wouldn't do.

Except that his hands weren't inclined to listen to his head, and they pulled away from hers to land on the lush, feminine curve of her waist instead. She wasn't wearing any stays beneath her dressing gown. By Deus, she felt decadent. Like something rare and special and in the wildness of that forbidden moment, like *his*. His hands molded to her, traveling over her softness as if he might imprint the feeling of her upon his palms. But it wasn't enough, touching her, holding her.

Her eyes were wide on his, her pretty pink lips parted.

And with one swift tug, she landed across his thighs in a heap of warm, delicious woman.

CHAPTER 8

Pamela was in Beast's lap. He had somehow deftly maneuvered her so that she was sideways. Her hands had found their way to his broad shoulders. This was decidedly not what she'd had in mind when she had been attempting to make him appear less foreboding so that she might sketch him.

Admittedly, inviting him to linger had been a mistake.

So, too, had the notion that she would be capable of sitting in the same room as him in the midst of the night, when the rest of the household was abed, with the warm glow of a brace of candles flickering around them, and not desire him. That she would have been able to stare at his handsome face without longing to trace the slash of his jaw and the finely molded sculpture of his lips with her fingertips. Without wanting to kiss him.

His scent, already familiar, crept over her like a lover's caress.

"What do you think you're doing?" she demanded, struggling to maintain her fast-fleeing control of the situation.

Of the man.

But that was foolish, wasn't it? No one could truly control a man like the one on whose lap she was seated.

His cool gaze melted all the ice inside her.

"Relaxing," he said slowly, "as you suggested."

There it was again, the hint of an accent flirting with his words. She wondered again at where he was truly from, with his unusual features, the traces of a foreign tongue lacing his speech when he forgot himself. Wondered at his secrets. At the reason why he never smiled.

Foolish, dangerous thoughts she couldn't afford to entertain. She had to escape his sinful clutches before she did something even more reckless than inviting him to stay whilst she sketched him had been. Pamela shifted on his lap, intending to remove herself and stand.

But that was when she felt it. Felt *him*. Thickening and stiffening beneath her. An answering ache throbbed to life between her thighs. That part of him felt quite the opposite of relaxed. And Pamela knew she ought to be scandalized, but she had always been a woman with a keen sensual nature. Something about this man had brought it back to life from a years-long slumber.

"This was decidedly not what I had in mind," she informed him as cooly as she could manage with so much fire licking at her from the inside, heating her blood. "You are once again being far too familiar with my person, sir, and this time, you haven't even the excuse of a fire iron."

"Wasn't it?" he asked softly, his eyes dipping to her lips. "Did you not think it reckless to invite me to linger alone with you at this hour of the night?"

What could she say? Of course she thought it reckless.

He was going to kiss her.

She knew it. Could see the intent as clearly as she could discern the flecks of gray and green in his irises. His head lowered slowly, slowly. He was giving her time, she realized.

Granting her the opportunity to push away from him and stand, just as he had held her before in a grasp she could have so easily slipped from, after their initial sparring.

Closer, his warm breath fanning over her mouth in a prelude that had her moving to meet him instead of retreating. She tipped her head back, waiting. Through the dark wool of his coat, his warmth seeped into her. But he stopped just short of taking her mouth.

Stopped and stared, as if challenging her to deny him.

But the fight was gone from her. She was once again a weak-willed woman who longed for a man's touch.

Not just any man's, she acknowledged silently. Only this one's.

"For a woman who has demonstrated remarkable prowess at speaking her mind, you have gone suddenly quiet," he observed, a mocking edge to his words.

He knew how greatly affected she was, the scoundrel. Knew it and was savoring her vulnerability. Enjoying it, quite clearly.

The realization had her finding her tongue at last.

"I had no intention of repeating what happened last night, if that is what you are inferring," she informed him as coldly as she could muster.

To demonstrate the veracity of her words, she shifted again, attempting to remove herself from his person. The action proved her second great mistake of the evening, the first having been asking him to stay. Because her movements only served to nestle his rigid cock more firmly against her. So firmly that if there hadn't been any garments separating them, he might easily have entered her. And much to her shame, he would have found her body welcoming and wet. Starving for his claiming.

He made a low sound of need, and it made an embarrassing surge of desire sluice through her.

"You have a damned odd way of avoiding an encore, Marchioness."

She swallowed hard. "You are a—"

His mouth took hers, silencing the rest of what she had been about to say. It was not the kiss of a tentative suitor but the kiss of a passionate lover. It was hard and demanding, carnal and wicked. His teeth raked along her bottom lip, and she opened for him, their tongues tangling together with eager abandon.

She was lost. Awash in sensation, drowning in him. Her arms wound around his neck, her fingers tangling in the silken strands at his nape, and she kissed him with all the abandon she'd once embraced, what seemed like a lifetime ago. Kissed him and felt an answering hunger within herself. The need to devour him, to be devoured in turn.

She had forgotten what it was like to kiss. How thoroughly rousing it was to lose herself to the sensation of a knowing mouth on hers, the taste of a man on her lips and tongue. Had forgotten what it felt like to ache, to need, to have someone stoke the flames of her desire ever higher until she was willing to be burned.

But she remembered now.

Heaven help her, she remembered.

She kissed him with every bit of passion she had kept ruthlessly suppressed. Kissed him until she was breathless. And not even then did she stop. She kissed him until there was wetness and salt on her lips and tongue, the lash of hot tears trailing down her cheeks. It shocked her to realize she had been weeping.

He jerked his head back, as if just making the discovery himself, his expression harsh. "Tears?"

She released her hold on him to dash at the wetness on her cheeks, struggling to explain, to understand herself. For they weren't tears of shame over her reaction to Beast. Rather, they were tears of relief.

"I had forgotten what this felt like," she told him.

What it felt like to desire a man.

To be desired in return.

It was powerful and wonderful and frightening—all the more so because of the man she desired, the man whose kisses had brought her back to life.

"What is it you had forgotten?" he asked quietly, almost tenderly.

The harshness had leached from his expression. Even the angles of his face seemed to have softened. He was no longer the aloof, cool-eyed stranger who had entered the salon. Instead, he was the passionate man whose mouth had moved over hers with such masterful promise.

And whether it was the lateness of the hour or the intensity of the desperate yearning she felt for him, she found herself answering his question.

"What desire feels like," she answered, searching his countenance for a hint of mockery and finding none. "I haven't allowed myself to feel it…to feel anything…in a long time."

"How long?" he asked.

She knew what he was asking—how long she had been a widow.

"Four years."

The admission made heat rise to her cheeks, for she had revealed a great deal to him with those two words. She waited for his censure. For mockery.

Instead, he leaned into her, pressing his forehead to hers. For the span of a few moments, he remained silent. Did nothing more than inhale slowly and exhale, as if he were taking in her breaths and feeding her his own.

"It has been longer for me," he said at last.

His own confession startled her. "Are you a widower?"

"No." He shook his head slowly, then rubbed his cheek along hers, the bristle of his whiskers somehow enticing and comforting both. "It's not a woman I mourn, but the man I once was."

His answer was not what she had expected, and in typical Beast fashion, he had left her with more questions than answers. She suddenly wanted to know everything there was to know about him. And that was frightening and foolish, for his presence in her life was temporary. He was not the sort of man to whom a respectable widow should grow attached. He was a gruff, mysterious enigma who would disappear into the shadows from which he had emerged whenever this terrible business with Ridgely was at an end.

"Who were you?" she dared to ask, leaning back so she could study his face.

A muscle clenched in his jaw, his beautiful lips set in a firm, almost angry line. "It doesn't matter. I am the man you see before you now."

So he hadn't always been Beast, then. It was what she had suspected. What she had known instinctively. But who was he truly? What secrets was he hiding? She wanted to understand him.

Pamela did something even more dangerous than what she had already done. She took his face in her hands, holding him still, and then she kissed him. Kissed him not because it was dark and he had kissed her first, not just because she was burning up with need, but because he had shared a part of himself with her that she couldn't help but to think he didn't readily reveal to anyone else. And because he had ridden to her rescue earlier that night. She didn't think now that it had been mere duty which had prompted the gesture.

Nor was it duty that had him taking command now. He angled his lips over hers, deepening the kiss as his hands slid up her back. Just as he had the night before, he cupped her nape, his long fingers cradling her head and holding her as he wanted so that he could feast on her mouth. He made her feel so wanted, so lovely. Made her feel like a woman again instead of a widow who had locked herself away from the world.

Her body hummed with yearning as she moved her lips in tandem with his, taking everything he had to give and demanding more. Of their own accord, her fingers threaded through his thick hair, and she raked her nails lightly over his scalp, a ravenous need to consume him overtaking her. To mark him, to claim him. To make him—even if only for this moment—hers.

After suppressing this part of herself for so long, she was suddenly hopelessly beyond any attempt at reining in her desires. She was a runaway carriage speeding toward a cliff and imminent destruction. But it didn't feel like she was about to fall to her doom when Beast suddenly rose from the chair as one, holding her in his strong, muscled arms as if the effort scarcely strained him.

She broke the kiss as she felt his footfalls carrying them forward. Such a strange sensation, floating above the air, propelled by a locomotion that was not her own. No one had carried her since she had been a child. And even then, her mother had only deigned to scoop her up and send her away to the nursery. She had most definitely not been treated to such reverent care. Had never felt protected the way she did in Beast's arms. Not just protected, but coveted, too.

Not even with Bertie had she felt such a stirring, intense passion. She didn't think it was time which had faded her memories. She and Bertie had been very much in love, but he had been sunshine and ease, sweet smiles and soft touches. Their lovemaking had always been tender and pleasant and lovely in its own way. But it hadn't been the maelstrom that afflicted her whenever Beast was touching her.

"What are you doing?" she asked, breathless from their kisses and from her reaction to him. "I must be heavy. Put me down."

He didn't obey. Of course, he didn't.

"You're perfect, Marchioness," was all he said as he carried her the rest of the way across the salon, until they'd reached the chaise longue she had so recently vacated, what now seemed a lifetime ago.

A lifetime in mere minutes. The woman who had been clinging to her convictions and the weighty guilt of the past had somehow disappeared the moment he had pulled her into his lap. It was as if he possessed some sort of dark, magical powers, some claim on her that was fated.

She thought again of his words, the starkness of them sending shivers through her as she recalled them. *It's not a woman I mourn, but the man I once was.*

So many secrets, so many mysteries.

Wrong and right blended together in the dancing shadows of the candlelight. She would fret over them in the morning. Tonight, there was no one but the two of them, no past, no future. Nothing but the present and the desire burning ever hotter and brighter.

He deposited her on the chaise longue slowly, reverently.

At first, she thought he intended to retreat and leave her as he had found her. A protest started in her throat but died when he dropped to his knees on the carpet before her. Holding her gaze, he cupped her face and drew her to him. The kiss began innocently enough, a few chaste brushes of his lips over hers. But then her arms twined themselves about his neck, and she made a soft sound of need that couldn't be contained, and his mouth changed. It became firmer, more demanding. His tongue swept over the seam of her lips, and she opened for him again. Opened for the taste of sin and tea and Beast, for the wet, velvet glide of his tongue over hers. The kiss turned filthy, erotic. They were making love with their mouths.

The last thread of her control, already frayed beyond redemption, broke.

She was a widow. She was not an inexperienced debutante. She could take a lover. Just this once. Could take what she wanted, what she needed. There were no emotions here, no betrayal of the love she carried in her heart for Bertie. This was nothing but pure, unadulterated lust. Bodily needs, as simple and elemental as breaking one's fast.

She surrendered, fingers sliding under Beast's coat to push it down his shoulders. She was rewarded with fewer layers, the corded vitality of his muscled arms covered only by a thin layer of lawn. He shrugged the coat away but when she caressed over his broad chest, fingers seeking the buttons of his waistcoat, he stopped her, ending the kiss and rocking back on his heels as he caught her hands in his.

"No," he said.

His denial quelled her ardor, brought embarrassment rushing over her. Had she misread him? What was she doing? She had never taken a lover. How could she have allowed things to progress so far? She had attempted to disrobe him, for heaven's sake.

"Forgive me," she blurted, cheeks hot with shame. "I shouldn't have been—"

He stopped her apology with his lips, kissing her slowly, languorously. Showing her without words how wrong she'd been to leap to conclusions. Chasing her worries. Seducing her again. He released her hands, his fingers working on the line of buttons bisecting her dressing gown. Beneath it, she wore nothing more than a thin night rail. But she was every bit as eager as he seemed to shed this extra layer keeping her skin from his.

She felt her dressing gown gaping as he progressed, stopping to brush his knuckles over her aching nipples through the fine linen of her night rail. His touch sent a sharp edge of desire through her. It felt so good, better than she could have imagined. All her misgivings were banished beneath the rising tide of sensation.

There were more buttons than she recalled. It seemed an eternity to wait for him to peel away the ruffled layer, leaving her in nothing more than a filmy white gown. He tore his lips from hers to survey what he had revealed. His eyes consumed her as thoroughly as his mouth had owned hers.

She slid her arms from the dressing gown, aware of the cool night air on her flesh. But his hands were on her, chasing the chill, warming her in a way that nothing and—she very much suspected—no one else could. Callused fingers rasped over her, sending fire in their wake from her wrists to her forearms.

"You bewitched me in the darkness," he murmured so quietly she could scarcely hear him, "but nothing compares to seeing you in the candlelight."

Her heart was pounding fast, her breathing shallow as she held herself still for his touch. He swept up her arms and her shoulders, traced over her collarbone with agonizing slowness, as if he were committing every moment, each touch, to his memory.

She grew impatient, wanting to explore him, but when her fingers lodged in the knot of his black cravat, he stopped her again, more tenderly this time, taking her hands in his and kissing her fingertips.

"Not now, Marchioness."

She wished he would call her Pamela. The need to hear her given name in his low, decadent baritone suddenly preceded all else. Surpassed the need to strip him free of the pretense of civilization keeping his masculine form from her avid gaze. She licked her lips, about to tell him, but then he groaned and took her lips with his again, and she forgot everything she'd been about to say. Instead, she surrendered to the madness, to desire.

To Beast.

Lady Deering's lips were hot and soft and supple beneath Theo's, and when he coaxed her to open for him, her tongue entered his mouth first, writhing against his. The wet heat of her and the feminine sound of need she made had his cock even harder than it had been when her bottom had been in his lap, taunting and teasing as she had shifted against him. Lust unfurled like molten honey, coursing through him, banishing every rational thought. He could spend forever kissing her, and he still would not have enough.

Her hands had settled on his shoulders, and he was at ease with them there. She had wanted to remove his layers, and he couldn't blame her for the natural instinct, but he'd had ample time during their ravenous kisses to make peace with the fact that he could not have her as he wanted. He could not strip himself bare, feel her hands on his skin. Couldn't bear to see the disgust in her eyes when they fell upon his ruined body, the lashes and burns that had grown over in a hideous patchwork that time could never truly heal.

Thankfully, he had distracted her from her course. And he would continue to do so, for there was great reward to be had in spoiling her with pleasure. She was a woman who was desperately in need of embracing her sensual nature. She deserved to be worshiped and savored, and although he couldn't allow her to undress him, he could give her this.

But who was he fooling? Pleasing her was every bit as much a gift to himself. Yes, he was selfish and greedy, and he intended to give her everything she deserved. He would make her forget about him, make her focus only on her own body's needs.

He indulged in her lips for another indeterminate span of time, kissing her hard and deep as he banded his arms around her and held her close. Her breasts were full and round, her hard nipples prodding him through her night rail and his shirt and waistcoat. He wanted them in his mouth. Wanted to suck them and bury his fingers in her cunny and work her sweet nub with his thumb. Wanted to hear her moan and whimper, wanted to watch her come undone. Wanted his tongue on her, in her, wanted the taste of her on his lips, the scent of her feminine desire surrounding him.

If he didn't take care, he was going to spend in his trousers, all without his lips ever leaving hers.

Theo tore his lips from hers and dragged them along her jaw until he found her ear.

"I want this off you."

As he spoke, he caught the thin garment she wore at her shoulder and plucked, showing her what he meant lest there be any question.

And then he caught her earlobe in his teeth, nipping her, before swirling his tongue against the soft, sleek patch of skin directly below until she made a breathy little gasp, and then a sigh.

"Yes."

That word on her lips. Damnation, it was the most potent aphrodisiac he'd ever known. Because he knew how much it cost, how much she must want him, for this icy, prim widow to agree to get naked for him on the chaise longue. Just because he had demanded it.

"Good," he said, and then he rolled back to his heels, catching a handful of the hem at her ankles and pulling it up.

No stockings. Bare feet. Delicate ankles. So much creamy skin exposed. For him, all for him. Theo stopped to caress her calves and knees, kissing every part of her he had revealed, like the greatest gift he'd ever been presented with. And in his former life, he had been given jewels and gold, priceless treasures. He'd had his choice of all the women in court to bed if he had wished. But none of that compared to the Marchioness of Deering lowering her guard and giving herself to him.

She grasped handfuls of the cloud-white linen in her hands, hesitating as the hem rose to her well-curved hips.

"You're beautiful," he told her, showing her with his lips. Worshipping her with his hands and mouth and tongue. Even his teeth, which he used to nip at the delicate hollow behind her knee, her inner thigh. "Like a goddess."

And he knew which of the old Boritanian gods he would compare her to. Elyrianna, the goddess of earth and abundance. Like Lady Deering, she had been golden-haired and beautiful, all lush, womanly curves. But his marchioness was more desirable, far lovelier than any cool marble statue or centuries-old oil painting could ever be. And she was warm and smoother than the finest silk. She was his, for these few, stolen hours only.

Perhaps it was his words, perhaps his caresses. Whatever the cause of her reassurance, the marchioness's hesitance faded. She shifted, pulling her night rail from under her bottom, and then up, up, over her head. It sailed through the night and landed somewhere on the Axminster.

He swallowed hard as he drank in the sight of her fully unclothed. The icy widow who lashed him with her tongue so easily. The cold, prim marchioness. With the candlelight playing lovingly over her every curve, she was a study in cream and pink. More than his wholly inadequate imagination could have ever conjured. He didn't know where to touch her, kiss her, taste her, first. She was like a feast laid before him, and he was ravenous.

"Sweet Deus," was all that emerged from him, part prayer, part plea, for he had never wanted a woman the way he wanted this one.

It was like the windswept waves crashing on the beach in a violent storm. Sudden and elemental and furious. Capable of anything, destruction or renewal, or whatever lay in between.

But just as swiftly as the thundering roar of desire hit him, the marchioness appeared to have second thoughts about her boldness. She pressed her legs together, looking suddenly young and uncertain, so different from her customary icy hauteur. More like an innocent newly making her debut than the experienced widow of the tart tongue who had delivered such withering set-downs. He couldn't shake the impression that he was seeing her as she truly was, bereft of all pretense and artifice. The woman beneath the mask she wore for the world.

"It has been some time," she said, her voice husky but hesitant. "If you do not find me pleasing, I shan't be—"

"No," he interrupted, not wanting to hear another word, because it was the opposite of what he found her. Deus, *pleasing* was a pale, unworthy attempt at describing the woman before him. "I find you so pleasing it hurts, Marchioness. Beyond pleasing. Now hush and let me enjoy the bounty you present to this most unworthy sinner."

It occurred to Theo that she had mistaken his awe for a lack of interest. When he had hesitated, her confidence had wilted, and that had not been his intention. Not for a single damned second. She had shown him the vulnerability hiding beneath her cool façade when she had shared with him that it had been four long, cold years since she had known a lover's touch. He was not going to take her for granted.

"You needn't charm me, sir," she said, some of the coolness returning to her voice. "I have already stripped myself bare before you. I am yours for tonight only, to take what you wish."

"Oh, but I do not charm," he reassured her. "I'm not, you'll find, a charming man."

He had been, once. But the prince was dead, and the scarred beast in his place had no use for pretty words or prettier women. At least, he hadn't reckoned so. Until he had spied Lady Deering sketching with the sun shining around her. Until he had known her lips beneath his. Now, he didn't know who the hell he was, other than a man who wanted this woman desperately.

He would show her how much. The time for talking was done.

Theo guided his hands back down her thighs, stopping at her knees, which he gently guided apart. When her legs opened, he moved between them, still kneeling before her. Golden curls covered her mound, the pink pouting lips of her cunny on display. He slid his hands higher, still marveling at the way she felt, her skin smooth and supple beneath his touch, and then he stopped at her hips, pulling her forward. When her bottom rested on the edge of the chaise longue, he tilted back his head and caught one of her nipples between his lips, sucking.

Yes, this was how they could communicate. Sensation, desire, mutual passion. He hadn't any words to say, and the ones that were crowding his mind now were love words from his mother tongue. Words he wouldn't dare say aloud, for fear of what he would reveal.

Lady Deering moaned, her hands fluttering to his hair, fingers sifting through the strands, back arching. The sensual abandon he had felt in her before had returned, and he intended to make the best of it. He flicked his tongue over the pert bud of her nipple, taking his time, caressing her thighs as he lavished attention upon her gorgeous breasts. First one, then the other.

They had hours yet until he needed to replace one of his men on duty. Hours until the sun rose and dawn chased his sensual goddess back into her stays and forbidding frown. He was going to put those hours to good use.

To that end, he buried his face in the hollow between her breasts, pressing his mouth to the soft skin there. He kissed her tenderly, slowly, making love to every part of her body. Because he felt to his marrow that he understood the Marchioness of Deering. She didn't have outward scars on her perfect, creamy skin. Hers resided on the inside, impossible to see and yet every bit as devastating. Oh, yes. He understood scars. He well knew the chains of the past, the pain memories continually inflicted, subtle as a knife's blade gradually cutting more and more flesh away until nothing was left but impenetrable bone. And even after, the bones still ached. They were capable of being broken.

Living in the past was slow torture.

To hell with that. All he wanted tonight was this moment. All he needed was now. For himself, selfishly, yes. But for her, too. For this beautiful, passionate woman who was clinging to what had come before as if it would save her instead of sending her beneath the flood to drown.

Theo's lips moved with a will of their own, down her stomach to her navel. Lower, to her hip bone. He kissed the gentle protrusion, thinking she had been made to worship, that each new place on her body that he explored was lovelier than the last. He kissed along her outer thigh first, all the way to her knee, his hands never leaving her, the connection unbroken. His every sense was heightened, like a berry almost bursting with ripeness. There was her jasmine and hyacinth scent, but as he parted her legs even farther, there was also the sweet perfume of her sex, musky and tempting.

Theo kissed the ridge of her knee, then moved to the softness of her inner thigh, dragging his lips over her. Higher, higher, higher. His hands moved, pushing her slowly wider, and she was like a summer bud unfurling into a decadent blossom. All pink, welcoming femininity, her skin sleek and glistening, ready for him.

"What are you..."

Her question trailed off as his head dipped, and he licked her seam, parting her folds with his tongue, finding her nub and stroking it lightly. The taste of her filled him with raw, animal lust. Feminine, sweet, forbidden. Fucking delicious.

Mine, he thought, drunk on the taste of her, on the way her hips bucked, bringing his face deeper into her heat. His cock throbbed in his trousers, and he longed to drive himself against something for mercy, but this was not about him. It was about his marchioness. He could tend to himself later, when he was alone. Or never. At the moment, his own release had ceased to matter. All that did matter was her.

She gasped from somewhere above him. "*Oh.*"

He had the presence of mind to tip his head back, seek her gaze. Her blue eyes were half-closed, shuttered by long lashes, and yet when her stare found his, it still seared him with its intensity. And in the violence of his need, it took a moment for the English words to filter through his mind, like sunlight through murk.

"It is good, yes?" he asked, noting the way he had spoken the words.

Not like an Englishman, he thought. But like the Boritanian he was. A man who didn't belong here, and who most assuredly didn't belong between this beautiful woman's thighs. Even if it was only his tongue he intended to sink inside her, rather than his aching prick.

"I..." Her words trailed away as she swallowed, and he

tracked the subtle movement in her pale, elegant throat, an indication of how thoroughly undone she was.

He felt victorious. This was how he imagined a general felt after emerging victorious from a tremendous battle. His chest swelled with pride, and his cock swelled in equal measure.

"No words?" he teased softly, blowing a stream of hot air on her sex.

She panted then, her hips rocking in a silent plea, lips parted.

It was wrong and wicked of him, perhaps, but he suddenly wanted to force her surrender from her entirely. To hear this proud marchioness beg for what she wanted. He watched her, running his hands up and down her inner thighs in a steady caress, content to make her plead. To show her who had won this little skirmish between them, even if he was the one on his knees.

"Tell me," he urged.

She whimpered, her even, white teeth sinking into her lush lower lip.

He flicked his gaze back down to her cunny, noting how she glistened in the candlelight, so very wet. Swallowing hard against a rush of need, he forced himself to take in the rest of her, the picture she presented. Deus, she was lovelier than any woman had a right to be, sitting somehow naked before him, as if he deserved the honor. Her folio and porte-crayon still lay abandoned and forgotten on the upholstered seat at her side, a slight recrimination he couldn't ignore.

This night had not begun in debauchery.

But that was how it was going to end. They had progressed beyond the bounds of propriety. The night before had been but a taunting prelude to now, and he intended to have his fill of her so that when sanity returned to them both with the morning's light, he wouldn't have a single regret over what he hadn't done.

Still, she hadn't given him what he wanted. No words. He needed to hear her say it.

"Do you want my tongue on you?" he pressed, using his nails to rake white trails up her inner thighs, all the way to where her legs and cunny met.

Ever so lightly, he dug his fingertips into her there, pulling her open, spreading her lips with his thumbs.

She swallowed hard and then released another gust of pent-up air. "Yes."

Permission.

Not enough.

"Say it," he demanded, drawn to her, his head lowering until his lips almost grazed her most-sensitive flesh.

"I want your tongue," she said in a rush.

But Theo wasn't done.

"Beg," he bit out.

This time, she didn't hesitate. "Please."

He smiled, and it was a true smile for the first time in as long as he could recall. Then, he lowered his mouth to her, intent upon giving her everything she had asked for and more.

Pamela was nothing and no one. She had ceased to exist. Or perhaps, more accurately, the woman she had been before Beast had crossed the threshold tonight had disappeared. In her place was a wicked wanton lost to any sense of guilt or conscience. Lost to everything but the moment.

And him. Oh dear sweet heavens, *him*.

Her mind and her body were fixated upon Beast's knowing mouth and tongue as they worked in tandem over her eager sex. Kisses were dotted over her folds, in a worshipful, slow manner that told her he had no intention of rushing this tryst to its inevitable conclusion. Rather, he wanted to savor. To prolong.

As he lashed her bud with quick, stimulating licks that sent sensation careening through her, Pamela had no complaints in the matter. She wondered if she might keep him forever on his knees before her, paying homage to her as if she were a worthy deity instead of a broken widow who had gone far too long without a man's touch. She, who had been unkind and cold toward him, even when he had driven her home so she needn't wait in a cold carriage alone whilst the repairs to the carriage wheels were made. She, who had questioned his name and everything about him and had meant to brain him with a fire iron.

For her, whom he had no reason to spare such gentleness and tender, sensual abandon, he licked and laved and stoked the fires of her desire ever higher. No one had ever pleasured her the way this man was, with a frank lack of inhibition or worldly cares. He was fully making love to her with his mouth, groaning into her as if he found her delicious. His hands caressed her hips as he held her still and fed off her as if he were starving, and ravishing her sex was the only relief that would sate him.

The rough stubble of his beard abraded her inner thighs, the intimacy strangely thrilling. His callused fingertips dug into her hips, then lower, cupping her bottom and pulling her to him. He drew on her pearl, using that hot, beautiful sinner's mouth to suck hard enough she would have thought it would hurt.

It didn't hurt, however. Instead, the sensations he drew from her were nothing short of exquisite. Her hips jumped from the cool upholstery of the chaise longue. A moan tore from her. Her eyes fluttered closed as she gave herself over to him completely. His tongue glided hot and sleek, licking her up and down, and when he sank inside her, the invasion made her gasp and shudder as a tiny spasm rocked through her.

It felt filthy and wrong, his tongue buried deep. But good also. So very, very good. Beyond good. How had she forgotten what sensual pleasure felt like, how she could wallow in its splendor? She had ignored her needs for so long, but now they were all loosed, and she was helpless to do anything but surrender herself to the bliss.

In and out he thrust, the wet sounds of his tongue plunging into her ready passage echoing in the quiet of the chamber, interrupted only by the crackle of the fire in the grate. Some fleeting part of her mind cautioned she should be ashamed of herself. That she *would* be ashamed of herself, with the rising sun and the return of her wits.

But Pamela was beyond the point of fretting over the inevitable regrets she would have when this shocking fever subsided and she was once more in possession of her faculties. How had she never known this existed, that this awful, wondrous pleasure could be had? And how could it be that this man, this near stranger, could visit such thrilling pleasure upon her, and she would not just welcome it, but revel in it?

She did not recognize herself, this woman she had become. This daring widow who could command her own pleasure, who would accept the shockingly rude demands of a man below her station, a bodyguard who haunted the halls of Hunt House by night. But she was beyond the point of caring. Perhaps this had been inevitable.

She had kept her true nature buttoned up, banished, hidden away, for four long and bleak years. Most women in her place would have taken a lover long before now. Perhaps even another husband. But no, she wouldn't think of that. All she wanted was this roaring, impossible flame of desire.

Pamela had planted her hands on the chaise longue's seat, but now she couldn't control the impulse to reach for Beast. Her eyes opened to the erotic, carnal sight of him, still fully dressed compared to her own shocking, pale nudity. She ought to be embarrassed for her having tossed away her night rail, for sitting in the midst of her brother's gold salon where she had spent countless hours on embroidery and other proper distractions, wearing nary a stitch. Nude, as a man she scarcely knew spoiled her with his clever tongue. For allowing Beast to pull her into his lap, to kiss her and touch her, to take what he wanted. To give her what she wanted, too.

Her fingers sifted through his hair, finding it silken and soft, so soft. Such a disparity between this man's cold, harsh mien and his hard, muscled body, that softness. Everywhere she touched him, she found not a hint of spareness. He was honed and sharp, all angles and ice. But for her, he was burning hot, and she wanted that heat, that flame. Wanted to pitch herself into the fire along with him.

She was on the edge, the knot of desire drawn taut deep in her belly. But she needed more. And as if he sensed it, he dragged his lips back to her swollen bud, sucking and laving, before one of his long, callused fingers found her drenched opening and slid inside.

Pamela cried out at the sensation, bucking her hips, drawing him deeper. In the dim recesses of her mind, it occurred to her that as delicious as he felt inside her, it still wasn't what she wanted most. That thick, long ridge she'd felt pressed against her was what she wanted, impaling her, filling her. Like everything else she was thinking and feeling, it was forbidden. She knew she mustn't. She had already come too far.

There was the sharp edge of something on her tender flesh. His teeth, she realized. He had nipped her there, and now he was drawing out the exquisite sensation, worrying her little bud, alternating between sucks and licks. A second finger joined the first, and he worked in and out of her, a slow and maddening rhythm that brought her quickly to the edge.

"Oh," she gasped, grasping handfuls of his beautiful hair now, gripping him because she knew that if she let go, she would fall backward over the opposite end of the chaise longue, go crashing to the floor.

She was like a wilting flower, bending to his whim, limp and helpless in the very best possible way. He growled, the vibration against her clitoris making her buck against him, seeking more. More friction, more of his tongue, more everything.

His fingers slid deep and then curled, stroking a place inside her that was so deliriously pleasurable that it almost bordered on pain. An intense quake began in her core and then released through her. He flicked his tongue over her, plunging in and out with quick, hard strokes as she splintered apart. Her body bowed forward, a moan forced from her, the intensity of her orgasm stealing all her breath.

His hands slid from her hips to her lower back, holding her to him, his mouth never leaving her as he drew the tremors of release from her body. Beast played her as if she were an instrument, as if he knew her better than she knew herself. When the last wave undulated through her, he withdrew, his fingers sliding from her cunny with a wet sound that would have embarrassed her had she the capacity to properly think.

Which she decidedly did not.

She was still grappling with the aftermath of her powerful orgasm, her heart thudding hard in her ears, pumping fast and furious. He pressed a reverent kiss to her sex, then another to her stomach, his lips slick with the unavoidable evidence of her own desire. Silently, he rose, and she took note of the fall of his trousers, the hard ridge of his cock plainly outlined, showing the effect she'd had upon him.

Pamela had never been a selfish lover. In her marriage, she'd discovered she greatly enjoyed the act of pleasing a man, found joy in exploring the masculine form, so different from hers. The urge to return the favor rose, but Beast was already moving away from her in neat, succinct strides. She clutched the end of the chaise longue, sanity gradually returning to her.

She was naked, and she'd just allowed a man to pleasure her for the first time since Bertie. What had she done?

As the ramifications swirled through her, Beast returned, carrying the gown she had discarded. Calmly, he drew the night rail over her head. Cheeks burning, she forced her arms through the holes, pulling the skirt down to cover herself.

She couldn't bring herself to meet his eyes, keeping her gaze upon her trembling hands twisting in her lap instead.

"That never should have happened," she whispered, as much for her own sake as for his.

Why, she knew not. The damage had already been done. Speaking her misgivings and guilt aloud did nothing to ameliorate her sin. She had been intimate with another man. He had brought her to climax with his mouth.

Dear God.

"Don't," he said, the authority in his voice forcing her to look up at him.

He stood tall and handsome, his lips dark and glistening from the pleasures he had just visited upon her. She forced herself to her feet, disliking the way he towered over her. Disliking herself most of all.

"Don't what?" she asked, frowning.

She had been intimate with this handsome, unnerving stranger. How absurd it all seemed.

He watched her, his countenance unreadable. "Don't feel guilty for living. It'll eat you alive, from the inside out." And then he bowed. Bowed as if they had just met and shared a dance in a ballroom instead of doing the wicked things they had done. As if he had not just seen into the heart of her where she'd believed no one else was capable of looking.

"Your servant, Marchioness," he added.

With that, he turned his back on her and walked from the salon, leaving her alone with her flickering candles and regrets. Shaken, Pamela retrieved her dressing gown and fastened it with trembling fingers. Her folio and porte-crayon mocked her from the chaise longue, a reminder of her true intention in coming to the salon. Grimly, she snatched them up before snuffing out the candles and making her way to her chamber through darkened halls.

Ensconced in her bed at last, Pamela fell quickly into a dreamless sleep.

CHAPTER 9

Another uneventful night—at least in terms of intruders—had passed at Hunt House. Theo finished speaking with the last of his guards stationed in the passages below the terrace, confirming that there hadn't been any attempts to enter the home through the evening and early-morning hours. Mind still preoccupied with those stolen, forbidden moments with Lady Deering in the salon, he thanked his men and told them to retire to their beds in the carriage house for a few hours' rest. He would watch the perimeter this cool, crisp morning because he needed the solitude, the chance for reflection.

Alone in the passage, he checked the three exterior doors, trying to keep his body and his mind equally occupied so that his thoughts wouldn't return to *her*.

His Marchioness.

Not his, not truly. He had left her in a furor of pent-up need, sought out his lonely bed, and had immediately stroked himself to completion before falling into a deep, sated slumber the likes of which he hadn't known in as long as he could recall.

His reaction to her vexed him. Because he saw himself in her, because he somehow, instinctively *knew* her. Not just the taste of her on his tongue, the way her body responded to his. But in a far-more-profound sense. And he couldn't afford to form attachments to anyone. Most especially not to brokenhearted widows.

As he reached the final door, the need to step outside and breathe in the moist, foggy air overwhelmed him. He thrust back the latch and found himself on one of the many gravel paths wending through the gardens. The erotic dream of the night had given way to a bleak morning. Mist was falling blearily from a leaden sky.

A cold breeze whipped his too-long hair across his face, and he found himself recalling Lady Deering's hands grasping the strands, tugging, the way she'd undulated beneath him with breathy gasps and low moans that sounded as if they had been wrung from the very depths of her soul. At the thought, his prick went half-hard in his trousers, despite all the reasons why he knew he must not surrender to temptation again.

If only she'd told him her given name. He wished to know her as something more familiar than Marchioness or Lady Deering. But that was a dangerous desire, too, one which should be ignored just like all the others in relation to her.

A sudden flurry of movement in his peripheral vision alerted Theo to the fact that he wasn't alone before the crunching footfalls did. He slid his hand inside his coat, hand unerringly finding the hilt of his dagger. And the instinct was a correct one, the urge to reach for his weapon, because the person who emerged from the other side of the boxwood hedge was indeed his opposition.

Lady Deering drew to a halt when she spied him on the path, the creamy jaconet muslin of her gown fluttering about her ankles. She was wearing a jaunty little bonnet atop her golden hair and a copper-colored spencer that only served to emphasize the luscious curves of her breasts. Scarcely any time had passed since they had parted in the candlelit salon, but his body reacted to the sight of her as if it had been starved.

He forced himself to bow. "My lady."

She was carrying a basket, the handles resting in the crook of her elbow as she dipped into a small, answering curtsy. "Sir."

Her formality did nothing to quell the rising tide of desire within him. He looked at her and recalled her sweet scent, the musk of her desire mingling with the clean, floral fresh soap she must use to bathe. He remembered how wet she'd been, sleek and hot, pulsing on his tongue.

Theo swallowed hard. "I trust I'm not disturbing you, Marchioness?"

She blinked, as if she too were caught in the same sensual spell. "Of course not. I thought to harvest some rosemary, thyme, and sweet marjoram before the frost takes it. I keep a small patch of herbs in the eastern corner of the garden."

She was speaking quickly, as if she were in a hurry to be freed of his company, and he did not miss the twin patches of pink staining her cheeks. But he couldn't blame her for the shyness; he was feeling a bit of his own this morning. He hadn't expected to cross paths with her again so soon either. Hadn't thought, last night, beyond the desperate need of those wild moments when his face had been between her legs and he'd been making them both mindless. He hoped to hell she didn't regret allowing herself the freedom of feeling. She'd been drawn tighter than a knot.

Theo seized on her words, trying to remain unaffected by the longing that threatened to consume him. "You keep herbs?"

The notion of her toiling in the soil intrigued him as

much as it surprised Theo. Many years ago, when he'd been a lad in Boritania, his mother had kept a small garden just beyond the royal apartments, in the inner courtyard. He harbored a few sacred memories of sunlight and salt air, his mother's lilting voice humming as she tended her flowers. When she had been imprisoned in the castle dungeons, the gardens had been the first of many things that were important to her which his uncle had destroyed.

"I do," Lady Deering said softly now, pulling him back from the relentless grip of the past and all its demons. "Would you care to help me with the cuttings?"

Her invitation shocked him as much as her appearance on the path had.

There was something about her this morning, he thought, that was different. There was a softness about her that had been previously absent. And he found himself wanting to conserve that softness. To keep it there. To please her any way he could. For he had the impression that the Marchioness of Deering was a woman who had denied herself far too many times in her grief.

"If you wish it, my lady," he allowed, not particularly eager for the memories he might have to confront watching her harvest her herbs.

He had not witnessed someone tending a garden since those days. But then, perhaps there was a rightness in seeing it again now. In the gardener being Lady Deering.

"Come," she said, part invitation, part demand. "Two pairs of hands are better in such instances than one."

She spoke lightly, as if there were no greater meaning in her invitation. But they both knew damned well that she would not have offered the same to one of his men, had it been a different guard upon the path. Theo said nothing of the sort, however, content to allow her to maintain her pride.

He trailed her along the path to the far corner of the

garden in careful silence. No sound between them but their footfalls crunching on the gravel, the occasional startled winging of a bird flying from the shrubbery as they passed. He was content to watch her, the sway of her hips beneath her gown, her graceful bearing, the peep of upswept locks from beneath her straw bonnet. How odd to think that mere hours ago, she had been naked and pliant beneath his questing mouth and hands.

They reached a small square delineated from the rest of the carefully planned gardens by a line of stones. The foliage was yet a deep, dark green, the leaves unmarred by the steadily cooler weather.

"Here it is," she announced, turning to him, her cheeks still fetchingly pink.

Whether it was from the cold or for another reason, he couldn't say. But he noted that her gaze was fixed upon something over his shoulder rather than upon his face.

"It's lovely," he said, but the praise wasn't for her herb garden, which he had scarcely spared a glance for. Rather, it was for her.

The misery of the gray day and the damp chill did nothing to detract from her beauty. As if she sensed the meaning behind his words, the flush on her cheeks deepened. He almost smiled—such shyness after her bold display last night. What a mystery she was, and one he dearly longed to unravel.

"You must think me silly," she said quietly, "keeping a garden when there's no reason for me to do so. The cook has a lovely kitchen cutting garden in the western corner, and of course, we have whatever we need sent from Ridgely Hall's orangery."

"I would never think you silly," he told her solemnly, and it was true.

Her gaze met his at last, as if she were searching for

something. Whatever it was, she seemed to have found it, for she nodded and said, "I brought two pairs of shears with me, thinking I might persuade Lady Virtue for accompaniment, but she didn't wish to venture into the chilly drizzle to indulge me."

Theo had the sudden thought that he would follow her into the fires of Hades to indulge her.

"Tell me what to do," he said, instead of blurting something so ridiculously foolish.

He wasn't dressed for the weather, and he wasn't even wearing a hat to shield him from the mists, but he didn't care about that either. Nor was he concerned about leaving his post. The garden was walled, and he would see anyone who crossed it in an effort to gain entry to the doors below the terrace.

Lady Deering flipped open the lid on her basket, reached inside, and extracted a pair of shears. She offered it to him, and he accepted, unable to resist brushing his fingers against her gloved ones. He didn't miss the way she paused for a moment longer than necessary before reaching inside the basket again and withdrawing a second pair.

"We will clip them close to the soil, but take care to keep some of the leaves remaining," she instructed, her tone no-nonsense as she placed the basket on the ground at her feet. "You may begin with the thyme, and I'll start with the rosemary."

His mother had grown thyme in her garden as well, and he recognized the foliage with bittersweet ease, bending down to perform his task. The marchioness moved to the opposite side of the square, putting some much-needed distance between them, and began clipping sprigs of rosemary. The fragrance of herbs rose, so redolent of his days as a young lad that it made emotion he hadn't allowed himself to feel suddenly well up, thick in his throat. Damn it, what was it about this woman that stripped him of every defense, made him so bleeding vulnerable?

They worked in companionable silence, their shears snipping, the sound metallic and sharp. The parts of London he frequented didn't have gardens. The distant memory of the Boritanian sun and the sandy soil beneath his fingers haunted him.

"Is something amiss, Beast?"

Lady Deering's question tore him from his thoughts. He looked up to find her watching him, an odd expression on her face. It startled him to realize how much he wanted his true name on her lips.

"Theo," he said before he could stop himself.

Her brow furrowed. "Theo?"

"My given name," he elaborated, his voice sounding rusty from the pent-up emotion. "You asked for it. Now you have it."

"Theo," she repeated, smiling softly.

It was a womanly smile, a smile that curved her lips but reflected in her eyes, and it made him want to kiss her again. But kissing her was dangerous, so he forced his gaze down and realized belatedly why she had asked him if something was amiss.

He had crushed a handful of thyme sprigs in his fist. "Memories," he bit out, flicking his glance back up to her. "My mother kept a garden. Forgive me for ruining your thyme."

"She is gone?" Lady Deering asked quietly, not mentioning the macerated remnants of the herb, mangled by his big paw.

Theo nodded. "Many years now."

But it was the manner in which she had been torn from this earth, from his life, that would haunt him forever. Her death had left a gaping void in his world, one which neither time nor distance could heal.

"Do you know why I keep the garden, Theo?" the marchioness asked suddenly.

Her use of his name had his head jerking up. "Why?"

"Because it brings me a bit of hope every time I see it, the reminder of life bursting from the soil, so green and vibrant, regrowth every spring." She cut another sprig of rosemary, eyes remaining downcast. "Death can make us forget the small joys, and I tend these herbs so that I remember them."

"I understand," he managed to bite out past the surge of feeling inside him at her words, her revelation.

His thoughts were suddenly painful as a bruise. He was thinking not just about his past, but about Lady Deering's as well. Wondering about what manner of man her husband had been. What it must have been like to have the love of a woman like her, one who had so mourned her husband's passing that she had hardened herself to anyone else for years.

It required all the restraint he possessed to keep his emotions locked away. He inhaled slowly, holding the breath in his lungs until his chest burned. Only then did he exhale, cutting a fresh sprig of thyme to replace the herbs he had crushed, then another. As he did so, he blinked against a stinging rush that felt alarmingly like tears.

He hadn't wept in years. Not since the palace guards had seized his mother and taken her to the dungeons for committing treason. And he wouldn't weep now. Not in the midst of a rainy London garden with a woman he scarcely knew, aside from the raw intimacies they had shared.

No, he would be far better served to keep in mind the true reason he was at Hunt House, and that didn't have a damned thing to do with finding solace in the past with the icy widow who had turned to flame in his arms. He was here to protect the Duke of Ridgely from whoever it was that was trying to kill him.

As he always did, Theo banished the past from his mind along with every last trace of emotion he possessed, turning his attention to the plants before him instead.

NEITHER OF THEM had spoken about the night. It lay between them, heavy as a boulder it seemed they both were seeking to avoid. For Pamela's part, she had already decided, when she had risen that morning and splashed calming water on her face to perform her ablutions, that what had happened could never be repeated. Indeed, she had promised herself, as she had solemnly dressed and prepared for her day, that she should avoid Beast at all costs. If she wasn't in his presence, she could hardly be tempted by him.

And yet, from the moment she had spied him standing in the mists of the garden, looking unfairly handsome in his black coat and trousers, his dark hair wet from rain, she had made the opposite decision. Her heart had given a pang, and the emotion that had coursed through her had been unexpectedly vivid. She hadn't expected him to agree to accompany her to her makeshift herb garden. She still wasn't certain why she had made the offer at all.

But she had, and here he was, working with her in the garden using efficient motions. Clipping, harvesting, tending. He had discarded his gloves at some point, revealing his long, capable fingers, now lightly kissed with smudges of dirt that made her long to clean them. He was such a mystery. Cold and walled off as a forbidding fortress, and yet there were glimpses of another man that shone through. *Theo.* He'd told her his name, had given her a small sliver of himself. A hint at who he truly was.

Did it mean anything, his revelation? She hardly knew. Good heavens, she didn't even know if their tryst in the salon had meant anything to him. To her. Whether or not she wanted it to.

One thing was painfully clear to her, however. The moment she was near Beast—Theo—her every good intention was hopelessly, thoroughly, recklessly dashed.

She finished harvesting the last of the rosemary, tucking it carefully into her basket. She would string it up in bunches and hang it to dry as she always did, from the ceiling in one of the unused guest rooms. Fortunately, Hunt House was massive and had no shortage of chambers. Her basket was quickly filling, and as she retracted her hand, Theo's was suddenly there, his fingers grazing hers and sending a warm flash of heat to chase the chill, even through the barrier of her dirt-stained gloves.

When she would have withdrawn, he caught her hand in his, staying her. Her gaze shot to his, finding his expression tense and harsh. Almost angry.

"Don't move," he told her curtly, and then he released her hand and was rising to his feet, moving with silent grace along the gravel path.

Confused and startled, she stood, shaking out her soggy skirts, wondering what had just happened. Where was he going? She dropped her shears to the ground alongside the sweet marjoram, which she had yet to cut. Trepidation rising, she caught her gown in her gloved hands, ignoring the stain she might leave with her dirtied gloves, and hastened after him.

He had rounded a bend in the path and disappeared around the tall, perfectly trimmed boxwood hedges that lined the outer walls of the gardens. Her misgiving growing, she hurried her steps, venturing across the garden until she was nearing the terrace. And still, there was no sign of Theo.

Where could he have disappeared to, and so quickly and thoroughly?

She was about to call out to him when a hand suddenly caught her elbow in a tight grip, and she was spun hastily against the stone wall beneath the terrace, her body trapped by a larger male form that was as hard as it was familiar. Her hands settled on his chest, anchoring her to him.

"Beast," she gasped, so startled that her mind reverted to the name he had given her that first afternoon. "What are you doing?"

"What are you doing, Marchioness?" he countered, his cool eyes blazing into hers.

"Looking for you, of course. You disappeared."

"I told you to stay where you were," he growled.

So he had.

Pamela blinked up at him. "I've never been particularly good at listening to orders."

"I wouldn't have guessed," he drawled, some of the tension draining from his countenance and shoulders.

"You might have said where you were going," she pointed out.

"And you might have remained where you were safe. I saw someone in the gardens. You could have been in danger."

"Who did you see?" Alarm coiled in her belly. "Not another intruder?"

"No," he hastened to say. "It was one of my men come to find me."

Another of the guards, then. Relief washed over her, chasing the worry that had never been far since the realization that someone was trying to do her brother great bodily harm. But just as quickly as the relief had arrived, it occurred to her that something could still be amiss.

"What did he want?" she asked. "Is something wrong?"

Theo hesitated, his lips twisting. "He had a message for

me. But, my lady, please. When it comes to your welfare, if nothing else, heed me. When I tell you to remain in one place, remain there."

"Are you concerned for me?"

The moment the question left her lips, she wished she could recall it. Likely, his nearness and the intimacy of his body pressing hers to the rough stone wall at her back was the source of her foolishness. That and what had happened between them last night. Her mind wandered, and heat flushed her skin at the memory of his mouth on her, the wicked pleasure that had ruined her every good intention.

"The duke has paid me handsomely to make you and everyone in this household my concern," Theo said coolly, frowning down at her.

Of course. But she hadn't required that particular reminder.

She pushed at his chest, her pride stinging. "As you can see, I am unharmed. Now, if you don't mind, I have herbs that need harvesting."

But he didn't move. His hands were still splayed on the walls on either side of her, keeping her there.

"You're unharmed this time," he corrected sternly, his lips flattening into a grim line. "But what of next time, my lady? Promise me that you'll heed me and have a care for your wellbeing."

"I don't heed anyone. I'm my own woman."

And how dare he tell her he was only concerned for her because he was being paid to do so, then make demands? He had no right. She had allowed his sinful mouth to rot her mind.

"Marchioness," he hissed, his tone warning.

"Beast," she returned, her tone biting. Because if he intended to act as if whatever this was between them didn't signify, then so did she. And he was keeping her from her garden. "Let me go."

His jaw tightened. "Not until I have your promise."

She pursed her lips, holding his stare. "I suppose you'll be here all day, then."

Theo sighed. "My lady, be reasonable, if you please. I'm only trying to protect you as I've been tasked with doing."

"You've been tasked with protecting Ridgely as I understood it," she countered, "and you've made it clear that protecting me is merely a duty you're being paid for. But I must thank you, truly, for your misplaced sense of obligation. I absolve you of it."

"Don't be so damned stubborn."

What did he want from her? It seemed that just as soon as the invisible boundaries separating them were crossed, he built them up again. They stared at each other, both of them refusing to relent, and suddenly the sky opened in truth, sending raindrops falling around them, loudly splattering on plants and hedges and gravel.

"It's raining," she said lamely, as if she were imparting a secret he wasn't privy to.

Thank heavens for the terrace above, the ledge of which stretched out overhead, keeping them dry.

"So it is." His gaze had strayed to her lips.

Pamela didn't miss it. She shifted so that she was pressed against him, from hip to chest, and she felt the evidence of his desire. He wasn't as unaffected as he pretended.

"Will you let me go now?" she prodded, even though remaining where she was appealed more and more by the moment.

"Don't think I will."

The hint of his accent had returned to lace his low, gruff voice. She shivered, but it was neither from the cold, nor the damp.

"My basket is likely filling with water."

He raised a brow, impassive as ever. "It has a lid."

Her patience had been tested and stretched beyond its breaking point. Something inside her snapped.

"Did last night mean nothing to you, then?" she asked.

For it had, she could acknowledge to herself alone, meant a great deal to her. Nor had the reason been pleasure alone. It was him, as well. Theo, whose surname she didn't even know, whose lips had taken hers with such tenderness and fierce hunger. Who had pulled her into his lap as if it were where she belonged. Who dared to make demands of her body and mind that she hadn't allowed from anyone else in four long years.

"Last night," he repeated, his voice low, and she felt it like a caress over her bare skin.

"Yes." Warmth flooded her cheeks. "You know what I'm referring to."

"Do I?"

"Of course, you do," she bit out, frustrated, grasping handfuls of his lapels and tugging. "Don't pretend as if you've forgotten. I trust I was the only woman you were kissing last night."

Kissing her *everywhere*, she might have added, but wisely did not.

It was scandalous enough, what she had done with him. What she wanted to do with him again.

"I'll tell you whether or not you were, but only after you give me your promise." His voice was smooth.

The scoundrel. He was doing everything in his power to extract the promise from her that she did not want to give. Not because she intended to cast herself headlong into danger, but because she didn't like the notion of answering to him, particularly when he remained so aloof. And because the way he made her feel was so very new. New and unwanted. Inside her, there brewed a confusing sea of longing and guilt. She had always done what she was supposed to do. She had been a dutiful daughter and wife, and later, a proper widow. But she'd forgotten herself somewhere along the way.

"I need to retrieve my basket and go inside," she lied, for in truth there was no hurry. She hadn't any pressing engagements this morning, and Lady Virtue was otherwise occupied until they paid calls later in the afternoon.

"Stubborn," he said, but there was an underlying tone of admiration in his voice that she didn't miss.

And her stupid heart leapt.

Conversely, the more he wanted her promise, the less she wanted to give it to him. This little verbal clash meant she could have more of his time, more of his attention. She hadn't remembered what it felt like to yearn for someone else, but she did now.

"Determined," she said, giving his coat lapels a gentle tug. "Besides, I hardly think you intend to keep me here all day."

He shrugged, as if they had all the time in the world and they weren't standing beneath an overhang while rain pelted the earth just beyond. "The notion has its merits."

His head dipped, bringing his mouth closer to hers.

"It's cold," she protested, breathless.

"I'll warm you," he said, and then he kissed her.

His lips were cool and soft. He angled them over hers slowly, tenderly. She didn't require any coaxing to open. When his tongue slid inside, they sighed as one, the kiss quickly deepening. He stepped forward, pinning her more firmly against the stone wall, and she knew she would never look upon Hunt House again without remembering how it had felt to have her mouth plundered by Theo beneath the terrace as the rain lashed the gardens behind them.

The scent of the earth rose around them, but there was

also him, citrus and damp wool and the sharp, clean tang of soap. She released her grip on his coat, her arms wrapping around his neck, fingers tangling in the ends of hair at his nape. He cupped her throat with one cool, bare hand, the kiss of metal against her skin as familiar now as his lips—the ring he wore on his forefinger. She tasted his morning tea as she ran her tongue against his, battling him without words just as she had verbally.

Between them, his cock was a prominent ridge, long and hard against her belly. The temptation to touch him there was strong, to cup her hand over the fall of his trousers, to undo the buttons, let him spring free. To lift her gown and petticoats and take him inside her right here, in the cold rain, nothing but the imperious stone wall at her back.

He was like a poison in her blood, and she very much feared there was only one way to cure what ailed her. More of him.

But then he broke the kiss and dragged his lips to her ear, breathing hot against it, catching her lobe in his teeth. "Your promise, Marchioness."

She wanted to tell him to call her Pamela.

Wanted far more than that.

His mouth went down her throat, licking and sucking until her knees threatened to give out and she was aching for him. She understood now what he intended to do. He was seducing the promise from her. And he was succeeding, too.

His other hand slid beneath her buttoned spencer to cup her breast, his thumb unerringly finding her stiff nipple. She gasped, arching into him. He rubbed his stubble against her neck, rolling the tender bud between his thumb and forefinger. Plucking and pulling.

"Promise me," he whispered against her skin.

She swallowed hard, unable to chase the rising tide of

desire. He knew how to make her weaken with scarcely any effort at all.

"I promise," she relented at last.

But the moment he'd wrangled the promise from her lips, he straightened to his full height, his hands leaving her bereft as they left her body. "Finally. I thought you would make me wait forever."

If only she possessed that much restraint where he was concerned. Or any at all.

"Stay here," he added sternly, and then he turned away, rushing into the slashing rain as she stared helplessly at his tall, broad form disappearing into the garden hedges.

The instinct to chase after him was strong, but she was nothing if not a woman of her word, and even if he had seduced the promise from her, she had made it. Trying to gather her wits and her composure both, Pamela remained where she was, leaning against the stone wall, awaiting Theo's return.

Somehow, she was not surprised to find him dashing back moments later, bearing her abandoned basket and thoroughly sodden.

"You didn't need to go into the rain to fetch my basket," she protested.

"If I hadn't, you would have done so," he said.

And he was not wrong.

"Perhaps," she allowed, reaching for the basket. "Thank you."

"I'll carry it," he said. "Come with me. We'll use the tunnels leading from the gardens to keep you dry."

He didn't wait for her response, simply strode past her toward one of several large doors on this side of the edifice. It startled Pamela to realize Theo knew the passages which ran below Hunt House better than she did. But then, she supposed it should hardly come as a surprise. She had a distinct suspicion that the darkened halls within weren't the only thing this mysterious man knew better than she did.

Bemused, she trailed in his wake, following him to the door and stepping past him, into the coolness of the stone passage. He joined her inside, the door shutting and quieting the rain outside. A row of high, arched windows brought faint light into the musty-smelling corridor, illuminating the passage enough for her to watch Theo bar the door they had entered and make certain it was secured. He must have entered the garden through it, she realized.

He turned to her, still holding her wet basket over his arm. Sprigs of rosemary and thyme protruded from one corner, his hair was slicked down his forehead, he was soaked from the rain, and there was no reason why he should be so unfairly beautiful standing there before her.

And yet, he was.

"Do you know your way, or shall I guide you to the main hall?" he asked, having no notion of the reckless thoughts flying through her addled mind.

Which was just as well. She didn't understand them herself.

"Perhaps you could guide me," she managed.

Eschewing the servant halls, he guided her deftly through the passageways until they reached a stairway that led to a small, hidden door in the entrance hall. She had traveled the halls before, of course, but it had been many years since she had done so with the abandon of a young woman eager to explore.

"Here you are, my lady," he said, offering her the basket as he stood before the door. "I'll take the passages to the servants' quarters."

She accepted the basket, so many emotions fluttering inside her, like the wings of frantic butterflies. "Thank you."

Pamela wanted to say more. Longed to, in fact. But in the

end, she knew it wasn't wise. Instead, she skirted him, reaching for the latch on the door.

"Lady Deering?" he called out, staying her.

She cast a glance over her shoulder, finding him watching her in the shadows, wet and handsome and mysterious.

"I owe you your answer," he said. "Everything. Last night meant everything to me, and that's why it mustn't happen again."

He bowed, and then hastily took his leave, disappearing into the darkness.

For a long time after he had gone, Pamela stood there, looking into the empty space where he had been, wishing she'd had the courage to chase after him. Knowing he had been right.

What had happened between them mustn't happen again.

But that didn't mean she didn't want it to, and more than she wanted to take her next breath.

CHAPTER 10

By the time Theo arrived at Archer Tierney's town house, he was drenched from the rain and thoroughly irritated with himself for the lack of control he'd been exhibiting whenever a certain gorgeous marchioness was within reach. He hated himself for wanting her, and yet, he couldn't seem to stop himself where she was concerned.

Although the distraction and opportunity to leave Hunt House and Lady Deering behind in favor of answering Tierney's summons should have been welcomed, Theo was undeniably grim. Tierney's man answered the door with his customary scowl.

"You again," was all Lucky said.

"Tierney asked me to call," he offered in explanation as rivulets of water ran off his hat.

Behind him, the din of the street was unusually quiet. The chill in the air had only grown colder as the day had progressed, and the rain showed no sign of stopping. Likely, others had possessed more common sense than Theo and had decided to remain at home and dry.

Lucky's lip curled into a sneer as he stepped aside with

what appeared to be reluctance, allowing Theo *entrée*. "Come."

Theo entered and removed his soaked hat and greatcoat, not wishing to drip all over Tierney's fine floors. He hadn't an inkling why he'd been summoned again so soon, but he feared it was somehow related to Stasia.

He followed Tierney's man to the study and waited as Lucky knocked at the door.

At the curt voice on the other side bidding him to enter, Lucky swept the portal open, raking Theo with a disdainful glare as Theo slipped past. He'd never understand the man's dislike of him, and nor would he understand Tierney's loyalty to the brooding guard. But when he made it two strides across the threshold and he realized Tierney wasn't alone, he forgot about everything else.

There, by the roaring fire in the grate, wearing a gown the deep, majestic hue of the St. George family colors, stood his sister. Theo stopped, his gut clenching. It had been ten long years since he'd seen her last, and she'd been little more than a child herself then, but he would recognize her anywhere. She had their father's blue eyes and cold, compassionless demeanor. But she looked like their mother, too.

For a moment, he felt as if he were staring at a ghost.

The past came rushing back to him like a pair of hands wrapped around his neck, threatening to choke.

"Theo," she said, moving toward him, a gold necklace at her throat catching his attention, for it bore the coat of arms their mother had been given at her marriage to the king.

A coat of arms which had been banished and outlawed by the king's deathbed decree so that anyone caught wearing it would be punished by death on the gallows.

He jerked his gaze from her, saying nothing for fear of what might emerge, looking to Archer Tierney, who stood with a hip propped against his desk in a deceptively indolent pose, watching the drama unfold. His expression was unreadable as ever.

"What is she doing here?" Theo bit out.

"You may speak to me directly, brother," Stasia said in flawless English that, had he not known better, would have convinced him she had spent all her days in England rather than trapped in Boritania beneath the thumbs of their uncle and brother.

He glared at Tierney, who shrugged his shoulders. "I delivered your message. The princess is deuced persistent."

Theo didn't care how persistent she was. She had come to the wrong man.

He turned back to her with great reluctance, noting she had stopped a few feet away. Close enough to bring all the memories of their youth which he had fought to banish from his mind.

"You should have listened to Tierney when he told you that your brother is dead," he told Stasia coldly. "You've wasted your time in seeking out a man who doesn't exist."

"But I can see you, living and breathing before me," she countered, looking so elegant now and like a woman fully grown. Every inch the princess she had likely been forced to become. "How do you dare to lie to my face, after everything I've endured to find you?"

He wondered for a moment at what she could have endured. He saw no marks on her arms. Her skin was far too golden for London drawing rooms, which suggested she'd recently been in Boritania.

"I never asked anyone to find me," he snarled.

"Well, Christ, does this mean you *are* a Boritanian prince, Beast?" Tierney drawled.

"No," he said.

"Yes," Stasia answered simultaneously.

Their eyes were locked. Emotions he had buried deep, so

deep, were rising, and he didn't want them. Didn't want to feel them.

"I shudder to think what the rest of your siblings are like," Tierney said, humor lacing his voice. "Just how many of you are there?"

"I haven't any family," Theo denied, shaking his head. "No siblings."

"That's a lie." Stasia's chin tipped up, her expression stern and demanding and familiar. He'd seen it before on their mother's face whenever she refused to relent. "His name is not Beast. He is Theodoric Augustus St. George, and the true and rightful king of Boritania."

Her words shook him. Was this some manner of trick? Perhaps their uncle had sent her here to lure him back to Boritanian shores so he could finish what he had begun ten years ago. Gustavson wouldn't have been wrong in choosing Stasia. Of all his siblings, he had been closest to her, before his imprisonment. They had been near enough in age. He'd been protective of her, knowing their uncle's intentions of selling her off as a bride at the earliest opportunity, using her to increase his influence.

"Reinald is the true and rightful King of Boritania," he said, speaking of their brother.

The one who had taken his place.

The one it had taken him years to forgive for believing their uncle's lies. For doing nothing to stay Theo's torture until it had almost been too late.

"That is why I've come looking for you," Stasia told him quietly, looking far too solemn for a woman of her years. For a princess who should have had every opportunity in the world presented to her.

"Because Reinald has demanded my return?" Theo would have spat in the old Boritanian way, to show his disgust, but he didn't think Tierney would take kindly to spittle on his

Axminster. Instead, he snorted. "The only way I'll go back to Boritania is as a dead man. Or perhaps, sister, that's why you've come." His mind spun. It would make sense. He had always known that if his uncle and brother would have sent an assassin for him, it would have been someone whom he least expected.

Someone like Stasia.

"Now you acknowledge me, when you accuse me of plotting your murder?" Her blue eyes bored into him, accusatory.

"Gin?" Tierney interrupted, offering a glass to Theo by pressing it into his hand. "Go on, old chap. I know you don't ordinarily imbibe, but you look as if you need it."

Theo's fingers curled around the cool glass. Inside, he was cold. Cold and angry. His chest was tight. Ten long years he'd struggled to find his place outside Boritania. Ten years of building himself up from the beaten and broken man he'd been. And now, here was the past, standing before him, reminding him precisely of who he was.

"Am I not to be offered any?" Stasia demanded of Tierney.

Theo raised the glass to his lips and took a slow pull of the liquid, relishing the burn as it slid down his throat. Something passed between his sister and their host, a wordless challenge of power, perhaps. And then Tierney relented, bowing.

"Whatever Her Royal Highness desires," Tierney said, his tone mocking.

He rose to his full height, stalked to the sideboard, and poured an amount of liquid into the glass that was far, far too much for a lady. Theo wondered if he should object, but then he quickly quelled the protective brotherly urge rising within, for he owed Stasia nothing. He didn't even know if he could trust her. Indeed, he was reasonably certain he should not.

Tierney brought her the gin, and she accepted it, raising her glass in Boritanian tradition.

"*Saluté*," she said, using the traditional Boritanian toast, and then she took a large pull from the glass.

Theo had to credit her—she showed nary a hint of dislike. Her expression remained perfectly unaffected as she swallowed the gin.

"There," she said triumphantly. "Now we will speak."

"Stasia," he protested, not wanting to hear what she had to say. It had been too long, and this business with Lady Deering had brought vulnerabilities to the surface which he'd already believed long buried.

"Reinald is missing, and Gustavson has assumed the throne," his sister said in Boritanian then.

And just like that, the careful world he'd built for himself in London splintered into jagged shards and disintegrated into dust.

Pamela and Lady Virtue returned from their evening engagements that night with mutual sighs of relief as they alighted from Ridgely's carriage and made their way up the walk. The rain of earlier in the day had given way to blustery cold, but at least the sky was clear for now. It wasn't the weather which had left her weary, however. Instead—and much to her shock—it had been one of the few refuges in which she'd found comfort following Bertie's death: society.

The dinner held by Lord and Lady Cunningham and the ensuing musical evening had been—

"Dreadfully boring," Lady Virtue murmured at her side, quite as if she had been somehow privy to Pamela's thoughts and was completing them for her aloud.

"Are you referring to my companionship or to our host

and hostess's entertainments this evening?" she asked the younger woman, all too aware that as the matron charged with shepherding her brother's ward through the *ton,* she was meant to encourage the girl.

Not agree with her assessment of an evening during which there had been excellent food—which may as well have been sawdust for all that Pamela had tasted it—and ample opportunity for Lady Virtue to make a match. All of it dull. She'd been able to think of nothing but returning to Hunt House and the possibility she might see Theo again.

"I was referring to the dubious evening's entertainments," Lady Virtue told her as they approached the imposing front door and it swept open.

"There was nothing dubious about them," Pamela felt compelled to argue, even though she agreed.

Mere days ago, however, she wouldn't have. Instead, she would have happily chattered about the fashion plates in the latest edition of *Ackermann's* and whether or not red Morocco slippers would best pair with a morning dress of cambric muslin or black kid. She would have whispered with Lady Dilmont about the shocking way Lord Pinehurst had flirted with Mrs. Aylesbury. She would have taken solace in listening to some raucous Scottish reels sung at the pianoforte. She wouldn't have spent every moment distracted, thinking of a place she would far rather be.

And that was a problem. A very large, very much unwanted, sinfully handsome bodyguard-shaped problem.

"If one doesn't find engaging in meaningless conversation with tedious people dubious, I suppose," Lady Virtue grudgingly allowed as a servant came forward and took their wraps.

"One cannot forever have one's nose buried in a book," Pamela pointed out crisply, ever cognizant of the fact that she was meant to be encouraging her brother's ward to wed.

Lady Virtue was a bluestocking who preferred the company of books to the company of others.

"One cannot have one's nose in a book at all at the moment," Lady Virtue groused. "Particularly when one's arrogant, meddlesome guardian has confiscated them all."

They moved into the entrance hall, and Pamela found herself casting glances about.

Searching for Theo.

"Ridgely has taken all your books?" she asked quietly, frowning at her brother's high-handedness.

It was quite unlike him to be so overbearing. Indeed, it was quite unlike him to take note of anything that wasn't directly related to his own pleasure. It wasn't that he was selfish; it was merely that he was a hedonist. He was almost never serious about anything. But he had been quite serious about Virtue. And there had been that dreadfully foolish incident in the library.

Hmm.

"Yes, he has." Lady Virtue was frowning at her. "Do you think you might speak to him, persuade him to see a bit of reason? He has also forbidden me from entering the library."

Pamela was about to retort that staying away from the library was likely a fine idea for her. But then she felt the unmistakable sensation of someone watching her. She turned her head ever so slightly and her stare meshed with a cool, hazel-gray gaze.

Theo stood in one of the doorways in the entrance hall, no longer soaked to the skin as he'd been when they'd last parted that morning after he had rescued her basket and herbs from the rain and then led her through the passageways. The connection, even with others surrounding them, separated by a vast marble floor and the watchful eyes of servants, made a jolt go through her. It was as if they spoke to each other with that look.

She was recalling his words in the shadowy halls belowstairs. Remembering his deep, accented voice telling her that last night had meant everything to him.

"Lady Deering?"

Lady Virtue's questioning voice broke through Pamela's thoughts, and she reluctantly forced herself to look away from Theo, back to her brother's ward.

She forced a smile, hoping she hadn't been caught. "Yes, my dear?"

"Would you speak to His Grace on my behalf about returning my books?" she repeated, still frowning. "I would ask him myself, but I haven't seen him since…in a few days."

Yes, dear girl. Wise not to mention when you last saw Ridgely or what you were doing with him before the servants, Pamela thought grimly.

Or ever.

"I'll speak with my brother," she chirped brightly, trying to pretend as if she didn't feel Theo's eyes on her, following her, just as surely as if he were running his callused hands all over her bare skin.

Oh dear heavens.

That was what she wanted.

She wanted him to touch her everywhere. She wanted more of what had happened last night. Only, this time she didn't want him to stop until he was inside her.

The wicked notion made liquid heat pool between her thighs and a strange, shivery feeling tickle her belly. The reaction was so sudden, so intense, that she nearly tripped over the hem of her gown. All whilst she was calmly escorting her charge through the entrance hall. Because she was supposed to be the proper, staid widow. She was supposed to be the voice of reason. The collected one. The one who didn't cause scandal but snubbed it out before it could begin, like a candle's flame extinguished beneath a sturdy snuffer.

"Thank you," Lady Virtue said softly, giving Pamela a searching look that made her wonder if the younger woman had seen her eying Theo.

Heat crept over her cheeks, but she forced her smile to remain on her lips even though it felt more like she was grimacing. "Of course, my dear. Now, then. We should get some rest. The hour is late."

Pamela's thoughts wandered where they shouldn't again, back to Theo, as she and Lady Virtue climbed the spiral staircase. Would she see him again tonight? Had he been awaiting her return home this evening? Was she the reason he had been in the entrance hall? Had he been lingering in the hope that he would see her?

Just as quickly as the questions bubbled up within her, Pamela dismissed them. How foolish she was, harboring all these forbidden thoughts. She had already risked far too much with him. No, she would far better serve herself by keeping her mind where it belonged—on the task of seeing Lady Virtue married to a respectable gentleman.

"What did you think of Lord Saltersford?" she asked Lady Virtue as they climbed the stairs. "It seemed the two of you were engaged in an engrossing conversation at dinner."

"He wanted me to pass the peas," Lady Virtue said succinctly.

Well. It would seem Pamela had been rather distracted at dinner as well. She could have sworn Lady Virtue and the earl had been enjoying each other's company. Hopefully her brother's ward hadn't taken note.

"Was that all he said, my dear?"

Lady Virtue sent her a tight smile. "Quite."

They rounded a curve and proceeded to the next floor. "Perhaps it was Lord Silvertry I was thinking of, then. You were seated next to each other for the musical entertainments, were you not?"

"There was a fellow seated to my left who I do believe fell asleep during Lady Anne's turn at the pianoforte," Lady Virtue said with a sniff. "I heard him snoring. Was Silvertry his name? I confess, I was introduced to so many gentlemen this evening that I cannot recall them all."

The younger woman wasn't making Pamela's efforts to see her married any easier. Indeed, she had made it abundantly clear that she had no wish to marry at all. But Ridgely had other plans for her, and Pamela liked to think Lady Virtue would find happiness in a marriage with a loving husband. As it was, the girl was an orphan, with no home or family to speak of.

"Many excellent prospects for marriage," Pamela forced herself to remind Lady Virtue. "Are there any beaus who have captured your attention?"

"None," Lady Virtue denied with a beleaguered sigh. "I do so wish you and Ridgely would cease all attempts at forcing me into marriage. It isn't a husband I want. All I wish for is to return to my home."

Poor, dear girl. Lady Virtue was having difficulty accepting that her father's unentailed estate, Greycote Abbey, was being sold. Pamela understood all too well the pains and changes that came with death.

"Give yourself time," Pamela advised her, thinking of how happy she'd been in her own marriage with Bertie. Yes, it was best to think of that. To remember the lasting love she had found with her husband instead of the fast-and-furious lust she felt with Theo.

"I fear no amount of time shall change my mind on the matter," Lady Virtue declared. "The sooner His Grace realizes it, the better off we all shall be."

They reached the top of the stairs and carried on down

the hall, Pamela seeing her brother's ward to her chamber door. Impulsively, she reached out and gave the younger woman's gloved hands an affectionate squeeze. "We only want what is best for you, my dear. Both His Grace and myself."

She thought of her brother's scandalous behavior toward Lady Virtue in the library then and frowned. Well, perhaps Ridgely wanted what was best for himself, but she had no doubt that her anger at what she'd witnessed had cured him of that particular selfishness. He knew as well as Pamela did that he didn't want to take a wife. But if he dallied with Lady Virtue again, then a wife he would have.

"That is the trouble," Lady Virtue said with a sad smile of her own. "Everyone always thinks they know what is best for me, that I don't know what is best for myself. All my choices have been taken away from me."

A pang grew in Pamela's heart at those words, for she well understood them. Felt them to her core. Her own choices had been taken from her when she had been a debutante faced with the pressure to marry. She'd been fortunate indeed to find love with Bertie. But then after his death, her choices and her life had yet again ceased to be her own.

"All we want is for you to find your happiness," she told Lady Virtue through a throat gone thick with emotion. "Now do get some rest, my dear. Tomorrow we've the Marquess and Marchioness of Searle's ball to attend."

"Another ball?" Lady Virtue's nose wrinkled in disgust.

"Yes, another ball," she said, pretending as if she were overjoyed by the notion, when in truth, she had no desire to attend either.

She released Lady Virtue's hands, feeling suddenly older than her years. It hadn't occurred to her until this moment that she had thrown herself into the social whirl after her period of mourning was over out of a sense of obligation as much as the need for distraction. She was the dutiful daughter, the good wife, and now the proper widow, always doing what she had been told she must do. Living for everyone else and their expectations, never for herself.

Good heavens, little wonder Lady Virtue was rebelling against the life in which she now found herself. Pamela was shocked to discover how much they had in common.

"Is something amiss?" Lady Virtue's concerned voice interrupted Pamela's thoughts.

She forced another smile, wondering how much her countenance had betrayed her. "Of course not. I'm merely weary as well. Good evening, my dear."

After making certain Lady Virtue was safely ensconced in her chamber, Pamela hesitated in the hall, tempted to seek out Theo before retiring for the night and yet knowing she should not. Her lady's maid would be awaiting her to assist. And going to Theo would only lead to more dreadful decisions, she was sure of it.

Still, the part of her that longed to live for herself again remained persistent, tugging at her. But she was stronger. Pamela forced her feet to carry her to her chamber. Forced herself to perform the necessary evening ritual. Her lady's maid took away her gown and petticoats and helped Pamela with her hair. Her jewelry was returned to its case, her gloves and stockings taken for laundering.

But when she was alone again, having dismissed her lady's maid for the night, she found herself pacing the sumptuous carpets instead of seeking her bed and the rest she knew she should likely obtain. Particularly after her sins the night before had kept her awake so very long.

Don't go to him, she told herself one step.

I must find him, she thought with the next.

No, it is wrong.

I'll never forgive myself if I don't.

And on and on, until finally, she went to the door and tore it open, her body moving of its own volition, taking her where it wished to go. Which, as it turned out, wasn't far.

Because not two paces away from her door, Theo stood in the darkened hall, his familiar figure a welcome sight as he strode toward her with the same purpose she'd felt inside. It was inevitable, inexorable, this pull between them.

He stood before her, his eyes blazing into hers, his expression raw and unguarded. He waited on the threshold, the candlelight and fire from her chamber lovingly illuminating all the stark angles and planes of his beautiful face.

She took a few steps backward into her chamber, not in retreat, but in welcome. He'd made her decision for her. Or, it would seem, they'd made it together. It was a decision that had been put into motion that first afternoon they'd met. One that had continued with each passing interaction. Every kiss, touch, longing look. All the words said and unspoken.

Theo crossed the threshold and slowly closed the door at his back with quiet care, his gaze never leaving hers. When it was all the way shut, he remained there, staring at her, his broad shoulders taking up nearly all the paneled wood.

"Theo," she said softly, a rush of tenderness blossoming inside her, rivaling the desire.

He appeared somehow vulnerable. Although, perhaps it was a trick of the light. Or a trick of her own mind and the frustrated musings that had been occupying it ever since that morning's stolen kisses beneath the terrace. She wanted to kiss him again now.

She wanted those unsmiling lips on hers.

"Lady Deering." He held two fingers to his mouth, and then, as if they were in the most formal of circumstances, he offered her a courtly bow.

It was elegant and practiced, that bow, as if he had bowed in countless drawing rooms and ballrooms beneath glittering chandeliers. But she had never seen the distinct salute, the kissing of fingers as he had done. The act seemed somehow intimate. Erotic, although they were both fully clothed and not an untoward word had been uttered.

She touched the buttons at her throat, the frills on her dressing gown.

"Are you on duty this evening?" she asked.

But truly, she was asking so much more, and he knew it as well as she did.

He had straightened from his bow. "Not now, my lady."

She was already plucking the buttons from their moorings, her fingers trembling. "My given name is Pamela."

"Pamela," he repeated softly, somehow making her name sound carnal.

Heat unfurled low in her belly, and lower still. "Will you stay with me?"

For a long moment, he was silent, his eyes watching the progress of her fingers, undoing that long line of buttons. Her dressing gown was gaping, parting to reveal her thin night rail beneath. She didn't stop, and nor did she hesitate. She reached her waist and continued down, holding his stare.

The only sound was the soft rustle of linen and the crackle of the fire in the grate.

At last, he spoke, uttering the single most beautiful word she'd heard from his sinful lips, aside from her name. "Yes."

THEO'S COCK strained painfully against the fall of his trousers as Lady Deering—he had to think of her as Pamela now, a strange, intimate luxury—shrugged. The action sent the ivory confection that was her dressing gown from her shoulders. He should not have come to her. He should have stayed away. But everything was falling apart around him, and somehow, she was the only source of solace. It scarcely made any sense, and yet, when he looked into her eyes, he knew she felt the same.

If they were drowning in the world, then they might drown together. Sink beneath the stormy waves in each other's arms.

His booted feet were carrying him across her fine Axminster floor in muted thumps before his mind had even formed the thought to move. His body was governing the rest of him, taking him to what he wanted, what he needed most.

Her.

They collided, her soft, smooth arms twining around his neck and her full breasts crushing into his chest. Her exotic scent surrounded him, chasing dark thoughts from his mind. The unexpected meeting with Stasia and the revelations she had made fell away. There was only this moment, this next breath, the frantic beat of his heart, the woman tilting her head back to look up at him with so much hunger that his knees actually trembled.

He, who had been tortured nearly to death in his uncle's dungeon, who had survived the ugly sea crossing from Boritania, followed by a decade of living dangerously as a cutthroat mercenary, was shaken to his soul by one woman whose ice turned into flame. Flame he wanted to be burned in. Flame to make him forget, even if only for one night. Even if only for one hour. By Deus, he would pitch himself into a raging fire for one second with her. That was how strong his need for her was.

Theo lowered his head and buried his face in the fragrant hair at her temple. Unbound, the burnished waves glinted in the warm glow of the candles. He took a moment to inhale, to savor her.

"I saw you," she murmured, fingers toying with the ends

of his hair that he'd thought to cut until he'd known how good it felt for her to tangle her dainty hands in it. "In the entry hall when we arrived home this evening."

He had seen her too. It hadn't been his intention; he'd been committing a final tour of Hunt House before turning the reins over to his men for the night. What he'd meant to do was avoid her. To return to his room and think about what he must do with the information Stasia had imparted.

But the commotion in the front hall had told him that someone was arriving, and he'd lingered stupidly and recklessly in the hope that it would be her. When their gazes had met and clung across the space, he had known that he wasn't going to his chamber. There was only one place he could go, given the torment eating him from within, and it was to her.

"You looked beautiful," he told her, lifting his head to survey her anew. "But you are even more glorious now, like this."

She gave him a small smile. "I'm not nearly as beautiful as Lady Virtue. She is young and innocent."

He hadn't had eyes for the lady accompanying her. She may as well have not been present for the attention he had paid her.

"You were all I saw," he told Pamela. "You're all I want to see."

There were other ways he could elaborate, other means of explaining himself to her. And yet, the emotions inside him were too strong, too overwrought, and the only words he could find were Boritanian. So he held his tongue.

"You needn't woo me," she said softly. "You've already won me."

But had he? Not truly. He'd won her for this night. Fate had never been kind to Theo St. George, and he knew that cruel, fickle mistress had no intention of changing her ways now. He would seize the night. Make her his while he still could.

"I'm not wooing." He kissed her lips lightly, just one chaste buss before ending it. "I'm telling you the truth."

Her hands slid from his nape to cup his face, her palms smooth and warm. "Who are you, Theo? Who are you truly?"

He could never tell her that. If he did, there was the very real possibility that she would be in danger. If what Stasia had said was true, then there were already Boritanian spies infiltrating London, and they knew who and where he was. But he wouldn't think of that now. Not with Pamela caressing his face. Tomorrow, he would contemplate the repercussions. He would make decisions. Tonight, he was where he needed to be.

He turned his head, kissing her palm. "I'm your lover."

"Oh," she whispered, lower lip trembling.

She likely hadn't expected such a frank response. She'd wanted more, his full name, his past. Perhaps calling himself her lover had been careless of him. She was akin to a shying horse just now, and he had no wish to spook her further and send her bucking and galloping away.

"If you wish it," he added quietly. "Or the man who holds you in his arms whilst you sleep if you wish for that instead."

He didn't tell her that he would be fully clothed whilst he did so, in either event. It wasn't a subject he'd broached with lovers in his past for there'd been no need then; he'd been unscarred. But with Pamela, it would be different. She would want everything from him, and he could not give it. Anything else, yes. But not that last part of himself, the part he loathed, the part where his demons lurked.

"I don't want to sleep," she said.

"You are certain?" he pressed, because her words had made his cock throb.

She licked her lips, the sight somehow innocent and

alluring all at once. "Yes. I want… I want what happened last night, only more."

The lust coursing through him was instant and intense.

He took her lips with his, telling himself that he would kiss her slowly and failing the moment she opened for him. The kiss turned hard and hungry, their tongues tangling. He poured himself into the movement of his lips over hers, telling her everything he couldn't put into words.

She tasted like wine, and he wondered where she'd been this evening. Whom she had spoken with, danced and flirted with. For a moment, he wished he'd been a guest there. Wished he was the suave courtier he'd once been, just so that he could meet her in a setting where they were equals. So he could bow over her hand and sweep her into a waltz and woo her as she deserved, instead of with stolen kisses and furtive touches, hidden away from the world.

At least this evening, they would have the comfort of a bed, though he hadn't minded being on his knees for her. Not for a single second. She deserved to be worshiped, not just because of how lovely she was, but because she had ignored her own needs and desires for far too long. Perhaps they were well matched in that, for he had grown accustomed to isolating and denying himself.

Her hands slid to his coat, pulling at the lapels, trying to work it from his shoulders. This, he allowed, shrugging it away. But when she moved to the buttons of his waistcoat, he stopped her as before, catching her fingers in his.

Theo raised his head, his breathing ragged. "It stays."

Her brow furrowed, but she didn't question him. "Your boots?"

He swallowed hard, a rush of tenderness rising up within him at her calm acceptance. "I'll remove them."

Although he had cleaned them after his return from Tierney's, they weren't unsoiled. He wouldn't drag the street muck into her bed.

"Let me help you," she said, surprising him with the offer.

The very notion of Pamela on her knees before him, helping him to remove his boots, brought a multitude of wicked thoughts to his depraved mind.

"You needn't," he rasped, not certain he would be able to control himself.

"I want to." Smiling shyly, she took his hand in hers, linking their fingers before guiding him to an overstuffed chair by the hearth. She placed her hands on his shoulders, urging him downward. "Sit."

There was nothing to do but obey. Theo sank into the chair, mesmerized as she smoothed back a lock of hair which had fallen across his forehead. She kissed his cheek, his jaw. The corner of his lips.

He gripped the arms of the chair and made a frustrated sound low in his throat, sounding more beast than man and feeling the same. "You shouldn't—"

Two slim, elegant fingers pressed to his lips, silencing his protest. "Hush. Let me tend to you."

No one had tended to him in years. And even when they had, women had fawned over him because he was the prince. Servants had attended him because they had been paid to do so. But here was a woman who wanted to show him care simply because she could. A woman who knew nothing of him, nothing of his past.

To her, he was a mercenary, a man for hire.

He kissed her fingertips, then caught her in a gentle grasp and turned her palm over so that he could set his lips to the silken skin of her inner wrist. "Thank you."

She withdrew from him and sank to her knees on the Axminster. Grasping his right boot in her hands, she gave a firm, swift tug that bespoke experience with such a task. He wondered briefly if this was a chore she had undertaken for her husband and then tamped down the question and accompanying surge of jealousy as unworthy.

The worn leather boots that had stood him in good stead for years now were no match for her surprising strength. The first boot was off, neatly laid aside. Next came the second, which was also pulled away and placed by its twin.

He sat before her in his stockinged feet, watching the play of the firelight in her tresses. Her hands settled on his knees lightly, bearing no more weight than butterflies, before sweeping higher.

Sweet Deus. His cock twitched.

She wasn't going to...

She was.

Her fingers moved to the fall of his trousers, finding the round discs of his buttons. He was gripping the arms of the chair so hard that he wouldn't be surprised by the sound of splintering, snapping wood as he tore the piece of furniture apart. She hesitated, her hair falling like a veil over part of her face as she glanced up at him, as if asking permission.

She needn't have, not with that part of him, which was pulsing and stiff, jutting against his trousers in crude invitation. His ballocks were heavy and drawn tight, his entire body on the razor's edge of sheer erotic splendor.

"Pamela," he said on a groan as another button slid free of its moorings.

Deus, her name felt good on his lips. Just as her hands felt good on his body. But he suspected they could feel even better without barriers between them. Just his cock, nothing more. He could allow that much, if only so that he could relive the pleasure of this night long after it was over and he was gone from her life forever.

"Just the fall of your trousers," she said softly. "Enough to free you."

It was as if she understood his misgiving without him needing to explain. Gratitude and lust slammed into him with equal force.

"Yes," he hissed out as her fingers grazed lightly over his cockstand. "Though nothing more."

Her expression didn't change, though he knew she must wonder at the cause for his refusal to disrobe. If she did, she didn't give voice to the question, and he was damned thankful for that as well.

But then, he forgot to be thankful. Forgot everything, including his own name. Because she undid the last of his buttons and with a bit of encouragement from her, his cock sprang free of his trousers and drawers both. He no longer had to wonder about how good her hand would feel on him without cloth separating them. Her fingers wrapped around his length, stroking him from base to tip.

A breath he hadn't realized he'd been holding escaped in a hiss. She swirled her thumb over his cock head. He was already leaking, and she slicked the pearly drops over him before taking him into her mouth.

His hips bucked, his white-knuckled grip on the chair going tighter still. Wet heat bathed his shaft as she drew him deeper and sucked. And then her tongue. Dear, sweet Deus, her tongue. It whorled over him, traveling the same path as her thumb had, before running along the underside, finding a place where he was particularly sensitive. All the while, she held him in a relentlessly firm grip, stroking and sucking, stroking and sucking. Her other hand had moved to his thigh, then higher, to his hip, caressing him as she took him down her throat.

He couldn't resist another second. He had to touch her. His fingers slipped into the softness of that blonde cloud falling around her face and down her back. He sifted it through his fingers, and it was like spun gold, and everything was too much. Her beautiful mouth wrapped around his cock, the sweet suction as she threatened to drain him dry. The breathy little moans she made as she spoiled him beyond any bliss he had known with another lover.

She was ruining him. Destroying him. He didn't deserve her. He couldn't get enough of her. And if he allowed her to remain as she was, those pretty pink lips stretched around his cock for another moment, he was going to spend down her throat.

He wanted that, but not if this was to be their only night.

If he never knew the glory of making love to her again, he wanted to be inside her, buried ballocks deep. Wanted to feel her tight heat welcoming him, her body thrusting to meet his.

"Enough," he managed to say, gently disengaging from her sinful, wonderful mouth.

She released him with a lusty, wet pop that somehow made him even harder. His prick bobbed, glistening with a mixture of her saliva and his leaking mettle, and the hunger in her face as she looked up at him, on her knees with the glow of the fire framing her and her lips swollen from taking his cock between them, was the single most erotic sight he had ever beheld.

"Did you…did I please you?" she asked hesitantly.

"You please me," he said, his throat thick, his voice strained. "You please me far too much. I want to be inside you."

She swallowed, her eyes darkening, and nodded. "Yes. I want that, too."

He had wanted to make love to her slowly, sweetly. But after she had taken him in her mouth and brought him to the brink of release, he wasn't certain how long he would last. Moving swiftly, he hooked his hands in her elbows and helped her to her feet. He kissed her again as he led her to the bed, tasting himself on her tongue, mingling with wine and Pamela and forbidden desire.

Every step, each eager stroke of her tongue against his, chiseled away at his control. They made it to the edge of the bed, and there was no restraint remaining. He lifted his head, breaking the kiss, breathing hard.

"Turn."

She did as he asked without hesitation, spinning away from him and facing the bed. His heart thundering in his chest and his cock aching for release, Theo took her hands in his and braced them on the pretty coverlet which had been drawn back, likely by a lady's maid. Then, he drew her night rail up to her waist, revealing the firm, pale globes of her backside. The urge to drop to his knees and sink his teeth into that sweet, tempting flesh was strong. But not as strong as the fiery need pumping through his veins.

He nudged her legs into a wider stance with one foot, making enough space for himself between them. Holding the hem of her nightgown in one hand, he palmed her rump with the other, squeezing lightly as he pressed his mouth to her ear.

"Are you wet?"

She nodded, face turning toward his, looking as if she were drunk on him, on pleasure. "Yes."

Theo dragged his fingers over her seam, parting her folds. She was soaked, and the knowledge that she was in such a state from sucking his cock made him groan. He teased her opening and then moved to her clitoris, strumming over the swollen bud lightly at first, and then with increased pressure as her hips moved.

"You're dripping, Marchioness," he said in her ear, before tonguing the whorl.

He wanted to lick and kiss and touch her everywhere. Wanted to fill her and fuck her and never let her go. Wanted to bury himself inside her and make her his not just for one night but for forever.

"Mmm," she said in wordless assent.

He teased his way back to her entrance, his fingers dipping into her in a shallow thrust that had her hips pumping backward, grinding her buttocks against his rigid cock. He was on fire for her, but he also wanted to prolong the moment, to bring them both as close to the edge as possible before they went over. In and out he stroked, loving the way her inner muscles gripped him, clinging, the wetness of her dew dripping down his hand, to his wrist where the sleeve of his shirt absorbed it.

He kissed her throat, sucking on the sensitive skin, and then licked the hollow behind her ear. The erotic sounds of his fingers moving inside her filled the air, along with her sweet, musky scent. Her breaths were coming in pants, her head tipped back as if she could no longer bear to hold it up, falling against his shoulder.

How delicious it was, the most potent aphrodisiac, to know she wanted him every bit as much as he wanted her.

Theo nipped her ear.

"Did sucking my cock make you this wet?" he asked wickedly, some deep, dark part of him reveling in the power he had to make her weak.

To melt her ice and turn it into fire.

"Yes," she murmured, breathy and desperate.

His in every way.

Deus. He had to be inside her now.

He withdrew his fingers and gripped his cock, coating himself in her wetness before he guided himself to her delicious, wet heat. "You want me inside you, don't you?"

"I do."

Ah, hellfire. He was going to die if he couldn't move. She was there, kissing the head of his cock, beckoning with her hot wet cunny. But if this was to be all they had, he intended to wring everything from her that he could.

He teased her entrance, then withdrew, rubbing himself up and down her slit. "Tell me. Say my name."

"Theo," she gasped out, hips circling, seeking. "I want you inside me."

And then she surprised him by reaching behind her with her right hand and grasping his wrist, urging him on. Showing him with her actions as well as her words just how desperately she needed him. The feeling was mutual.

"Brace yourself on the bed," he warned. "I'm not a gentle man."

Gentleness was no longer in him. But he would take care with her. He would see to her pleasure. Still, this would be no meek and mild coupling, and he wanted her to know it.

"If I wanted a gentleman, I wouldn't have chosen you," she said, clearly mistaking his words.

But that was well enough. He wasn't gentle, and nor was he a gentleman. He was a law unto himself, a man of shadows and darkness, forever running from the past, belonging nowhere and to no one.

And he liked her words. Liked that she had chosen him, of the many lords and dandies she no doubt could have had, as her first lover as a widow. He was humbled that a proud woman like her, so proper and careful in her mannerisms and dress, would not just choose him but want him. Desire him. Need him, even.

Her hand returned to the bed, fingers splayed. He nudged her legs a bit wider, notched his cock to her beckoning cunny, and slid inside. One fast, hard thrust, and he was fully seated, so deep inside her. The momentum carried them both onto the bed, her feet leaving the floor as he covered her body with his, pinning her to the mattress. Theo buried his face in her hair, breathing deep as he struggled to regain possession over himself.

But it was difficult. Damned difficult.

She was all tight, silken heat, so deliciously wet, gripping him so hard he thought he might explode after just one pump. He regained his footing, withdrawing from her slightly, his hands finding her lush hips and holding her to his liking. Another thrust, and she cried out.

Loudly.

The sound was throaty and steeped in ecstasy too long denied, and there was no doubt that if anyone overheard it, they would know exactly what was happening within the widowed Marchioness of Deering's bedchamber. That wouldn't do. Theo cared for her far too much, and he knew she guarded her reputation fiercely.

"Hush," he murmured, almost reverting to Boritanian. To the word for *princess*.

He was so lost in her, so far gone, that he had nearly forgotten himself. But the name suited her. It was right. It felt right.

And she felt right.

So right.

Fate had brought them together.

"You'll bring the house down upon us," he crooned into her ear, reminding her, reminding himself.

He kissed her cheek, the corner of her lips. She turned her head and kissed him too, her tongue thrusting into his mouth, and like every other exchange between them, Theo couldn't be sure who was seducing whom.

He had to move.

Without breaking their kiss, he rolled his hips, using short, quick thrusts. In and out, quick and hard. He had warned her he wouldn't be gentle, but she was meeting him halfway, using her balance on the bed to move in time with his hips, bringing him deeper. She was slippery, her cunny clenching on him with such delicious pressure that she nearly squeezed him out.

Pamela moaned into the kiss, and he realized she hadn't come yet. But she was close. He glided his hand from her hip to her mound, parting soft curls to find what he sought. The throbbing bud was sleek and hot. He pinched it between his thumb and forefinger, fucking her faster, deeper. Kissing her, his own breaths as ragged as hers.

He played with her clitoris, listening to her cues, strumming harder when she moaned into his mouth and her tongue slid almost drunkenly against his. By some sheer miracle of determination, he remained on his feet, cock sliding rhythmically through her wetness, hand working her nub, mouth feasting on hers.

She spent with a strangled cry that he swallowed, her cunny clamping on his cock so hard that little black stars dotted his vision. In his former life, he had always bedded his lovers with his eyes closed. But he wanted them open now. He didn't want to miss a single second of making her his.

When the last ripple of pleasure had been wrung from her, she partially collapsed to the bed, all without ending the kiss. He plunged in and out of her. Again. Again, so close, one more time, and…

"Pamela," he growled against her lips.

And then he jerked his mouth from hers and withdrew from her body, gripping his cock hard as he spent, his seed shooting across the perfect, creamy skin of her bottom as his heart pounded in his ears.

CHAPTER 11

Pamela woke in the darkness to the unfamiliar sensation of an arm slung protectively over her waist and another body curled against hers. The body was warm. And hard. And separated from her naked skin by barriers of cloth. And decidedly male.

The fire had long since burned low in the grate, and it cast scarcely any light.

Not that she needed light to know who it was holding her in his arms, his even breaths coasting over her ear. She would know him by his scent, by the way he felt, by her body's reaction to his. But more than that, she knew because her body was still tingling from making love with him earlier. She ached in places she hadn't ached in years.

But more than that, she wanted.

Desire still resided low in her belly. Her sex still felt heavy and eager. Fulfilled and yet desperately wanting. Had she thought that taking Theo as her lover once would satisfy her? If so, her body was making a thorough liar of her as she lay there in the quiet stillness of the night, listening to the comforting sound of his rhythmic breaths and loving the way it felt to be so near to him.

As near as he would allow her.

For he had secrets aplenty, her lover. And one of them was the reason he refused to disrobe before her. She could only guess at why. When she had first married Bertie, he had been painfully shy. He'd spent the first year of their marriage hiding beneath a banyan under the cover of darkness. It had only been with much coaxing on her part that he had become comfortable with his body. They had both been virgins on their wedding night, and they had taught each other how to love. Finding pleasure together had been a great joy.

She didn't think it was shyness, however, that was the reason Theo refused to remove his clothes. Indeed, there was nothing timid about him. His words, his touch, his voice, his kisses were all so very confident. So brazen and bold and commanding. He was a skilled lover who knew how to bring her to ecstasy, who took care and listened to her body when it told him what she liked.

Why then, would he hide himself away?

She yearned to ask, but everything about their relationship—if she dared even refer to it thus—was yet so new. So entirely unpredictable and unlike anything she'd ever known. So unlike herself, too.

"What are you thinking?" he murmured, his lips grazing her ear.

And to her shock, there was nary a hint of slumber in his voice, quite as if he had lain there with her in his arms for however many hours had passed whilst she slept.

"You're awake," she said stupidly, feeling suddenly shy herself, for she was naked beneath the counterpane.

After they'd made love, he had tended to her, cleaning her with a cloth and water from the basin on her rosewood table.

And then, he had stripped her of her night rail and slid into bed beside her, wearing everything but his boots and his coat. He hadn't even loosened the knot in his cravat.

"As are you." He pressed a kiss to her temple, the gesture so tender that a strange new emotion came loose inside her.

She refused to examine it just yet. Too new. Everything was so different, so strange. Perhaps she would feel differently by morning light. For now, Theo was here, and he was hers, and that was all she would think of.

"I fell asleep, however," she reminded him. "Have you not slept at all?"

"I rested."

She noted the clever manner in which he had evaded her question. He was a man of so many mysteries she longed to unravel.

"Resting and slumbering are two different states," she said tartly, taking care to keep her voice quiet so that it would not carry.

With so many guards traversing the halls and her brother's chamber not far, she had no wish for suspicion to be raised.

She wanted these private moments alone with Theo while they lasted.

And if she were brutally honest with herself, she would admit that she never wanted them to end, even if the rational part of her mind knew they would. That they would have to.

"Are you worrying over me, Marchioness?" he asked, his voice teasing.

"Someone ought to," she said, before thinking twice about her words, her assumptions. And then it occurred to her, in one shocking, terrible moment, that she had never asked him if he had anyone worrying over him. If he had someone. A wife, a lover, a betrothed. "Of course, for all I know, you have a legion of women worrying over you. It would hardly be surprising if you did."

He kissed her cheek, his fingers lightly stroking her forearm beneath the covers. Bare skin on bare skin. "There are no other women, Pamela. There is only you."

She believed him. And the way he said her name. *Swoon.* She felt like a young woman again instead of a widow fast approaching thirty years old.

"I should have asked sooner," she forced herself to say. "What must you think of me? A proper widow who takes a lover within days of meeting him, who never asks—"

Gentle fingers caught her jaw, turning her face toward his, and his mouth covered hers, swallowing further rambling. Which was just as well. He kissed her deliciously, slowly, wonderfully, before taking his lips from hers.

"I think you are the most incredible woman I've ever met," he said softly. "And I think I'm so damned fortunate you chose me as your lover."

"Oh," she breathed, for his words were so profound and yet so simple, and they made her feel terrible and wonderful and frightening things all at the same time.

Yes, she knew quite suddenly why she felt like a young debutante again. It was her heart. Theo was capturing it as surely as Bertie had years ago, when they'd been young and innocent and naïve, thinking they had the rest of their lives together. But she wouldn't think of that now, and nor could she allow her heart to be so freely given. She would have to guard it well.

He nuzzled her cheek, the gesture every bit as tender as the others which had preceded it. "I've stayed for longer than I should have. I'm likely soon due to replace one of my men."

Of course he couldn't stay here with her all night, and yet Pamela couldn't contain the pang of regret at his words. It was too soon. She felt as if she had scarcely had him to herself at all. And when he left her chamber, they would go back to being strangers, unable to freely touch or be at ease with each other unless they were certain they were hidden from others. How she dreaded it.

"But you haven't slept," she protested, despite knowing it likely wouldn't do her one whit of good.

"I don't require much sleep," he said softly, kissing her throat.

"Why not?" she dared to ask, for she knew the reason she avoided slumber.

The dreams that haunted her. Dreams of the crushing losses she had suffered.

His fingers stilled in their restless skimming over her arm and she felt him tense.

"Doesn't matter."

And just like that, she knew that her charming, tender-hearted lover was reverting to his curt, brooding self. She was losing him already. He was withdrawing from her and yet he still held her snug in his arms.

"It does matter," she countered quietly, tangling her fingers in his. "To me."

You matter, was what she meant, but she was too wise to utter such damning words aloud.

He was silent for so long she feared he wouldn't answer, but he didn't withdraw from her touch or leave the bed.

Finally, he answered her. "When I sleep, my mind travels to dark places. Places better left forgotten."

It didn't please Pamela that she had been correct. And she suspected it had something to do with his reason for not disrobing. What had happened to him in his past to make him so aloof and cool, to make him fear falling asleep or removing his clothes with a lover? Her heart ached for him despite her all-too-recent reminder to herself that she must protect it.

"What places?" she asked.

"You don't wish to know, Marchioness."

Ah, but she did. Because she cared for him.

"Please," she said softly, knowing it likely wouldn't be enough.

That some secrets would remain his to keep.

"I must go." He kissed her cheek, the corner of her lips. "Sleep well."

He rolled away from her then and slid out from beneath the bedclothes. The hushed sounds of him slipping his arms back into his discarded coat and then pulling on his boots filled the night. And then, just as quickly as he had arrived at her door, he was gone, his booted feet carrying him quietly over the Axminster, the paneled mahogany clicking closed.

Pamela shifted into the warmth he had left behind, absorbing this small piece of him, breathing in the faint traces of his scent on her pillow. Longing to go after him and knowing she could not. That what they had shared was temporary and fleeting, even if her heart longed for it to be more.

EVER SINCE HE had forced himself from her bed in the depths of the night, Theo had been sternly admonishing himself that he had to keep his distance from Pamela. But despite his best intentions to avoid her, they were still beneath the same roof, and it was inevitable that their paths would cross.

In a diaphanous blue gown that made her eyes seem even more vibrant than they ordinarily appeared, she bustled down an upstairs corridor toward him. Her golden hair was swept back, a few curled tendrils falling over her forehead and framing her face.

She appeared utterly unfettered, and he thought of how

she would look, barefoot in a traditional gown of white lawn with her hair unbound and coming to him on a sandy beach in Boritania. But he banished the notion as quickly as it had arrived, for it was a moot point. Boritania was no longer his home, and if he crossed those shores he would be imprisoned and killed.

Pamela could never truly be his, and he knew it.

Forcing his expression to remain a calm, impassive mask, he offered her his most elegant bow. "My lady."

"Sir," she said, curtsying.

They stared at each other, and he couldn't help but to see her as she had been last night, on her knees before him, those pretty pink lips wrapped around his cock. Ah, damnation. Longing was a ferocious ache lodged somewhere behind his collarbone. He wanted to touch her more than he wanted his next breath.

But he had already risked far too much by indulging in their mutual passions the night before. He didn't dare do so again.

"Good day," he said, intending to pass by her and carry on with his duty, regardless of how much he wished to linger. To touch her again. To kiss her.

"Theo," she said quietly, a question in her voice.

"Marchioness," he returned, determined to remain cool and polite. Impervious. He was a stone wall and she could not conquer him, not even with her midnight-sea eyes and her soft, parted lips. "Is there something you require?"

It should be enough to see her, should it not? He had already made love to her once. Their coupling should have been enough to remove her from his blood. To lessen the wildness of his need for her.

But no, of course, it wasn't.

Deep in his marrow, he understood that nothing would be enough when it came to Pamela, Lady Deering. Not ever.

He wanted every hour of her day, every minute, each second. But that was impossible.

She sighed, her breasts moving beneath her becoming blue gown, catching his wandering eye a moment longer than was polite. "Yes, there is something I require."

"How may I be of assistance?"

He was calm. Formal. He was not the impassioned lover who had unwisely gone to her door the night before. He could control himself where she was concerned. He could resist her.

At least, he thought he could if he repeated it enough within his mind.

I can resist her.

I can resist her.

I can—

Pamela took his elbow in a determined grasp, pulling him along with her. "Come with me, if you please."

How like her, to feign manners. To pretend as if he had a choice in the matter. He'd never had a choice where she was concerned. His body and his soul had recognized her from the moment their paths had first crossed. He understood now, the old ways he had once scoffed at. How inevitable and right it had been between them from that initial meeting, even when it had been wrong.

Even though it was *still* wrong.

"Where are you taking me, my lady?" he asked as she tugged him down the hall.

She led him as if he were a child who needed governance instead of a man who was desperate to haul her into his arms and kiss her senseless. And then, with an abrupt haste that was rather unlike her, Pamela opened the door of an empty guest chamber and led him inside.

She released him quickly when they were ensconced in the room, and he mourned the lack of contact. "I hope you don't mind my familiarity. I merely wished to speak in a more private setting than the hall."

It was on the tip of his tongue to tell her that she could be as familiar with him as she liked, as often as she wished. But he swallowed down those impossible words, along with his many regrets. He would be cold. He would send her away from him. There was no future for a man with no name and a proper widow. She was made for marriage, not fleeting trysts, and he would sooner leap from the roof of Hunt House than bring even the slightest hint of danger to her door.

"Wouldn't do for the marchioness to be seen speaking with the lowly bodyguard, would it?" he asked her. "Are you ashamed for wanting me, now that you've had your fill last night?"

"You're angry with me."

She said it as a statement rather than a question.

His words had been cruel, and he knew it. But it was better to create distance between them now. To cut the ties whilst he still could. That was what he had to do for both their sakes. Last night, he had allowed himself far more than he should have. He would atone for his sins, beginning now.

Theo forced all expression from his face. "I'm not angry, my lady. I feel nothing."

Confusion swirled in her eyes. "After last night, how can you possibly feel nothing?"

"Last night didn't change a thing for either of us. I'm still the nameless bodyguard charged with your brother's safety, and you're the proper widow who should avoid me at all costs."

What a liar he was. Last night had changed everything. *She* had changed everything. But he couldn't let her know it.

Her sultry lips flattened into the line of disapproval he'd come to know so well. "You're being deliberately unkind."

Theo told himself this was what he had to do. She was not for him, and nor was he for her.

"I'm not a kind man," he told her harshly, anger at himself lending a sharp edge to his voice.

"That's not true." She shook her head, curls bobbing in her agitation. "You are a man of great compassion and kindness. I know because you have shown me both."

Damn it. She brought out parts of himself he'd thought long gone, and now she sought to use them against him. But he would bury them again. Mercilessly suppress them. Destroy them if he must. It was for the best.

"Is that how you see me?" he asked. "Is that what makes my touch palatable to you, that you believe I'm kind? Because if so, allow me to disabuse you of that notion. I've done things that would shock your fine sensibilities. I'm a mercenary, my lady, capable of doing anything for a price. Why do you suppose they call me Beast?"

"I..." she faltered, her brow furrowing. "I don't know."

"Because I *am* a beast, my lady, and you'd do best to remember it. Now say your piece, so I can return to my duty."

And he had never felt more like one than this moment, with naked hurt on her lovely face.

"What has happened since last night?" she asked, her gaze searching.

What had happened was that he had rediscovered his sense of reason. Last night, he'd been stripped bare of every defense, his guard lowered. And when he'd seen her standing at the threshold of her chamber, he hadn't been able to resist. But the sun had risen on a new day, and there was nothing like slipping from her bed in the darkest depths of the night to remind him that there was no future for them.

He gave her a careless shrug. "Perhaps I'm the one who

has had my fill, and now that I've had your quim, the fever in my blood has been cured."

She went pale, and he wished he could withdraw his words. But Gustavson's men could already be in London, searching for him. And he had no doubt that they would harm anyone close to him. They would stop at nothing in their quest to destroy Theo. He'd be damned before he allowed anything to happen to Pamela because of him.

"You would reduce what happened to mere lust?" she asked, a tremble in her voice that almost broke him.

Damn it, how was he to remain unyielding? How could he keep his distance when the yearning to touch her was clawing him apart inside?

"Yes, lust," he bit out dismissively. "What else is there between a man and woman?"

"Tender feelings. Emotions. There is love."

Of course, she must have been in love with her husband. A sudden, painful stab of envy hit Theo then.

But he couldn't allow himself to dwell on the way she made him feel. Moving nearer to Pamela, he intentionally crowded her with his body, clinging to the dynamic that had existed between them before last night.

The one in which she viewed him with icy distaste and he toyed with her like a cat batting at a mouse. Because that was far safer than what they had become. Lovers who possessed tender feelings for each other. No, better to return to what they had been: enemies at daggers drawn.

"Do you know what I think, Marchioness?" he asked.

"No, and nor do I care to know what you think," Pamela said, some of her flagging hauteur returning as she tipped up her chin in defiance. "You, sir, are a brute."

He *was* a brute. He felt like one, and he hated himself for it. Hated that his past had chosen now to return. Hated that he couldn't have this woman the way he wanted her. That they had been reduced to one night of secrets instead of something more.

"A brute whose mouth you fully enjoy," he told her cruelly anyway, unable to keep from reminding her just how responsive she was to him.

It was foolish and reckless, he knew. They were nearly pressed together now, and the scent of her, sweet temptation and jasmine laced with hyacinth, filled his senses. She reached for him first, her arms curling around his neck as her breasts crushed into his chest. He banded an arm around her waist, holding her tight, loving the way her curves molded to his hardness. Suddenly, all his intentions to drive her away were swallowed by a flood of desire.

"You are vile," she said, but there was more desperation and hurt in her voice than true bite, "to taunt and tempt me so."

The last few words were whispered so quietly he scarcely heard them. But it hardly mattered, for she tugged his head down to hers, and then her mouth was on his, and all the reasons why he should keep her at a distance fell completely away. There was nothing but the softness of her lips, the sweet demand of her kiss, and the driving need to be inside her again.

CHAPTER 12

Pamela had been correct early that morning when Theo had left her bed. The tender man who had made love to her so passionately had again been banished behind the impenetrable mask of the brooding stranger. The harsh man who had faced her in this guest chamber and in the hall had been cold and indifferent, fashioned of stone instead of warm flesh and bone.

It was as if there were two different parts of him, one hiding behind the other, and only in rare, sweet moments did he reveal his true self. Moments like last night.

Moments like now, his lips moving over hers, making a mockery of all his cruel disinterest. He could tell himself anything he liked, but his body didn't lie, and all the heat pouring off him and the thick ridge of his cock pressing into her told her that last night hadn't been enough. That he wanted her every bit as much as she longed for him.

Pamela threw herself into this kiss, showing him without words what she felt for him. Far more than lust. She was not a woman who cared lightly or easily. She had guarded her heart well for four years after Bertie's death, and only Theo had decimated her defenses. Theo, with his secrets and cool eyes and haunted past he wouldn't speak of.

She hadn't intended to kiss him when she'd seen him in the hall; she'd only meant to talk to him. But now that his lips were on hers, it felt as inevitable as the sun in the morning sky. And like the sun, he warmed her, brought her to life.

She was new again in his arms. And she was on fire everywhere he trailed his touch. His hands caressed her from hip to waist, then higher. Pulling her into his solidly muscled form as he traced over her spine. One of his hands cupped her nape, the scrape of his rough hands on her sensitive skin lovelier than she could have imagined. The other cradled her face, holding her still as he feasted on her mouth, feeding her long, carnal kisses that made wetness pool between her thighs.

Last night had been foolish and daring and most unwise.

But this afternoon was reckless and dangerous.

Anyone could come upon them. Heavens, she wasn't even certain if they had properly closed the chamber door. And yet, she didn't care. Not with his lips moving over hers and his tongue sliding hot and wet and possessive into her mouth. He kissed her thoroughly, claiming her, until all she could taste was him and all she knew was the vibrant, pulsing need to be one with him.

The kiss had begun in angry frustration, but it gradually changed. They were no longer two people at war, but two lovers savoring each other instead. His lips gentled on hers, his thumb sweeping over her cheekbone, the hand at her nape clasping her in a tender hold that made her melt against him. The fight fled her, and she was no longer furious with him for mocking what had happened between them.

Instead, she understood he had been clinging to his icy mask, doing everything in his power to ward her off. Like his refusal to disrobe before her, his cutting remarks and chilly indifference had been a means of protecting himself.

His lips left hers to trail a path of fire along her jaw, then lower. Down her throat. "Pamela." He whispered her name against her skin, part curse, part raw plea. "What do you do to me?"

She hoped she did to him what he did to her. That she made him desperate with wanting. That he could scarcely think for the need coursing through him. That when he finally slept, he woke with a body hungering for hers and an ache that could only be assuaged one way.

Her head fell back, far too heavy, giving his wicked mouth more room to explore, and found her voice. "Tell me again that it's only lust, what we feel for each other. Tell me that this is meaningless—that I am meaningless—to you."

His mouth opened, sucking on her skin, the action hot and wet and so very carnal. "If I did, it would be lies."

Some vindication, then. She moved her hands, which had settled upon his broad shoulders, to his back, caressing him in slow and soothing motions. How she wished for the barriers of cloth to be removed, to touch his naked skin. But more than that, for him to trust her enough to take off every layer keeping his body from hers.

"Why then?" she asked quietly. "Why did you say what you did to me? Why were you so cruel?"

He tensed beneath her questing fingers, the muscles of his back going tight as he raised his head to gaze down at her with stormy eyes. "Because you deserve better. I'm not the man you think I am."

"Why should I not decide what I deserve?" she asked. "It seems horribly arrogant of you to choose for me and tell me what I want when I already know."

"And what is it that you want, Marchioness?"

The hand cupping her cheek moved, gliding down her

throat in a smooth caress that turned her knees into liquid. How easily he could turn her fury to longing, her outrage to desire. He had such power over her. She was helplessly, hopelessly in this enigmatic man's thrall.

But how could that be? The knowledge was unwanted and altogether terrifying. She had never thought twice about a man after Bertie, and yet she could see now how easy it was, once her heart had cracked open, to let someone inside it again. And that was most frightening of all, not the physical intimacy she had shared with Theo, but the greater intimacy, the deeper feeling dwelling within. One could give one's body, lose one's self to pleasure. But it was the heart, that stubborn, wondrous muscle, that wasn't penetrated with ease. And once it was...

She held Theo's stare, her heart thudding hard. He had asked her what she wanted, and the truth was, she wasn't sure. She had never thought to want happiness for herself again. But perhaps she had been wrong, closing herself off. It seemed to her quite suddenly that she had spent so much time mourning Bertie that she'd forgotten how it had felt to simply be herself. She had buried her grief in dresses and fans and frippery, in society and her reputation, and she had lost the Pamela she had once been.

The Pamela who still longed for kisses and a man's reassuring touch.

"I want to remember what it's like to live again," she told him bravely. "I want passion and happiness."

"You should find it," he said, his hand lowering until it splayed over her heart, so big and warm.

She wanted to tell him that she had, that he had brought both back into her life, but she sensed that he wasn't ready to hear such a confession. There remained what she left unsaid: *I want you.* And neither was she bold enough to reveal everything to him. Not now. Not yet.

She covered his hand with hers, keeping it pinned in place, asking the question she dared. "Will you come to me again tonight?"

"You should find it elsewhere," he said gently, sliding his hand from beneath hers. "I'm not the man for you, Marchioness."

And once again, he was rejecting her. Not as callously as before. His words were soft. But he was rejecting her, nonetheless. It stung. Not just her pride, but her foolish heart.

"Why not?" She held his gaze, challenging him with hers, still holding him in her arms. It gratified her that he did not withdraw. "Why do you insist on pushing me away?"

"It's for your sake," he rasped, jaw tight.

His answer frustrated her. He had admitted that what was between them wasn't meaningless, and his kisses and touches told her the same. And yet he still denied them both.

She sighed, the sound heavy, torn from deep within. "You asked me what I wanted, and now that I've told you, you say I am wrong for wanting it."

"Not wrong. But there are things you don't understand, things I cannot explain, my lady."

Pamela shook her head. "Don't do that. Do not reduce us to formality. Not after everything that has transpired."

"Our stations are different." The hand at her nape moved slowly down her neck, caressing between her shoulder blades.

He hadn't released her yet either, and she could sense his reluctance, for it was the same stubborn feeling inside her. *Don't do it,* she thought. *Hold me. Stay with me. Never let me go.*

She clung to him, absorbing his heat and strength through his coat, still rubbing up and down his back. "I don't care about our stations. That means less than nothing to me."

"What would your brother the duke say if he were to discover his proper widowed sister has taken one of his guards into her bed?" he asked sharply. "Do you imagine he would be pleased to know it?"

She hadn't thought about the repercussions she would face with Ridgely. All she had been thinking about was Theo. But his words gave her pause as she considered them. Her brother was far from a saint. He was a known rakehell, and his actions with his ward were ample proof of that.

"It isn't any of his concern what I do," she denied, though she knew in truth that there was a possibility he wouldn't be pleased. "I am far from a virginal miss."

And if gossip were to spread that she had taken a lover... well, she would fret over that eventuality when she came to it, rather than now. She could be discreet. She would hardly be the first woman in her position to take a lover.

"And what of your charge, Lady Virtue?" he pressed. "Do you reckon you will be able to squire her about society if there are whispers you've taken a ruffian into your bed?"

She disliked the way he spoke of himself, with such deprecation, as if he were unworthy. Where did his ill opinion come from? What had happened to him, to make him believe himself so contemptible?

"You're not a ruffian," she denied.

"You don't know that, Pamela," he said intently. "You don't know me."

"Then tell me who you are," she begged. "Tell me why you hide yourself from me. Tell me what you haven't said. Tell me *everything*."

"Deus," he gritted, lowering his forehead so that it pressed to hers.

The gesture was somehow every bit as intimate as a kiss.

"Tell me, Theo," she repeated. "You came to my door last night. You kissed me first. You started this."

He closed his eyes, shuttering the impenetrable, gray orbs

for a moment before he opened them again. "I shouldn't have."

"But you did."

She wasn't going to allow him to withdraw from her so easily. Pamela cupped his face, the stubble of his whiskers pricking her palms, and fused her lips with his. He didn't push her away. Instead, he returned the kiss with a low growl, his arms going around her to hold her tightly to him, as if she had broken the last of his restraint with her mouth.

Good, she thought. She would smash it to bits. Break down every barrier and wall he sought to erect between them.

His hands clamped on her waist, his hold possessive and firm, and oh how she gloried in it, in the urgency she felt, the subtle pressure of his fingers nipping into her through her gown and stays. He was losing control.

Theo tore his lips from hers, chest heaving, staring down at her with such intensity that it robbed her of breath. "I'm a danger to you. You shouldn't be here, alone with me. You should go. Run. Stay in your safe little world of drawing rooms and balls and musicales."

"My world isn't safe," she argued, her lips still tingling from his kisses. "Your presence here at Hunt House is evidence of that."

She had not forgotten the reason for Theo and the other guards. Someone wanted Ridgely dead. If he wished to speak of danger, well, she was already surrounded by it in ample measure, and none seemed more concerning than the threat to her heart that Theo presented.

"I can't give you more than fleeting pleasure," he said, his voice low, all silk and velvet-covered steel. "That is all there can be between us."

Did he think to quell the fire burning inside her with such a warning? If so, he was mistaken.

"I want what you can give me," she said.

He began moving them as one, backing her toward the door of the chamber, which was still ajar. Anyone could have come upon them. It didn't matter. All that did matter was that she seemed to have won this little battle. He was holding her in his arms. He was here with her.

Theo pulled the door closed and latched it. And then she was trapped solidly between his big body and the paneled mahogany, and there was no place she would rather be. He hadn't told her his secrets, but that no longer signified either.

She could be patient. She would wait. He wasn't trying to push her away any longer. Now, he was holding her close. His cock pressed into her, and she rediscovered the boldness that had made her bare her heart to him and banish her pride.

She reached between them to graze the fall of his trousers. He groaned, hips chasing her touch. She molded her fingers around that pulsing ridge, stroking his thickness until an answering ache began to swell like a rising tide. Here was all the evidence she required of what he felt for her—the same deep and abiding yearning. If the rest of him was stubborn, his body, at least, was not.

"Pamela," he ground out her name in warning.

She found a button on his falls, plucking it free. "I want you inside me."

How freeing it felt, that confession, taking command of her body's needs. Taking command of herself after so many years of denial.

"Then take what you want."

He kissed her deeply, his tongue tracing the seam of her lips. More buttons slid open, and then she was freeing him, his cockstand springing hot and urgent into her waiting palm. She grasped him, stroking slowly.

Did he intend to take her against the door? His lips left

hers and he raised his head, watching her with burning, raw hunger, his gaze darkening as it fell between them, to where her hand stroked his cock. She looked down too, mesmerized by the sight, the feeling of him. How beautiful he was by daylight, big and hard, his skin smooth and ruddy and stretched taut. The slit in his crown leaked a pearly drop, and she used her thumb to swirl it over his cock head as she had last night. Her cunny pulsed in an echo of readiness. She was hollow and aching and only he could fill her. Only he could give her what she needed.

But how? Her marriage bed had not been particularly inventive, though it had brought her pleasure. Was it even possible for a man and woman to make love whilst standing up thus, aligned against a door?

"Can we?" she murmured, licking her lips, recalling how it had felt to take him in her mouth, to breathe in the musky scent of him, to feel the controlled thrust of him sliding over her lips and tongue. "Standing?"

He caught a fistful of her gown and petticoats in answer, dragging it to her waist. "Hold your hems."

She did as he asked, clutching the fabric with her free hand, cool air kissing her stockinged legs as she bared herself from the waist down for him. Theo's fingers dipped unerringly, finding the center of her need, working over her swollen bud. She was almost unbearably ready for him, their lovemaking the night before and impassioned kisses leaving her body flushed and impatient. So desperately aching for more.

He painted her dew over her folds, then glided his fingers lower, finding her entrance and slipping inside. "Hook your leg around me."

She did as he asked, the shifting in positions opening her to him more fully. He slid inside her, stroking deep, his fingers filling her in rhythmic pulses that had her breaths coming in uneven gasps and her body arching into his. Her world shrank to nothing more than the two of them, to the connection of their bodies, the pumping of his fingers. To the sound of her own readiness, lurid and loud in the chamber, filling her with more wetness and heightening her need to a pulsing, raging crescendo.

When his fingers curled, pressuring so deliciously the sublime, secret place inside her, everything burst. A cry tore from her lips, and he swallowed it with his mouth, kissing her as her body simultaneously tightened and flew apart. He kissed her hard and fast, so deeply that her head knocked against the door. But she didn't care, because in the next instant, the firmness of his cock was at her entrance.

In one thrust, he filled her. Filled her so completely and fully. She was pinned to the door by his body and his cock, the hand holding her hems up trapped between them, the other landing on his shoulder for purchase as she raised to her tiptoes and met him thrust for thrust as he began to move. They made love furiously, bodies pounding together, straining, seeking. She wasn't sure which of them was more desperate for the other.

He moved inside her with glorious precision, finding the same place his fingers had so masterfully stimulated, each pump of his hips angling against her pearl with delicious friction. Faster and faster, the door thumping behind them with each stroke. But she was too far gone to care if anyone passed in the hall and wondered at the noises emerging from the empty guest chamber. Too far gone for anyone who wasn't him.

Theo broke the kiss and buried his face in her throat, his mouth moving over her skin as if he were ravenous for her. As if he could not have enough of her. She was in an agony of ecstasy, desperate to find release again, twining her body around his, using the floor and her position against the door to move in time to his body's frantic thrusts. Deeper, higher, harder. It was pain and pleasure united, every stroke through her wetness undoing her more than the last. Until she came undone a second time, her cunny clamping on his cock in a series of spasms that had her body bowing from the door.

She lowered her face to his shoulder as her climax twisted through her, her teeth finding the solidness of his shoulder and sinking in without regard for whether or not she would leave a mark. He moved into her in frantic, quick bursts, and then his body stiffened against her, and he was frantically withdrawing, gripping his cock as his seed spurted all over her inner thigh in hot bursts.

He collapsed against her, a beloved, solid weight, their hearts pounding in unison, both of them breathless and spent. She held him tightly, until the sound of bustling in the hall beyond had them breaking guiltily apart. Hastily, he withdrew a handkerchief and tended to them both, his countenance an impenetrable mask as he met her gaze.

"I must go," he murmured, his voice hushed so that it wouldn't carry. "I've a duty to attend."

"But you will come to me tonight?" she pressed. "Later. I've a ball to attend this evening, and I won't be back until well after midnight."

How she wished it were a ball at which he would be in attendance, and that they could whirl together in a waltz. But that was a foolish desire, and she knew it.

"Later," he agreed, unsmiling as he gently pulled her away from the door and then left her without a backward glance.

CHAPTER 13

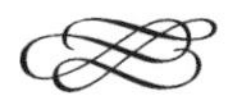

Alone in the cavernous Hunt House drawing room, Pamela was attempting to distract herself from thoughts of Theo and failing abysmally. Because when she had finally set her porte-crayon to paper to sketch following their unexpected interlude in the guest chamber, only one face had emerged.

His.

She stared down at the rough facsimile of his handsome countenance looking back at her and sighed. The hours until she could see him again stretched before her, unwanted and daunting. And she realized, quite suddenly and forcefully, that the diversions she had used to soothe herself in the years following Bertie's death were no longer sufficient. She didn't wish to draw, and she didn't want to shop. Nor was she enthused about losing herself in the societal whirl this evening at the Searle ball.

Everything she had so thoroughly lost herself in failed her.

And her heart? He had thoroughly melted every last hint

of ice she had built around it. It was terrifying, because she hadn't an inkling what to do with these inconvenient feelings. Not just base lust, but something far stronger. Something bigger. Something terrifying.

Something that felt quite a lot like love.

A creak in the hall floor alerted her that she was not alone a moment before a maid appeared in the doorway, offering a perfect curtsy. "Lady Deering, pray forgive me for the interruption, but His Grace has asked me to inform you that he wishes an audience with you in his study."

Ice slid down her spine. She slammed her folio closed, banishing Theo's face. Hands trembling, she rose and smoothed her skirts, clutching her folio and porte-crayon. Had her brother seen her leaving the guest chamber earlier? Had a servant?

"Of course." She forced a smile for the girl's sake, not wishing for the maid to see how very affected she was by the unexpected request. "Thank you."

Another curtsy, and the maid disappeared down the hall. Pamela made her way to her brother's study, her stomach tightening into a knot as she wondered what he would do now. There was only one reason he could wish for a private audience.

He *knew*.

Would he ask her to leave Hunt House? If he did, where would she go? To Mother, she supposed, in the country. If Mother would have her. Or perhaps she might beg the hospitality of friends for a time. Mayhap Selina. Certainly, Ridgely would make sure to cut off her accounts at the shops if he were angry enough. She couldn't blame him. She could only blame herself. It had been wrong of her to take a lover at all, let alone at Hunt House. Particularly with Lady Virtue in residence.

Mind reeling with the implications of what she had done, she knocked at his closed study door, waiting for him to bid her enter. Hesitantly, she stepped inside, finding him standing sentinel at a bank of windows, raking a hand through his dark hair and leaving it in disarray.

"Ridgely," she began, thinking that she ought to offer an explanation. Anything to blunt the sting of his outrage over her scandalous actions.

"You are to wish me happy," he blurted before she could continue. "I am about to enter into the vaunted institution of marriage. Otherwise known as the parson's mousetrap."

She blinked, staring at him, utterly shocked.

He didn't know, then. This meeting was not at all about herself and Theo. Relief washed over her like the cold rain lashing against the window panes behind him. She swayed on her feet, thinking that if she were of weaker disposition, she might have swooned from the force of it.

"Marriage," she repeated, finding her voice. "You?"

"Me," he agreed wryly, inclining his head as if to acknowledge the irony. "Marriage. To Lady Virtue."

To Lady Virtue?

No. She had been so careful in her chaperoning of the girl after that dreadful incident in the library. Had she not? Or had she been too caught up in her clandestine affair with Theo?

Guilt twisted through Pamela.

"But…you…she…" she sputtered, words eluding her.

"Yes. I intend to marry her." Ridgely paused, then sighed heavily. "I *must* marry her."

"You must, you say." Understanding dawned on her. Good God. Something else had happened. He had ruined Lady Virtue. Pamela had to move. To walk. Her feet began carrying her down one length of the chamber, closer to her brother, that she might better read his expression. "What have you done this time?"

She marched toward Ridgely, her fear of being caught supplanted by outrage on behalf of her charge. Was it her imagination, or was her careless rakehell brother flushing?

"I have compromised her," he said simply, moving away from the window and stalking toward the hearth, where a black ink stain remained on the bricks, mocking her for her inability to control her fury the last time they'd had such a tête-à-tête. He turned back to her, looking rather shamefaced. "Quite beyond repair."

Dear heavens. She *had* been so caught up in her own affairs, then, that she had somehow failed at her duty.

"It has only been three days since the last incident," she said lamely.

"Four," Ridgely muttered.

As if it mattered. She was not sure which of them she was more disappointed in, herself or her brother.

"You *promised*," she reminded him. "You swore you would keep your distance from her."

"Apparently, I'm no better at keeping my word than our father was."

Their father had not been a good or kind man. He'd been selfish and greedy, and he had compromised their mother to secure her dowry for himself, only to carry on with a string of mistresses after he had what he wanted. Pamela couldn't blame their mother for her bitterness, but neither did she want to believe her brother was anything like their sire.

"Your lack of control is appalling," she agreed coolly. "Truly, Ridgely. Could you not have found one of your lightskirts and dallied with her instead?"

"I am a scoundrel," her brother said. "It is one of the reasons, I dare say, why my own family reviles me."

What tomfoolery was this? Despite her vexation with him for his failures where Lady Virtue was concerned, Pamela loved Ridgely dearly.

"We do not revile you," she denied.

"Mother does," he argued.

Their mother was an unhappy dragon, the product of her life with their father and the loss of her favorite sons, Bartholomew and Matthew.

"Mother reviles everyone," Pamela pointed out.

Ridgely quirked a brow. "I challenge you to find someone she reviles more than I."

"Why are we speaking of our mother when the subject at hand is your egregious conduct?" She sighed and shook her head, turning her mind to where it was better served—limiting the spread of the damaging fire about to burst forth. "Tongues will wag quite furiously. Everyone will assume you have ruined Lady Virtue."

"Let them wag." Ridgely waved a dismissive hand. "I don't give a damn about gossip. I never have."

Naturally not, being a man. But Pamela did. She had to, as a widow with nothing to recommend herself save her good reputation. One she had been doing a quite excellent job of ruining on her own without this added muddle.

"But *I* do," she countered. "Of course, you have not thought of the effect this news will have upon Lady Virtue or myself. I have been acting as her chaperone, and I have failed quite abysmally at the task of keeping her safe from you. She will be scorned in polite society if there is the slightest whiff of scandal."

"She will be a duchess," Ridgely said. "Surely that will ameliorate the pain of having to marry a rogue. As for you, no one will find fault with you for the match. You have performed your duty as chaperone well, and you're a paragon of virtue. Everyone will have no doubt I am to blame."

Her cheeks went hot as she thought of the reason she had failed as a chaperone—her own wayward yearnings and a man she couldn't resist. Perhaps she and her brother were not so very different in that sense. For she could not seem to keep her distance from Theo any more than Ridgely had been capable of being a gentleman with Lady Virtue.

"I do try, but I am far from perfect," she conceded. "I fear I have been remiss in my duties."

"You have hardly been remiss. I am at fault. Not you."

"Nonetheless, it shall reflect on me."

"I will do everything in my power to make certain no hint of scandal taints either of you," her brother vowed. "You have my word."

She believed him. Ridgely was many things, but liar was not amongst them. Still, a sudden compromising and an unplanned marriage between himself and Virtue…she loved her brother, and she had grown to care for her charge very much. She wanted happiness for them both. She wanted for them the love and contentment she had known with Bertie, only she didn't wish for it to end abruptly in sadness and grief.

"You will make a good husband for her, will you not?" she asked Ridgely.

Her brother swallowed, looking more serious than she had seen him, even on the night when the mysterious man had broken his neck falling down the staircase. "I shall try."

"Try?" She resumed pacing. "That is hardly reassuring."

"If you intend to throw something, please reconsider," Ridgely drawled in an attempt at a jest. "I've only just replaced the inkwell."

"I was overset when I threw the inkwell," Pamela defended herself, though she did regret her hastiness and flare of temper. "And it was your fault then," she added for good measure. "Just as this is your fault now."

Ridgely had returned to his vigil at the window, and he stood there, hands clasped. "As we have already established, I am a rogue."

His calm acceptance of whatever it was that had transpired between himself and his ward nettled. He did not have to be a rogue. He chose to be one. Just as Theo did not have to keep his secrets. He chose to do so. Why did men have to be so blasted stubborn?

"And one who is utterly without compunction," she told her brother tartly. "Where is Virtue now? I will need to speak to her."

The magnitude of what faced them—a wedding to plan, scandal to avoid—hit her just then.

"I'm afraid she isn't entirely pleased with me at the moment, having just learned that Greycote Abbey has been sold," Ridgely said with a wince, referring to his ward's former home and the one place she was determined to return to at any cost. "She has refused my suit, and quite soundly, too."

Oh dear.

"If she is displeased with you, how did you also happen to compromise her?" She frowned then, a terrible thought occurring to her. "Surely you did not *force* her?"

"Saint's teeth, Pamela." Her brother scowled. "What do you think of me? I would never harm a woman. You bloody well ought to know that."

Of course, she did. This was Ridgely. He may be a devil-may-care rake with a collection of bedmates as large as the Serpentine, but he would never do something so unconscionable. She felt guilty for even considering it for a moment.

"I should hope not." Pamela sighed. "Forgive me. This is

all quite a shock. Not entirely a surprise, given what I witnessed in the library. But a shock, nonetheless." She paused in her pacing, the rest of what her brother had said about Virtue sinking in. "What do you mean she has refused your suit?"

Ridgely turned away again, staring out the window, still grim. "She says she has no wish to marry me. Apparently, she intended for me to send her back to Nottinghamshire."

Heaven preserve her from rebellious debutantes who thought they knew better. The world was made to eat up ladies like Virtue and swallow them whole.

"She cannot refuse you," she said. "She hasn't a choice now."

"Then perhaps you might have a talk with Lady Virtue," he suggested cheerlessly, "and persuade her to see reason."

"You have created quite a disaster, brother." And naturally, it was down to her to help him fix it.

But then, she was beginning to fear that she had created a disaster all her own. One that was brewing painfully in her foolish heart. And that particular disaster...well, she didn't know if it could be fixed at all.

"THERE'S nothing I can do, Stasia," Theo told his sister flatly.

She had come to the Hunt House mews, demanding to see him, refusing to leave unless he met with her again. It had been either stand there before a host of curious grooms or follow her to her waiting carriage. After making certain his men were in place, he had settled for the latter. Now, they were rumbling over the streets of London in a carriage Stasia had borrowed from Archer Tierney after once more escaping the palace guards their uncle had sent to watch her.

The distraction from endlessly churning thoughts of

Pamela was welcome. He'd spent every moment since they had parted in the guest chamber earlier chastising himself for just how ineffective his attempts at keeping her at a distance had proven. Loathing himself for wanting her so badly still.

"You can come home," Stasia said now in their native tongue, her voice and her eyes crackling with an intensity that couldn't have been stronger had it been fashioned from true fire. "You can come home to Boritania, where you belong."

Home.

A bittersweet word, and with it a rush of unwanted sensation, and for inexplicable reasons he couldn't define, it brought to mind a golden-haired goddess he longed for far more than was wise. But no, despite the desire that he couldn't seem to control in Pamela's presence, she was not for him, and he would never have a home with her.

He hadn't had a true home in years. But whereas once, he would have shed every last drop of his blood to return to Boritania, he was no longer the cossetted prince he had once been.

"I don't have a home," he answered Stasia in Boritanian, "and nor do I belong anywhere."

"Lies." She shook her head, stubborn and persistent as ever. "You belong in Boritania. You are a prince of the blood."

"I've been banished," he reminded her. "My return is punishable by death. If you don't think Gustavson would have me arrested, imprisoned, and send me to the gallows as quickly as you can blink an eye, you're deluding yourself."

"You know that your exile can be renounced by someone of royal blood," his sister countered, unwavering in her determination. "I could revoke it now, here, in this moment."

He had thought of it. Many times, over many years. Until he had eventually accepted the fact that what remained of his family had to stay loyal to Gustavson or fear a fate similar to his own. That no one would revoke his exile. Still, that Stasia offered it now made some old, lost part of him come to life. Pressure built inside him, but he ruthlessly banished it.

"Renouncing my exile would be dangerous for you," he said. "Our uncle would have you imprisoned and tortured, just as he did to me."

"I'm not concerned with what our uncle would do to me. Saving our kingdom is far more important than saving myself could ever be."

"You *should* be concerned," he ground out, struggling to keep the memories of his days in the dungeon from rising in his mind.

Doing so required great effort. His hands were balled into fists at his sides, his palms sweaty. It was always worst in the darkness, the shadows threatening his sanity, but when he was forced to remember, his panic heightened until his throat went tight and he almost couldn't breathe. He hadn't suffered from such fits in years. He'd believed himself cured of them.

But this discussion with Stasia, all the reminders of the past, proved he was not.

"Theo." Her voice was in his ear, concerned.

Her hand on his arm made him flinch. He caught her wrist. "Don't."

"Brother." She withdrew her touch. "What is wrong?"

The words clamored, rising in the language of his homeland and youth. "What they did to me in the dungeon…I wouldn't wish it upon my mortal enemy, and most certainly not upon you, Stasia. I'll not allow you to renounce my exile at your own expense."

"I know they hurt you badly." Her voice broke. "Reinald said you were near death when they removed you to the ship's hold that day."

He closed his eyes against the sight of her anguish, the tears glistening in her eyes and rolling down her cheeks. Theo couldn't bear pity. Inevitably, it made the old anger rise inside him. Anger over what had been done to him, over everything he'd lost, over the scars it had left him with, both inside and out.

He clenched his jaw hard, forcing the emotions to wither inside him and turn to ash. "I survived."

"But did you, truly? I scarcely recognize you as my brother. Indeed, I wouldn't have known it but for your ring and mother's eyes."

Yes, he had their mother's hazel eyes. And the ring he bore on his forefinger had been all he had been allowed to take with him, aside from the clothing on his back. He'd buried the ring in the dirt floor of the dungeon, and he remained amazed he'd possessed the presence of mind to scratch it from its hiding place before he'd been hauled from the dungeon. Mother had given him the ring. He wore it in remembrance of her.

"You see me before you," was all he said. "I'm alive."

"But a part of you died in that dungeon," she whispered. "I can see it, and I hate him for it. Do you not despise Gustavson too, for everything he has done to us, to our family? To our mother, our brother?"

"I loathe him with the fires of a thousand burning hells," he said.

For many years after his exile to London, Theo had dreamed of returning to Boritania beneath the cover of darkness. Of stealing into the palace and creeping into his uncle's chamber. And then bringing a blade to his throat, draining the lifeblood from him. But such a death would be too merciful.

"Then return home," Stasia urged. "You can fight him and win."

"I won't place you or our sisters in that kind of danger. I'd sooner go back into the dungeon myself."

"I am betrothed to a monarch far more powerful than he is, and Gustavson would not dare to imprison me. He needs my marriage to King Maximilian far too much."

King Maximilian was indeed wealthy and powerful, and Stasia's betrothal to him was the reason she had been able to come to London. But Gustavson was cunning and vicious, and he was willing to commit any sin to retain his power.

"Our uncle would never honor your renouncement." Theo shook his head. "Gustavson won't allow anyone to take the power from him. He was planning to overthrow Father before you and I had even been born, and when Father died, it spared him the trouble. He'll stop at nothing to keep the power he's seized for himself. He'll have my head if I return, and then he'll have yours."

"What if I promised you his head instead?"

There was no one's death that Theo would celebrate more than their uncle's. Not just for the torture he had ordered inflicted upon him, but because of what the bastard had done to their mother. The last true Queen of Boritania.

"You can't promise me that, Stasia," he said quietly. "I'm sorry you've risked so much in search of me during your stay in London, only to find disappointment. But I'll not return to Boritania. When I left there, I was nearly dead, and I promised myself I would never go back."

"I've already set the plans in motion."

She was serious. Deadly serious.

His heart pounded at the realization, his palms going sweaty.

"You've made a plot against him, Stasia?"

"I'm not the only one who wishes Gustavson dead," she said calmly, as if they were discussing something of negligible importance instead of a plot to have a usurper to the

Boritanian throne killed. "There are many of us, united for a common goal. Our kingdom has suffered under his tyrannical rule. His soldiers plunder villages and bring the spoils back to him. The farmers can no longer bear the taxes being levied upon them. Our people are poor and hungry and mistreated, and Gustavson has turned the capital into a haven for prostitution and other vices. He has killed nearly everyone close to him. Those who are alive have been tortured in his dungeon. He has almost certainly killed Reinald. If I don't marry as he has chosen and follow his demands, he will kill me as well, and then he will do the same to our younger sisters."

Damn it. He didn't want to hear this. Didn't want to think about the devastation their uncle had caused in Boritania. Didn't want to have to worry about Stasia, their sisters, their people. But he was worrying now.

"This plot of yours," he began, his voice thick, because Deus, to have his revenge upon the bastard who had seen him cut and burned and forever hideously scarred, the bastard who had killed their mother… It would be everything he could have ever wished for and then more. "What is it?"

"It isn't my plot alone," Stasia said quietly. "King Maximilian has offered me his aid. I've accepted on behalf of our sisters and our people, but we need you, Theodoric. When Gustavson is killed, the rightful heir must ascend to the throne, or the kingdom will be plunged into chaos. I'm not sacrificing myself and my future to a union that I do not want merely so that Boritania can descend into civil war. I would have explained all to you before this meeting, but I didn't dare to reveal the full plot before Mr. Tierney. No one can know what we are planning. Not a word of this must reach Gustavson."

Her reason for using their native tongue occurred to him.

She didn't want to risk any of Tierney's men overhearing and carrying tales. And he couldn't blame her, because what she had described would be considered treason. She could be arrested by their uncle's men, even in London, and returned to Boritania so that Gustavson could make an example of her. And he wouldn't stop at torture in his dungeon.

A shiver passed down Theo's spine. He was cold and hollow and numb all at once as the full ramifications of everything she had just told him hit him like a blow. Returning to Boritania? Could he bear it, accept the risk? And if he could, what would happen if he were to assume the throne? His mind inevitably wandered to Pamela. To whatever it was that was between them, something much bigger than he had ever known. And he didn't have an answer for his sister.

"I need time, Stasia," he said.

Time to ponder everything she had just revealed to him. To consider whether or not he was capable of returning. To contemplate the risks and the rewards of going back to Boritania to defeat his uncle and assume the throne if he survived.

Sweet Deus.

"We haven't much," his sister warned. "My betrothal to Maximilian will be announced in a fortnight, and you would need to travel to Boritania soon after. For our sisters' sakes and for the sake of our kingdom and our people, I pray you will make the right decision."

"I will send for you when I've decided," he told her grimly. "But know this. If I decide to return, *I* will be the one who kills him."

"For Boritania," she said, raising two fingers to her lips in traditional salute before lifting them into the air.

"For Boritania," he repeated, returning the gesture solemnly.

She rapped on the carriage roof.

"Return to Hunt House, please," she called in English to the coachman.

The man shouted down his response, and the carriage turned, lumbering back in the direction from which they had come. Theo couldn't help but to think it prophetic.

CHAPTER 14

Pamela swept into Virtue's room immediately following her interview with Ridgely, a new sense of urgency washing over her as she took in the state of the younger woman—gaping seams at her sleeves, wrinkles where they didn't belong, and terribly mussed chignon. In a word, her charge looked thoroughly ravished. Compromised indeed. No question—marriage was absolutely necessary.

But if the stubborn expression on Virtue's lovely face was any indication, Pamela would have to proceed delicately.

"What has happened to your gown?" she asked her gently.

Virtue glanced down at herself, her cheeks stained pink. "My gown was caught. I will have to repair it."

That explanation wouldn't do. She had come here to persuade her brother's ward that she must accept her fate, and that couldn't happen if they both pretended that she hadn't just been thoroughly compromised.

"Caught?" she repeated archly. "By whom?"

Lady Virtue wrapped her arms around her waist in a defensive gesture, chin tipping up. "I suppose he has sent you here to me."

"He has." Pamela approached her charge, hoping she could make her see reason. "There is no alternative for the both of you now save marriage."

Virtue's answer was instant and vehement. "I'll not marry him."

Just as Pamela had suspected. It would seem she had quite a challenge awaiting her. But then, it was either carry on with saving Virtue from ruin or spend the rest of the afternoon and evening pining after a man who had made it clear to her that his heart was unavailable. Yes indeed, this was the far safer course.

"You haven't a choice," she said calmly, giving the younger woman's shoulder a consoling pat. "You've been compromised."

"No one knows," Virtue countered with stubborn insistence.

"Yes, but *I* know." Pamela frowned at her. "There also remains a possibility that the servants are aware as well. All it requires is one person to whisper a hint of scandal. Believe me, my dear, bad news travels with far greater alacrity than good."

Still, Virtue's expression remained impassive. "I won't marry him, my lady."

Her heart softened for the young, headstrong lady who was now destined to become her brother's duchess. She recalled all too well being Virtue's age. She had been a shy debutante once, doing her utmost to please everyone but herself, thinking that doing her duty and marrying well would somehow earn her mother's love. It hadn't, although she couldn't have known it then. Fortunately, she had found love with Bertie, and their marriage had given her a sense of purpose, if not the family of her own she had dreamed of.

Until the day it hadn't.

"If we are to be sisters, you should call me Pamela," she

told Virtue, giving her another shoulder pat. "And you *will* marry Ridgely, dearest. You must now, after today's indiscretions."

"From the moment my father died, I have been told what I must do. I must have a guardian, I must go to London and leave Greycote Abbey and the only home and family I've ever known, I must find a husband, and now I must marry Ridgely. I am sick to death of hearing what I *must* do. What about what I *want* to do?"

What, indeed? Pamela's heart gave a pang, for she understood Virtue's plight more than she dared reveal. What she wanted was to find happiness again. To live again. But what had happened today between Virtue and Ridgely while Pamela had been distracted—making love with Theo in scandalous fashion—served as a bittersweet reminder that she could not have what she wanted. She could not openly take a lover, and Theo had made it clear that he had no wish for a future with her. All they had was stolen moments before he disappeared from her life forever. And when he was gone, she would return to being the icy widow, guarding her heart and living for the past.

A dutiful widow, who lived a life above reproach.

"I am afraid ours is a life of duty rather than wants," she told Virtue.

"Did you never want something more than the life you were told you should lead?"

Pamela thought of Theo again. Of his kisses and knowing hands, the way he held her in his arms. The way he felt inside her.

"It wouldn't signify if I did," she said hastily. "We are, all of us, governed by society. We must follow its dictates or suffer the consequences. I do not think you are prepared to pay the price, Virtue."

"What price is dearer than marriage?" Virtue shook her

head, as if she couldn't bear to contemplate it for another second. "No, I'll not marry him. Not after the way he sold Greycote Abbey without a word of warning to me. I didn't have a chance to say goodbye, nor to see it one last time."

The younger woman blinked, her eyes shining brightly with tears, and Pamela felt her own eyes welling in response. She hated to see Virtue so distraught, and she knew what her home had meant to her. Even if Ridgely's hands had been tied in the matter—Virtue's father's will having decreed that it be sold and the funds used for her dowry—it hardly seemed fair.

"I understand you are frustrated with my brother," she said. "However, he was only acting in your best interest as he was charged, carrying out your father's wishes. As Greycote Abbey has been sold, and you have been compromised, there is nothing that can be done to change what has been set in motion."

Virtue started across the Axminster. "He cannot force me to marry him. I'll leave Hunt House and absolve him of all duty related to me."

With that pronouncement, she opened her wardrobe and began pulling her belongings from it and draping them across her neatly made bed. It appeared as if she was intent upon fleeing. However, any such attempt would prove even more ruinous than what had already come to pass. Pamela couldn't allow it.

She followed Virtue, placing a staying hand on her arm. "Don't be foolish, my dear. Where would you go, a young lady alone in the world, with no one to protect you? You haven't even access to your own funds."

Virtue collapsed onto the bed in dramatic fashion, draping herself over her morning gowns and petticoats.

"You will accustom yourself to the notion of marriage," Pamela suggested with a reassuring tone.

"I won't," Virtue said to the ceiling.

She settled herself primly on the edge of the bed. "I do believe he possesses the ability to be a good husband to you. He has been wild, heaven knows, but I've never seen him so attentive with another lady before you. When you are in a room, you are all he watches. His reputation is well known, but it isn't like Ridgely to dally with innocents. He usually prefers widows and unhappy wives."

"I shouldn't like to think of anyone else the duke has preferred just now."

She couldn't blame Virtue, because heaven knew that she didn't want to think of any lover Theo had taken before her. Most especially not the lovers he would take after her.

"No other will be his duchess," Pamela told her. "That right will belong to you alone."

Virtue turned to face Pamela. "He will take mistresses, you mean."

She couldn't speak for her brother. But yes, it was the world in which they lived.

"He may," Pamela allowed. "It would be his right."

Although that didn't mean she wouldn't personally box his ears if he chose to do so, or if he hurt Virtue in any way.

Virtue sat up, her brown eyes intent and searching upon Pamela's. "Did Lord Deering have mistresses?"

Her cheeks went hot at the question, quite unexpected, and at the realization that during most of her conversation with Virtue, it hadn't been Bertie occupying her mind, but Theo. "No, he did not."

"How would you have felt," Virtue asked, "if he had taken one?"

She had an easy answer for that question, at least.

"It would have broken my heart. Ours was a love match. But you are not in love with Ridgely, are you, dear?"

"Of course not!" Virtue scoffed, with rather telling

emphasis. "And what would my match to Ridgely be? A pity match? I'll not do it."

"Not a pity match, but a match of good sense," Pamela said. "You require a husband. Ridgely must marry eventually anyway. The two of you clearly share some manner of connection, or else you would not have found yourselves in this predicament."

"I cannot forgive him for what he has done. Nor can I bind myself to him forever. We would never suit."

"Give yourself some time to contemplate the matter," Pamela advised. "I'd wager you will change your mind."

"Never," Virtue vowed firmly.

But no one knew better than Pamela that *never* and *forever* were two states always destined to be broken. Much like a heart.

Pamela returned from the Searle ball well after midnight, weary but hopeful that Theo would come to her.

He hadn't been awaiting her arrival in the entry hall.

Her faithful lady's maid helped her to disrobe and remove all her jewelry from the evening, returning the sapphire parure Bertie had given her early in their marriage—one of few gifts he had ever bestowed upon her, and the only one she had remaining—to its case. Everything was in its place, her hair down and brushed, and her lady's maid had taken her leave.

All was silent.

Almost eerily so.

After the evening's crush, her ears filled with the nebulous chatter of a hundred lords and ladies, the hush in her lonely chamber seemed to mock her. Oh, she had distracted herself as best as she had been able, fretting over Lady Virtue who had been unusually sullen and solemn given the events of earlier in the day and the impending nuptials she refused to acknowledge. But now, she was alone.

He wasn't going to come to her.

She told herself it didn't matter. Hadn't she convinced herself earlier when she had been speaking with Lady Virtue about the inevitability of her marriage to Ridgely that there was no future between herself and Theo? And hadn't he made it staggeringly clear to her that he wasn't willing to be the sort of man she needed in her life?

Well, perhaps she ought to have listened.

Because here it was, half past one, and she was staring at herself in the looking glass, scarcely recognizing the woman staring back at her. Tonight, she had worn Bertie's jewels at her throat and ears. But she had taken another man as a lover. A man who—she could not deny it—had made her feel again. Had made her live again.

Had made her love again.

The barest hint of a tap at her door reached her then, and her heart—her stupid, aching, longing heart—leapt at the sound. And she likewise jumped to her feet, crossing the room faster than she ever had. She drew back the latch and pulled open the door, and Theo crossed the threshold, his cool gaze filled with intensity, his countenance unusually unguarded.

There was something in his expression—turmoil, she thought, his jaw rigid, as if the weight of the world had suddenly fallen upon his shoulders. She'd never seen him so vulnerable, not even in the throes of passion when they made love. Pamela was scarcely aware of the door closing as she opened her arms to him.

He stepped into them, holding her tightly, burying his face in her hair.

"What is it?" she asked him softly. "Is something amiss?"

He inhaled sharply, as if breathing in her scent, and said nothing for a few moments. "How was your ball?"

Not an answer to her questions. Had she truly expected him to respond, revealing all? But then, it was sufficient that he had come to her. She knew she ought not to expect more. He had warned her against it, after all.

"Tiring," Pamela said.

She stroked up and down his back in soothing motions she sensed he needed, her hands gliding over the hard planes of his shoulders, the lean slabs of muscle below. His familiar scent mingled with the fresh, clean scents of rain and the outside air. She wondered if he had been in the gardens.

"Did you dance?" His voice was a low rumble.

"I didn't," she admitted.

"You should have."

"Why?" She tilted her head back, seeking his stare, searching. "There is only one man I wish to dance with."

He flashed her a charming and rare half smile. "A fortunate man indeed. Perhaps you can settle for me instead."

"I was speaking of you."

The smile faded, and he was far too serious, his customary gravity returned. He released her, taking a step back, and offered her the most formal, elegant bow of any she had ever beheld.

"My lady, may I have the honor of this waltz?" he asked softly.

"Now?" she asked. "Here?"

"Now. Here." He offered her his hand.

"But we haven't any music."

"Shall I hum?"

His offer was so unlike him, so unprecedented, that a laugh stole from her lips before she could stop it. Lighthearted, that laugh. It was the laugh of the woman she'd been before death had stolen her levity from her. She clapped a hand over her mouth to smother it, lest anyone overhear them.

One scandal in Hunt House was quite enough for the day.

Theo arched a brow. "Shall I keep from humming? I only wish to please you."

She lowered her hand, still sensing the sadness within him, knowing he needed a distraction as much as she did.

"You do please me," she said quietly, sobering. "You please me greatly."

And then she dipped into a curtsy as if she were a debutante making her presentation at court years ago, before placing her hand in his.

"Let me please you more, Marchioness." He pulled her gently back into his arms, holding her nearer than would have been considered polite in the ballroom, and yet, his form was quite perfect.

Had there been any ice remaining in her heart, it would have melted then and there, as he prepared to waltz with her in her chamber at half past one in the morning. What an astonishing man he was. How would she ever let him go?

He began humming and sweeping them about the room. She learned something new about him. Theo was an excellent dancer. But she supposed she should hardly be surprised. He always moved with such stealthy, innate grace. Of course, that same flawless, sleek motion would extend to dancing. But she couldn't help but to feel as if she had just discovered one of his secrets.

For no humbly born man would possess such undeniable skill at waltzing.

"You dance beautifully," she murmured.

His eyes burned into hers, glittering gray in the candlelight, their interlaced fingers sending heat skittering up her arm, past her elbow, and lower, to linger between her thighs, as they whirled together. His hums died, and yet they carried on without missing a step, gliding languidly together as if they had always been meant to dance thus.

"You sound surprised," he said, voice silken velvet. "Are all the London dandies so graceless, then?"

Dandies were not, nor had they ever been, the sort of gentlemen who spurred yearning in Pamela. But then, neither had Bertie. That had happened later, after their marriage. He had won her with his charm and wit. Her attraction to him had been so very different than what she felt with Theo.

"I wouldn't know," she replied as they spun together, "and nor do I care to dance with them and discover whether or not they are."

"And yet you dance with me, a lowly guard in service to your brother."

There was nothing about this man that was lowly.

"Surely you must know I see you as far more than that," she said softly.

He slowed their pace, bringing their linked hands low between them. "You shouldn't."

"Life is far too full of things we should not do." She paused, summoning her bravado. "For instance, I should not have fallen in love with you, and yet, I have."

Pamela hadn't intended to make the admission to him tonight. Perhaps not ever. But the difference in him this evening—the vulnerability lingering behind the mask—prompted her. Life was too precious to waste. Losing Bertie had taught her that. If she could have done, she would have told him how much she loved him so many times more before she lost him.

Theo stopped. His jaw was clenched, his expression all stern angles and planes.

"Love?" he repeated the lone word, as if it left a bitter taste in his mouth.

And perhaps it did. She did not know his past. For a long time, love had been nothing more than a pain residing inside her, sharp as a splinter, a reminder of everything she could never have. But that had changed somehow over the course of the last few days. Love felt like a second chance instead of a burden. It felt like hope again instead of agony.

It felt very much like something she wanted to tell him instead of keeping it trapped inside herself.

"I've fallen in love with you, Theo."

He worked his jaw. "You don't know me."

"But I do." She lifted a hand, cupping his stern, beard-covered jaw. "I know everything I need to know about you. I know what my heart feels."

"Marchioness." His eyes closed, as if he couldn't bear for her to see the emotion shining within their depths.

Too late. She'd seen the yearning there, the hunger. The need.

"Don't tell me I don't feel it, that I don't love you," she said. "Look at me. Please."

He opened his eyes at her plea, such indecision and agony on his face now, those full, sensual lips that had pleased her so well twisting with grim determination. "I'm new to you. You've buried yourself away in your grief for so long that you've forgotten what it felt like to be desired. You forgot to tend to your own pleasure. But you'll find someone else now, someone worthy of you, someone—"

"Stop," she commanded. "I don't want anyone else, Theo. I want you."

"You want the idea of me. You don't even know the true man I am."

"Then tell me," she entreated. "Tell me who you are."

"I'll show you," he said bitterly, releasing her.

He shrugged off his coat, discarding it on the Axminster, his long fingers moving to the line of buttons on his waistcoat. One by one, he plucked them free as she watched. He tore at his cravat next, plucking it away. By the time he reached the handful of buttons at the collar of his shirt, his eyes were blazing, and her heart was pounding for him.

She hadn't meant to push him so far.

"You needn't," she protested, guilt arcing through her.

"I do need," he ground out. "You say you want me. Here I am, the beast."

He caught fistfuls of linen and tore the garment over his head, throwing it at his feet. And then he stood before her wearing nothing but his trousers and boots and a scowl, daring her to tell him she loved him anyway.

The reason for his reluctance to disrobe was revealed to her at last. His beautiful, strong body was covered in scars. His arms, his chest, his abdomen. The only parts of him which remained untouched were his face, his neck, and his hands. Everywhere that he had been hidden by fabric was a mass of slashes and ridges and puckers and healed-over wounds.

But if he had expected her to be disgusted, he was wrong. Because he was gorgeous, his body a map of resilience and thick, corded muscle, all lean, masculine power. She closed the distance between them and wrapped her arms around him. Pressed her cheek to his bare skin. Breathed him in. Reveled in his warm, reassuring strength.

"Pamela," he ground out, her name sounding as if it had been torn from him, as if its very utterance caused him pain.

"You are not a beast," she said firmly, as loudly as she dared in the quiet of the night. "You are Theo, and I love you. I love the man you are, outside and in. Every part of you."

His arms came around her then, anchoring her to him, and he lowered his face to her crown, pressing a reverent kiss there. And she knew that she had won this part of the battle. All that remained was the war.

CHAPTER 15

She loved him.

It was all he could think as he lowered Pamela to her bed and covered her body with his. His mouth sought hers, and he kissed her deeply, slowly, ravenously. Showing her how much he desired her, how much he worshiped her.

They were naked, skin to skin, for the first time, and although his ruined flesh had lost sensation in many places, he could not deny how positively glorious having her beneath him felt. She was creamy and silken and warm and soft and curved everywhere a woman should be.

And she *loved* him.

When he had torn his shirt over his head for her, revealing himself, she had shown him neither revulsion nor pity. Instead, she had embraced him. And he had known with crushing certainty that he did not deserve this woman. But her arms had encircled him, her smooth hands traveling over his ruined back, over the hideous scars his uncle's torturers had left behind with their lashes, and he had felt whole for the first time since he had been forced from his homeland with nothing but the dirty, blood-stained clothes on his back and his mother's ring.

She made him forget.

But she made him remember, too.

Remember the man he had been, before. Not the seducer, not the prince who hadn't thought beyond his own pleasure, but the courtly gentleman. She made him want to waltz with her, to walk with her at his side, to charm her and woo her, to win her and wed her, to present her to his people as his bride. She made him want things he hadn't thought to ever want again.

A future, a home, a woman in his bed. One woman, for forever.

Her.

Pamela's fingers threaded through his hair, and she kissed him back, tongue gliding against his. Her scent was on the bedclothes, rising around them, floral and musky. Filling him with the driving need to possess her. His cock was painfully hard, trapped between them, but he wasn't ready to attend to his own pleasure yet. First, he wanted hers.

Wanted her wild.

Theo left her lips to kiss his way to her ear. When he found the sensitive hollow and licked, she gave a throaty moan of delight. She was so deliciously responsive everywhere, and he gloried in her sensual nature. Of all women on earth, no other could have been more perfectly made for him. She was his.

But words were beyond his ken now, so he would show her the only way he could, with his body loving hers. He was torn apart by twin desires: to slowly savor every bit of taking her and to be inside her immediately. He kissed his way down her throat, bracing himself on his forearms so that he could find the place where her pulse pounded with frantic beats. And then over the delicate ridge of her collarbone, trailing kisses to her shoulder. Creamy and rounded, it called for his teeth. Gently, he nipped her there, delighting in her response.

She was impatient, moving beneath him, her hand slipping between them to grasp his cock. "I want you inside me, Theo."

Grinding his molars against the sheer pleasure of her hand on him, stroking, he took her wrist in a gentle grasp. "Not yet, love."

He kissed the supple curve of her breast, then sucked the peak as he caressed her waist. She made another breathy sound of approval, so he laved her nipple with his tongue, ringing it with lazy swirls as he glanced up. A pink flush had swept over her, and her kiss-swollen lips were parted. He lapped again, and she arched her back, thrusting the pillowy softness forward like an offering.

One he accepted. He glided his touch to her hip then inward, over her thigh to her perfect, wet cunny. Deus, she was dripping, and all from him sucking on her pretty little nipples. He moved to her other breast, lavishing attention on the pebbled tip as he dragged a finger through her folds, parting her. When he stroked over her clitoris, she gave a throaty moan and pumped her hips, telling him wordlessly that this was what she wanted.

He stroked and sucked and she made sweet, soft sounds of surrender, her body his to claim. No jaded lady at court eager to bed him because he had been a prince had ever given herself to him like this, with complete abandon, nary a hint of artifice. Pamela was all flame, and he gloried in it as he dragged his finger lower and buried his face between her breasts, kissing that smooth expanse of flesh between.

He found her entrance and swirled more of her dew, teasing her with shallow dips until she was panting, her body bowing toward him as if she were an instrument only he knew how to play. For a moment, he leveraged himself up on one arm so that he could better admire her. Pale, sleek skin, generous breasts, hair unbound in glossy waves over her pillow. Decadent, womanly curves. And the glory of her thighs, parted to reveal the pouting bud of her pearl, the wetness on her curls, on his fingers.

Theo watched his finger disappear inside her, relishing in the tight, welcoming heat of her cunny. They both inhaled sharply, because it was good, so good, the feel of her, the grip, watching her hips roll to bring him deeper.

"Theo." His name was a frustrated moan now, and she clasped his wrist in a pleading grip, as if to make him move faster.

But no, he wasn't done tormenting either of them. Wasn't finished thoroughly enjoying every second of watching her fall apart. His finger still buried inside her, he kissed his way down her body, until his shoulders were between her parted legs and he could kiss each of her inner thighs.

He withdrew his finger slowly, then pushed it inside her again, reaching for the place where she was so desperately sensitive. He knew the moment he found it by her reaction, another gasp, her feet going flat on the bedclothes so she could thrust herself higher, meeting his motions.

Pleased, Theo lowered his head, unerringly finding her clitoris and sucking.

Fingers found his hair, his shoulders. Urging him on. Hips rocked beneath him. The taste of her filled him with fiery need. She was sweet and musky and delicious. He wanted to fuck her with his tongue until she screamed. Wanted to claim every part of her, to make her weak with desire. Wanted to see how many times he could make her come with nothing more than his lips and tongue and fingers.

Not enough. The fire inside him was burning bright.

He withdrew from her and dragged his mouth along her folds, until he found where he wanted to be. His tongue sank deep, and he stroked her, in and out, in and out, just as he intended to do with his cock. As he licked into her, he strummed her pearl, using tight circles and pressure until she cried out, shaking and shuddering beneath him, and her walls pulsed around his tongue.

And then he latched on to her bud again, sucking as he slipped two fingers into her, thrusting and filling her.

"Theo, sweet God."

He was ravenous. "Come again," he said against her slick heat, flicking her with his tongue and then using his teeth to gently nibble.

"More. Please. I need you."

Ah, yes. She was unraveling for him, his perfectly proper marchioness losing control. Her voice was breathy and sultry, her fingers grasping at him everywhere she could in plea. Fingernails raked over his shoulders, his scalp.

"Again," he repeated, then sucked hard on her needy bud as he sank his fingers in and out in quick pumps, giving her just what he knew she liked.

"I can't…I…*oh*!"

Yes, *oh*, he wanted to say out loud, but couldn't find the strength for anything other than lovemaking. He was proving her wrong, mercilessly licking, sucking, and thrusting. And she was wet and writhing beneath him, everything he wanted. He curled his fingers, caught her clitoris in a gentle bite, and she bucked against him, spasming around his fingers, her cunny and thighs quaking from the force of her second spend.

Triumphant and desperately hard, he rose on his knees, guiding his cock to her opening. With one roll of his hips, he was fully seated inside her, deep, so deep. And Deus, she felt better than she ever had, clamping on him so wet and greedy.

He urged her legs to wrap around him, and then he lowered his body over her until they were pressed as closely together as before, breast to chest, hip to hip, skin to skin.

No cloth barriers between them.

He hissed out a breath at how good it felt, how right, to be inside her and naked. So good that he lost himself for a moment, thrusting in and out of her, pinning her to the bed with his weight. Until belatedly, he realized he was being an oaf and used his forearms to prop his upper body up. Why had he waited so long to know what she would feel like—truly feel like—beneath him? It was heaven and hell in one.

He lowered his lips to hers, taking her mouth, moving faster, driving into her without regard for finesse. It was all about claiming her, feeling every inch of her, possessing her. He fucked her in such a frenzy that she slid across the bed and at the last moment, he ended their kiss to realize her head was about to connect with the carved wood of her headboard. Lacing his hands together atop her head, he continued his rhythm, using his fingers to blunt the impact with each thrust.

"Kiss me again," she whispered.

He gave her what she wanted. Anything, anything she wished, this perfect goddess who somehow loved him. This woman he didn't deserve. He thrust his cock inside her with all the desperate need within and sealed his lips over hers, feeding her the taste of herself on his tongue. She twined her arms around his neck, holding on tightly, meeting him thrust for thrust.

And then she cried out and her cunny clamped on him so deliciously, tightening like a vise. He swallowed her cry with his lips. He was close, so close. Just a few moments more…

Ah, Deus. He was going to…he couldn't…

His climax took him by surprise, roaring through him with such ferocity that he couldn't withdraw in time. Instead, he emptied himself inside her as he came so hard that tiny black stars speckled his vision and a rushing noise sounded in his ears. Came until she'd wrung every last drop from him.

Surrendering, he collapsed atop Pamela, her body a soft, divine temptation beneath his. She held him tightly to her, and he buried his face in her throat, inhaling her sweet scent, wishing he never had to leave her bed.

Realizing in the aftermath, in the painful thuds of his heartbeat, that he was in love with her too. Fate had brought them together. And now, it would likely tear them apart as well.

~

PAMELA WOKE to a thin trickle of dawn's light painting the ceiling of her bedchamber, her legs tangled with Theo's, his body pressed tightly to her back, his arms wrapped around her waist. To his deep, even breathing falling hotly on her bare shoulder.

Unlike all the other nights they had spent together, this time, he had stayed.

And not just stayed with her, but slept.

He had fallen asleep, and so had she, content in the protective circle of his embrace. Gratitude swept over her and something else, too. A bittersweet acknowledgment that her love for Theo didn't diminish her love for Bertie. That she could love them both. That Bertie would want her to find happiness again, not to force herself to live a lonely life for the rest of her days.

It hadn't escaped her notice, of course, that Theo hadn't returned her feelings. But she hoped that in time, he would lower his guard further. He had already shown her his scars. He had made love to her, without a stitch of clothing separating them. And then he had fallen asleep in her bed.

Beneath the covers, she gently traced over the scars on his forearm, feeling the puckers and smooth places, the deep grooves which had been caused by something sharp. Perhaps a blade or the lashes of a whip. Her heart ached to think of how terribly he must have suffered.

What had happened to him?

Had he been injured in a fire, perhaps? One of Bertie's uncles had been burned as a child, and he had suffered similar scars on his face. And yet while some of the scars looked the same, others were different. The deep gashes her fingertips traveled had not been caused by flame. Had a ceiling fallen in upon him? Had he crawled through a burning building and suffered horrific injuries on his way to safety?

So many questions swirled in her mind, but she would not ask them. Nor would she pressure him to reveal more to her so soon after he had shown her the most important part of all—himself.

He shifted behind her, and she knew he was awake by the change in his body. His cock was thick and stiff, gliding in the crevice of her bottom. But the arm holding her, the one she had been touching, tensed, although his hand sought hers, stilling her wandering fingers by tangling them in his.

"Good morning," she murmured softly, not daring to turn and face him, lest she break the spell that seemed to have fallen around them.

"Damn," he muttered, sounding grim. "I've lingered far too long."

"Or you haven't lingered nearly long enough," she countered, determined not to allow him to disappear with such haste.

For she feared that when next their paths crossed, he would once again revert to his cool, aloof self. That he would fight what was happening between them. That he would pretend as if they hadn't waltzed together in the sweetly glowing candlelight of her chamber, as if he hadn't stripped himself bare before her and made love to her until she had been nothing more than a limp, sated heap on the bed. As if she hadn't fallen in love with him.

He kissed her bare shoulder, his neatly trimmed beard rasping over her skin. "You know I've a duty to attend."

"Of course, and rest assured I do take the welfare of my dear brother quite seriously. However, I am selfish. Cannot your men carry on without you, just for another quarter hour?"

"And risk being seen leaving your chamber?" he rumbled in her ear, his lips grazing the shell. He slid his hand from hers, trailing his touch along her inner wrist in slow, maddening caresses that made her want him to touch her elsewhere.

Everywhere.

But he was right. They played a dangerous game, and the longer he lingered, the sooner the household would be alive again, the servants rising to perform their duties in the chambers and kitchens. Belowstairs humming quite like a hive of bees. Hunt House was immense by town house standards, and the veritable brigade of servants attending its gilded halls was proportionally massive. So many servants, so many chances to be seen. For ruinous gossip to spread.

"I wish I had a home that was mine alone," she said wistfully.

She had never longed for one, nor needed one, before now. Bertie's death had left her nearly destitute and without the home they had formerly called their own—a lovely town house belonging to his father the duke which had been subsequently inhabited by her heartless brother-in-law and his avaricious wife. But since she had left her beautiful home and all its pleasant memories behind, she had never truly required a home of her own. Rather, she had been content for companionship. To not be alone.

"Why do you not have one?" Theo asked her, his voice bearing the pleasant husk of a man who had recently awoken. "Are not widows of English lords ordinarily well provided for?"

"English lords?" she asked, clinging to this small hint, coupled with his occasional accent and unique features, that he was originally from elsewhere.

Somewhere far from London.

"What other manner of lords are there here?" he asked, deliberately misunderstanding, she thought, the unspoken question in her words.

Who are you? Where are you from? How did you find yourself here?

Oh, how she wished she could ask them all without driving him away. But their peace was too new, and waking in his arms after he had shown her his scars was more gift than she could have imagined possible. She dare not reach for more. Not yet.

"Occasionally, there are others from abroad," she said. "Foreign royalty, for instance, or dignitaries."

The caresses which had been working their way up her inner arm stilled, and she felt his hold on her tighten. "Indeed?"

Something had distressed him. But what? Surely he was not jealous of the few members of royalty who had visited London in her day, none of whom she had ever been introduced to.

"I have never made their acquaintance, of course," she hastened to add. "But I do hear the gossip, and I do read *The Times*."

"Mmm," he said, resuming his slow, maddening strokes. He was toying with her inner elbow now, and she had never particularly been fond of that part of her body as she was forever colliding with doorjambs with a complete lack of grace. However, when he touched her there, heat pooled low in her belly, as if he were stroking over her sex instead of a mostly ignored and derided portion of her anatomy.

The effect he had upon her.

Her nipples tightened into hard points.

His mouth found her throat.

"Tell me again," he said against her skin, "why your husband left you without a home. Why are you here, beneath your brother's thumb?"

"I'm not beneath his thumb," she denied, her pride smarting. "Ridgely is a generous brother to me."

More than generous. Yes, they had struck a bargain—in exchange for her chaperoning Lady Virtue, Ridgely paid for all Pamela's shopping expenditures. And quite handsomely. But her brother hadn't had to offer her carte blanche. And heaven knew she had squandered a small fortune on her expeditions. Before that, she had spent the entirety of her widow's portion. Countless bonnets and ribbons and gowns and fans and fripperies, all in the name of filling the chasm in her heart that Bertie had left.

"I didn't mean to suggest otherwise," Theo reassured her, his lips on her jaw now. "But your husband should have provided for you in his death. It would seem he did not."

"He did his best," she said, feeling herself grow defensive, as she always had of Bertie, before quelling the urge.

Again, Theo's fingers stilled. "You are protective of him, even in death."

An observation, not a judgment, she thought. And yet, for a moment, she was not certain if he questioned her loyalty. Or if she questioned her own. Was it possible to love two men at once, one who was long gone and another who was very solidly here, wrapped around her, his warmth burning into her body? Was it wrong to have loved a man with all her being and yet also understand his faults?

She swallowed hard, her emotions turning jumbled. "He was a good man. He…he gambled. Poorly. Frivolously. He once wagered his prized barouche and four blood bays over whether or not it would rain in the next half hour. Needless to say, he lost, for he had betted against the rain."

"Deus," Theo grumbled. "Did he not know the weather in his own homeland?"

"He was in his cups," she said, thinking upon how furious she had been when he had returned home to deliver the news. And what had happened next… No, she wouldn't think of it now. It was a terrible memory she had buried along with Bertie.

But still, it surfaced, despite her best intentions. And she remembered.

Bertie had been at his club, and he had come home with a tale of losing one of the few possessions of value he yet possessed. But he had laughed, as if it had all been one grand lark, and she had been so furious. It had been one of the worst days of her life. She didn't know why she had even mentioned it, for the recollection made her stomach tighten into a knot and unwelcome tears rise in her throat.

"I'm sorry," Theo said into the silence which had descended, bringing her back to the present with a jolt. "I didn't mean to cause you distress."

She blinked furiously, keeping tears from rolling down her cheeks, glaring at the sunlight growing brighter by the second. "You needn't apologize. 'Tis an unhappy memory, that is all. I was very angry with him. So angry that I shouted. I…threw a vase that had been filled with flowers, and it smashed to bits. I was quite overset. And when I was finished venting my fury, I proceeded with my day whilst he went to sleep. I had just returned to my carriage after paying a call to a friend and I began feeling quite unwell. I was aching, in pain, and I only learned later that I had been carrying a babe. I lost it, of course."

And she had never carried another.

She didn't know if she could.

Theo was quiet at her back, and a sudden flood of embarrassment mingled with sadness overcame her. "I don't know why I told you that. Forgive me. I shouldn't have done so. It is all in the past now."

"Don't." His voice was gruff, but his touch was tender as he rolled her until she lay on her back and he was hovering over her. "Don't apologize." He cupped her face reverently, his palm hot, his callused thumb stroking over her cheek. "Thank you for sharing this part of yourself with me."

She tried her best not to think of that day, that tremendous loss. How she had mourned for the babe. It hadn't mattered one whit that she had been so early on that she hadn't realized she was *enceinte*. But then, all too soon, she'd had Bertie to grieve for as well.

"I never told anyone," she admitted. "The fault was mine for growing so overset."

"No, love." Theo kissed her softly, reverently, a kiss of consolation rather than seduction. He raised his head, his hazel gaze burning into hers. "The fault was not yours. You mustn't blame yourself."

But she did. How many times had she wondered how different her life as a widow would be if she hadn't been left entirely alone, if she had been the mother she had always wanted to be?

Tears were rolling hotly down her cheeks now, and she couldn't stop them. "What a ninny you must think me, sobbing after all these years."

"I think you many things," he said, kissing the tears from her cheeks. "Strong, beautiful, intelligent, bold, selfless.

Ninny isn't amongst them. I'm sorry for the child you lost, for the husband you lost. Sorry for your sorrow. I wish I could carry it for you. Take it from you. Lift all your burdens."

She felt those words deeply, to the very marrow. Because she felt the same way for him. If she could take all his pain, the demons of his past that haunted him still, and lock them away, she would.

Her hands found purchase on his broad shoulders, his bare skin so warm and vital beneath hers, and in his tenderness and reassuring presence, her tears receded. "Now we have showed each other our scars."

He gave her another chaste kiss. "Yes, we have."

"What will happen when your time at Hunt House is over?" she asked, giving voice to the question that had been troubling her.

His expression changed, hardening, his mask slipping back into place. "I will move to the next duty."

"My widow's portion is small, but perhaps it might be enough for a cottage in the country," she ventured.

"What are you suggesting?" His gaze searched hers, his jaw tense.

What *was* she suggesting? He looked so beautiful in the early-morning light. Handsome and fierce and hers. She never wanted to leave this bed. She was speaking from the heart. Making plans that she was not even certain could ever come to fruition.

A lock of hair had fallen rakishly over his brow. She swept it away tenderly, love for him beating strong and sure in her heart.

"I don't want this to end," she confessed.

"Pamela."

She knew the tone in his voice. Knew what it meant.

"You've swept into my life so unexpectedly," she

explained. "I never thought to love again. To want a life with another man. But I do. I want to be with you."

A muscle in his jaw ticked. "You would give up everything for me? Your elegant gowns, your balls, your dinners, your shopping trips?"

Did he not believe her capable of such a sacrifice? For she knew she was.

"None of those things make me happy," she told him fervently. "They aren't you."

Something in his expression shifted. Hardened. "I make you happy?"

She smiled up at him, running the backs of her fingers over his rough, beard-stubbled cheek. "You cannot see for yourself?"

"I made you weep mere moments ago."

He was being stubborn. "It was not you who made me weep. Would you consider it, Theo? Consider running away with me to the country? We could be happy there. We could be together."

"I have to leave," he said quietly. "The sun is rising higher, and I've lingered for far too long as it is."

Not the answer she wanted, the answer she was desperately hoping for.

She swallowed hard against a rush of disappointment. "Of course. I don't know what I was thinking. Foolishness, really."

"Marchioness," he said sternly, urgently, taking her face in both hands and staring into her eyes, holding her captive. "I don't know what the future holds for either of us, but I do know one thing. I love you, too."

His declaration astounded her. For a moment, Pamela could not find sufficient words in her mind to cobble together into a sentence. He loved her.

Theo. This man, this cool, mysterious stranger who had made her realize she still had a life of her own worth living.

"You love me?" she blurted at last.

"How can I not?" Another quick, firm kiss. "But because I love you, I must go. I'll not be the cause of scandal for you."

She didn't want him to go. Not now, not ever, but most certainly not after he had told her that he loved her. What they had suddenly seemed fragile and precious, as if she must protect it with her very life. And she couldn't shake the fear that when he left this chamber, everything would change.

But she knew he was right.

They weren't tucked away in a little cottage yet. They were in Hunt House, surrounded by servants. She already had the matter of Virtue and Ridgely's scandal and upcoming nuptials to contend with. Not to mention the danger to her brother's life.

She had waited four long years to find happiness again.

Pamela could wait a bit longer.

She kissed Theo again. "If you must."

"I must."

He was already drawing back the bedclothes, letting in the morning chill. She shivered, hoping it wasn't a portent for their future.

If they could have one.

CHAPTER 16

Archer Tierney's carriage arrived at the appointed hour, hovering near the mews behind Hunt House, Venetian blinds drawn tightly closed to obstruct any view of the occupants within.

Stasia had come at his request.

With a deep breath for what he knew he must do, Theo stepped inside.

The day was lacking in sun. In the dim light, he took note that his sister was dressed in Boritanian purple, their mother's coat of arms again at her throat.

"Brother," Stasia greeted warmly in Boritanian.

"Sister," he returned solemnly.

At her command in English, the carriage rocked into motion, swaying over familiar roads that he would soon no longer traverse. The notion of returning to his homeland filled him with a terrifying combination of awe and dread.

Because doing so meant he would have to leave Pamela.

"You have made your decision?" Stasia asked shrewdly, reverting to their native tongue.

He wasn't prepared for the finality of admitting so just yet. For what it would mean.

"You are familiar with Tierney's carriages," he observed instead, finding it curious.

A small smile played at Stasia's lips. "He is a clever man."

"Too clever, perhaps," Theo cautioned.

"I enjoy his company," she said, as if that should dismiss his concerns. "The opportunity to slip away from the guards and be free of our uncle's watchful eye is a liberty I'll not apologize for."

He wondered what she had endured in his ten-year absence. "I didn't mean to suggest you should."

"You needn't worry I'll not do my duty to the kingdom," she said, and not without a trace of bitterness. "I know what I must do. The question is whether or not you do."

Again, the question. He wasn't any more prepared to answer it now than he had been when he had entered the carriage. Doing so would change everything.

"You do not want the union between yourself and King Maximilian?" he asked.

"Why should I wish it?" she returned. "But it is never a matter of what I want to do in this life. It is what I must do. It is what is best for Boritania."

He understood the faint resentment underscoring her words, for he felt it himself. Because doing what was best for their kingdom meant leaving behind the one true source of contentment he had known since his exile.

"For that reason, I have made my decision," he told her. "For many years, I was too angered over what had happened to me and what had happened to our mother to care about Boritania. But knowing that our people are suffering, and knowing how you and our sisters will suffer under Gustavson's evil rule, there is only one choice I can make. I'll return."

Some of the stiffness left his sister's bearing, her shoulders sagging beneath the weight of what must surely be relief. She looked, for a moment, much younger than her five-and-twenty years. She resembled the young girl he remembered instead of the stoic woman she had become.

"Praise Deus," she said. "You've made the right decision, Theodoric, although you don't look happy to have done so."

"It sits well in my soul, and yet it also sits heavy," he confided. "There is a woman I've fallen in love with, and I very much hate to leave her here."

"Ah," Stasia said, a wealth of meaning in her tone, in her eyes. "Who is she?"

"The widowed Marchioness of Deering." He hated referring to her by her title. Would have far preferred to make her his wife. But he knew that a hasty marriage was not the answer to his problems. He would not bind her to himself until he was assured of his fate, his future.

Pamela had known far too much suffering and loss in her life, and he wouldn't be the source of more.

"Does she know who you are?" Stasia asked softly.

Theo sighed, for the secrets he kept from Pamela weighed heavily upon him. "Not yet."

He knew he would have to unburden himself. She deserved the truth from him. Deus, she deserved so much more than that. However, it was the only thing he could give her. The promise of a future was beyond him.

"She loves you, then?"

Stasia's question cut through his churning thoughts. "She does." He couldn't bear to think of how desperately it would hurt to have to bid her farewell, without ever knowing if he would return. "How long are you to remain in London? It would please me if the two of you would meet."

Stasia pinned him with an arch look that reminded him

of their mother. "Perhaps it would be best for you to tell her who you are before we meet. She is trustworthy, yes?"

"I would trust her with my life," he said simply.

"She can't know the details of our plan, regardless of your confidence in her," Stasia cautioned. "Gustavson has trusted eyes and ears in London, waiting to carry the slightest hint of news back to him. If word reaches him of our plans, your return will be for naught, and she could be in danger as well."

His mind returned to the darkness of the dungeon he had been locked in. Of the sound of footsteps on stone as another of his tormentors approached. Perspiration beaded on his forehead, made his palms go damp. Could he face what he had barely survived all those years ago?

Theo thought of his mother. Of his brother. Of his sisters. Then he thought of his people, the proud Boritanians suffering beneath Gustavson's cruel rule. He thought of Pamela, her love, her strength.

And he knew he could.

He knew he *had* to.

He nodded. "I'll not risk her for anything, and nor will I risk our plan. Gustavson has been allowed to live for far too long, free of repercussions. He killed our mother, he is stealing from our people, and he deserves to meet his end by my hand."

"How I hate him for all he's done and everything he has taken," Stasia whispered. "I wish it were me going in your stead. I wish I were the one to rid the land of that merciless snake."

"We are doing it together," he said grimly.

"Together," she agreed, surprising him by reaching out, taking his hand in hers, her expression fierce. "I am so sorry, Theodoric. Sorry for your suffering, for the years you've been exiled."

"It isn't your fault, Stasia. You were naught but a child."

"I should have done something to fight him." Tears gleamed in her eyes. "If I had, then mayhap none of this would have happened."

"No," he denied softly. "You would have had the same fate as I did, or perhaps worse. I am glad it was me who went to the dungeon. I'm glad it was me who was tortured, who bears the scars. Did he ever hurt you? If he did, you must tell me now, so that I can revisit the same suffering upon him, only a hundred times worse. I'll not be merciful."

"The hurt was a different kind," Stasia explained. "He was cruel and controlling, but he knew he could use us to his advantage. He wanted to see us married to increase his power and fortune, and he didn't dare ruin his chances by beating us or sending us to the dungeons." She smiled bitterly. "Thank Deus for that."

"What of Reinald?" he forced himself to ask, though it pained him. Pained him mightily to think of their brother suffering as he had, to wonder what had become of him. "Did Gustavson harm him?"

"I don't know for certain. We were never free to speak openly with Reinald. Over the years, I saw very little of him. He was forever meeting with the council or our uncle, and many times, he would remain in the king's chambers for weeks at a time." She paused, shaking her head, looking distraught. "Knowing what I do now, I suspect Gustavson was somehow making him ill. And then, there came a day when Reinald was gone and our uncle declared himself king."

Fury rose inside him at the lives their uncle had destroyed with his corruption and greed. At the lives he would yet destroy if he wasn't removed from the throne.

"We will have vengeance," he vowed harshly. "That monster will be stopped, even if it requires my last breath to do it."

"I pray it won't be your last breath, brother," Stasia said. "Boritania needs you."

"I will do my utmost to see that it won't be. I've too much to live for." He had Pamela now. And he would do everything in his power to come back for her. "Now, tell me what must be done."

The carriage rocked through London, and their plotting began in truth.

~

PAMELA STOOD over Theo's shoulder, watching the masculine scrawl of his penmanship take shape on the register laid before him. He was about to give away another one of his secrets—his surname. But unlike the last occasion when he had made a revelation to her, this time, he hadn't a choice in the matter.

Ridgely and Virtue had married in a rushed little ceremony attended by two witnesses only—Theo and Pamela. Somehow, her brother had persuaded Lady Virtue of the wisdom of marrying him. Pamela didn't wish to hear what he'd done, for knowing Ridgely as she did, she was rather convinced it involved something positively scandalous.

But then, she could hardly claim to be innocent of all scandal herself. She and Theo had spent the last few days making love whenever and wherever they could. The music room, the library, her bedchamber. The tunnel leading from the gardens. The room he had been temporarily given. Although their conversations hadn't again drifted to the future, she had been content to sneak away to meet with him. To hold him close in the night before dawn inevitably put an end to their idyll.

She didn't wish to press him. He had already shown her

his scars. The rest, she was sure, would come, given the proper amount of time.

With a cool impassivity that belied the heated embraces and masterful kisses he had been bestowing upon her, Theo stepped to the side, allowing her to take up the quill and sign her own name on the register.

His full Christian name was there—Theo St. George.

He did possess a surname. A familiar one, at that.

Familiar for very good reason. The newspapers had been laden with reports concerning the visit of one of the royal Boritanian princesses, Her Royal Highness Anastasia Augustina St. George. But surely there could not be a connection…

Stomach clenching, Pamela dipped the quill into its ink well and signed her name in the designated space.

Her mind spun with the possibilities as the rest of the formalities concerning the wedding took place. Theo could not somehow be a relation of Her Royal Highness, could he be? Of course not. He would have told her. Would he have not?

Misgiving curdled the tentative happiness that had her in its grasp.

There was his accent. The way he had tensed when she had mentioned foreign royalty. The way he had spoken of English lords as if he hailed from a different land.

She swallowed hard.

Everything around her seemed to slow and blur. She was dimly aware of Ridgely politely asking Virtue what she wished to do following the wedding breakfast and Virtue responding that she wished to ride on Rotten Row despite it not being the fashionable hour.

"You will join us at the wedding breakfast, will you not, sir?" Ridgely asked Theo, drawing Pamela's attention back to the man she loved.

The man who she had secretly taken as her lover.

The man whose mysteries continued to unravel, one by one.

He was dressed impeccably, with his customary dark cravat tied in a simple knot, the crisp white linen of his shirt setting off his dark hair and hazel eyes to advantage. The ring on his forefinger caught her attention. He wore it always. What did it mean?

"I have duties to attend, Your Grace," he declined politely, and there it was again, that trace of a foreign accent in his velvet-soft baritone.

"Your duties can go hang for an hour or so," her brother said easily with a dismissive wave of his hand. "Pamela has ordered a feast prepared to make amends for her disappointment at not being able to plan a tremendous affair as she would have preferred."

It was true that she had wanted Virtue and Ridgely to have a lovely wedding. A proper wedding. One that was not nearly as hasty and dipped in scandal as that which had just occurred. However, her brother's will had prevailed, and here they stood.

She caught Theo's gaze, the same jolt of awareness traveling through her that always did whenever their eyes met. "You must join us at the wedding breakfast, Mr. St. George."

If her use of his surname affected him, Theo gave no indication. He wore the same impassive expression she had come to expect from him.

"Please do," Virtue entreated kindly. "It would be a pleasure to have you join us."

Theo bowed deferentially. "As you wish."

And still, no change in his countenance. Nothing to suggest that the small suspicions rising within her could possibly be true. Yet, they continued to grow as their unlikely little quartet was seated in the dining room, the sumptuous breakfast she had planned with Mrs. Bell laid before them. Hothouse fruits sent from Ridgely Hall, honey and plum cakes, Bayonne ham, an assortment of jellies, hot chocolate.

She wasn't hungry for any of it. She was, of course, happy for her brother, who she hoped would find contentment in marriage. Not long ago, she wouldn't have believed it possible for him to marry anyone, and most certainly not his spirited bluestocking of a ward. He had been adamant that he had no wish to take on such a responsibility.

But she could see the ease between the two. And she saw the way Ridgely looked at Virtue. It was undeniably the way a man gazed upon the woman he loved. And Virtue seemed happy as well, despite her initial anger with Ridgely and refusal to marry him.

Love, Pamela supposed, could work strange magic.

Was it that same magic which had made her fail to see what seemed so apparent to her now, that Theo was not at all who he claimed to be? And if he was indeed a member of the royal family of Boritania, what did that mean? Why was he in London, earning his living as a bodyguard?

"You are quiet, sister," Ridgely observed. "Are you still mourning the wedding you could have planned?"

He was teasing her, but for a moment, her mind went to a different wedding. One which would likely never occur—between herself and Theo. Had he been keeping the truth of who he was from her despite the intimacy they shared?

She forced a smile. "Of course not. I am merely shocked that you have finally married. I thought you would never settle down with a wife."

Ridgely grinned in his customary, devil-may-care fashion. "I reckon I was waiting for the only woman who could tame me."

Virtue's cheeks flushed with color, but she sent an arch

glance in her new husband's direction. "Have you been tamed? I hardly think it possible."

"You've taught me to believe in the impossible, my dear," Ridgely said, with eyes only for his new duchess.

Pamela forced down an unwelcome surge of envy.

She was happy for them both. Truly. The jealousy simmering within was for Ridgely and Virtue's ability to openly acknowledge their relationship, a luxury that she and Theo did not enjoy. That and the permanence of their union. She didn't know if she would have Theo beyond the next morning's light.

"And you've taught me that I need to take particular care when you've decided there is something you want," Virtue told Ridgely wryly. "Your persistence is unparalleled."

"Persistence is the only way to woo and win a woman," her brother quipped, turning his attention to Theo. "Would you not agree, Mr. St. George?"

Theo's gaze drifted to Pamela just for a moment, and she felt her cheeks go hot. To distract herself, she took a discreet bite of her hothouse pineapple.

"I'm afraid I wouldn't know, Your Grace," Theo said politely.

"Ah, is there not a Mrs. St. George, then?" Virtue asked.

"I'm not the sort of man a lady ought to marry," Theo offered.

Pamela stiffened. It was the first time she had heard him speak of marriage, and his response did not bode well for their future. Of course, it was possible that he intended to remain her lover. They hadn't spoken of permanency. They simply lived for stolen moments. So much of him still remained shrouded in secrecy.

But not his name.

She thought again of the coincidences.

"Why not?" Ridgely asked, sounding curious.

"It is the nature of my occupation, I suppose," Theo said smoothly.

"Yes, I can see that," her brother agreed. "Tierney never did tell me where he found you. There's a hint of the foreign in your accent."

Theo smiled coolly, and Pamela knew he wouldn't reveal so much as a hint to Ridgely. "A man must have his secrets."

And no one had more than Theo.

Doubt and dread settled in her belly, heavy as stones. He had told her he loved her, had he not? But what if loving her wasn't enough to make him long for anything more?

"You are astonishingly quiet again, Pamela," Ridgely said then, giving her a questioning look. "After all the tongue lashings you've delivered these last few weeks, I thought you would have something more to say. Or an ink well to smash. Surely even the smallest of harangues?"

Her brother didn't know what her temper had cost her that long-ago day. He hadn't referred to the ink well incident as anything other than a jest. And yet, she couldn't help but to think of the vase. How it had broken into so many jagged pieces, the flowers within it ruined, water everywhere. And later, the blood seeping from her body.

Beneath the table, she felt Theo's hand creep to her knee, comforting her.

He knew.

He understood.

She summoned a smile for her brother's benefit. "If you would care for a harangue, I would be more than happy to offer you one. I'm certain your wife could find any number of reasons for me to do so. Is that not right, Virtue?"

Virtue returned her smile, looking relieved at the confirmation she had someone on her side. Pamela recalled what it was like as a new bride, finding her footing in a strange and daunting territory. So many times, she had slipped. Bertie's family had never liked her, and when he had died, they had been only too happy to wish her well and send her from her home.

"I can think of at least half a dozen different reasons right now," Virtue drawled.

Her response earned a delighted laugh from Ridgely, and the remainder of the wedding breakfast resumed with a lighter air.

And through it all, Theo's hand remained, a steady, reassuring weight on her knee beneath the table.

CHAPTER 17

He was going to lose her.

Theo knew it with an awful, sickening sense of understanding that curdled in his gut like spoiled milk.

The wedding breakfast had disbanded, with the Duke of Ridgely and his new duchess excusing themselves to prepare for their ride on Rotten Row. Theo arranged for two of his guards to follow the newly married couple on their excursion at an inobtrusive pace.

And then he went in search of Pamela.

She had been distraught at the wedding breakfast, and he didn't think the sole reason for her upset had been her brother the duke's good-natured taunts. Theo suspected *he* was part of the reason. And there was also the memory of the miscarriage she had suffered, haunting her still. But there was something more that had been needling him all through the polite wedding breakfast and the fulfillment of his duties where protecting the duke and his duchess were concerned.

He had to tell Pamela the truth about who he was. He had kept it from her for far too long, not knowing how to confess. But every day that passed was another one that took him closer to the day Stasia's betrothal would be announced. Another day nearer to him having to make his decision about returning to Boritania and facing their uncle.

She was in the gardens, seated on the bench she often occupied whenever she sketched. Whenever she was in need of distraction, he'd discovered. For Theo, losing himself in tasks had always been an excellent means of banishing the demons. But for Pamela, it was shopping, society, and drawing.

She had shown him her sketches, including the rendering of him, and even if he hadn't fallen hopelessly in love with her, he still would have seen the undeniability of her natural talent. She drew with the same eye she turned to the world, seeing the best in everyone and everything, making even the mundane appear majestic and the unworthy laudable.

Theo made no effort to hide his approach, and at the crunch of his boots on the gravel, she glanced up from the sketch she had been frowning over, a small smile curving her lips.

"You've found me," she said softly, as if she had known he would.

"What are you drawing?" he asked, settling himself on the bench at her side, near enough that his thigh brushed hers through the morning gown she still wore.

"The duke and his new duchess," Pamela replied, opening her folio and holding it toward him like an offering.

And there indeed upon the page was the Duke of Ridgely and his new wife as they had stood together, speaking their vows to each other. It had been a sacred moment, one he hadn't expected to affect him as deeply as it had. Nor had he been prepared for the longing it incited within him, the thought that in a perfect world, it would have been himself and Pamela marrying instead. But the world was far from perfect, and so was he.

He stared at Pamela's sketch, noting how she had captured the intensity in the duke's expression as he had gazed down at his bride. "You've represented them very well, love."

As usual, she shrugged away his praise for her skill. "I've only just begun. Perhaps with a few more hours of work, it shall truly resemble them."

"It does resemble them," he told her firmly. "You are so very adept at creating sketches that come to life, Pamela."

"It is a middling talent," she persisted in her humility. "Which is just as well, for I am an utter abomination when it comes to embroidery and watercolors."

Damn it, he hated the way she refused to acknowledge how skilled she was. It was plain that she had spent all her life living for everyone around her instead of for herself, and he loathed that, too.

He took her chin gently in his thumb and forefinger, angling her head toward him so that he could see her blue eyes beneath the brim of her smart bonnet. "Nothing about you is middling."

She opened her mouth, looking as if she were about to argue.

So he lowered his lips to hers, smothering her protest. Just for a moment. And Deus, the way her mouth felt beneath his, all warm and welcoming, it was heaven. A heaven he didn't deserve. And just like that, his reason for seeking her out returned to him.

He broke the kiss as a light mist began to fall. The air was cold, the sky predictably gray. He wondered if she had not grown cold, sitting here by herself, sketching away. Pamela was forever looking after everyone else and neglecting herself. He had noticed that about her as well.

"I must tell you something." He forced the words out, so painful, past the fear that what he was about to say would ruin everything they had.

He reminded himself that it wasn't fair, continuing with her as if he had no plan of leaving. As if he would remain at Hunt House forever, and they could carry on making love in every corner without anyone ever growing the wiser. She deserved more. So much more than he could give her. But he could give her honesty. The truth. He could tell her who he was.

"You look so very somber," she murmured, her brow furrowing, her expression turning pinched with concern. "I'm not certain I should like to hear it."

"And I don't want to say it," he confessed, his chest tight and aching. She was the sun rising after a decade of darkness, and he couldn't keep her. But he was greedy and selfish, and he wanted as much of her as he could have, for as long as he could have it.

"Tell me," she whispered.

He took a deep inhalation, preparing himself, and then exhaled slowly. "My name is Theodoric Augustus St. George, and I was once in line for the throne of the Kingdom of Boritania."

There. He had done it. The impossible had been spoken aloud. He waited, his stomach in knots.

Silence greeted his confession.

Pamela's lips parted. In shock, he supposed. But she said nothing.

He hastened to fill the quiet. To explain.

"I was exiled by my uncle, Gustavson, who has assumed the throne after the disappearance of my younger brother, King Reinald," he added.

"My God," she said at last, her voice hushed.

Theo couldn't tell how she felt. If she was angry or

shocked or hurt. Perhaps a combination of all three. She sat there on the bench staring at him, pale and so lovely he ached just to look at her. Slowly, she closed her folio, and settled it in her lap.

"Do you believe me?" he asked, for there was also the possibility she would think him a liar.

And he could not blame her. His story was more tangled and twisted than vines.

"I suspected," Pamela murmured slowly. "When I saw your surname this morning, it reminded me of what I read in *The Times* about a Boritanian princess's visit to London."

"Stasia is my eldest sister," he acknowledged.

"Your accent, your secrets, your scars. My God, your scars, Theo. What caused them? Will you tell me now?"

He didn't want to.

Speaking of it to her…he didn't want that hideousness between them. But she had asked, and he had lied to her for far too long.

He scrubbed a hand over his face. "From my uncle's men. I was held captive in a dungeon before my exile for weeks, tortured slowly. I was whipped and beaten and cut and burned daily, on almost every part of my body, except the places that are deemed holy, for not even my uncle would curse his soul by angering the gods he worships. It was only by the grace of my brother Reinald that I was allowed to walk free, directly onto a ship that set sail to England. If I return to my homeland, the punishment is death."

She gasped as if he had caused her physical harm, pressing a hand to her heart. "Why? Why did they hurt you?"

So many reasons, all of which boiled down to greed.

But he had begun this, and he would finish it.

"My father was on his deathbed," he said quietly. "He had two living male heirs to take the crown, myself and Reinald, but my uncle Gustavson wanted the throne for himself. My father was not in his right mind when he lay dying. He would have agreed to anything, and I was…" His words trailed off as his throat grew thick with old emotion long suppressed. "I was not present in his dying hours. I will forever regret that, not just because of what happened afterward, but because I should have been there, at his side. I was his son. I loved him. But I was so terrified of losing him that I couldn't bear to go to his chamber."

Emotion made him pause.

"Theo," she said, her hand resting on his forearm. "You needn't explain."

"I want to," Theo told her. "I want you to know." Another pause, a fortifying breath, and then his history rose like a virulent wraith, and he was ten years in the past again, a twenty-year-old prince who had never bore a single responsibility suddenly faced with losing his father and becoming sovereign over a kingdom. "My uncle leapt at the opportunity. He closed himself in my father's chamber and emerged with an account of my mother's treason, claiming she had poisoned him. There was a royal decree signed by my father demanding that every child in his line must renounce my mother and demand her head."

"No," Pamela said, as if she couldn't bear to hear the rest, but suspected what she would hear.

He forced himself to continue. "I was the oldest. Twenty. I refused to renounce my mother. Refused to demand her execution. I knew it was all lies and that Gustavson had used our father's illness to seize the power he wanted. The others were younger. Reinald was thirteen. Stasia fifteen. Our sisters Annalise and Emmaline but ten. They didn't understand what they were signing until it was too late. I was taken to the dungeons, for I wouldn't sign our mother's death warrant. And no matter how they tortured me, I refused to renounce her."

"Theo." Tears were streaming down Pamela's cheeks. She didn't even try to dash them away or pretend as if they weren't there, as she ordinarily did. She simply sobbed.

For him.

For his mother.

For his siblings who had been too young and naïve to comprehend.

Deus, how he loved this woman. More than he had ever imagined possible.

"Don't cry for me, my love," he said, taking her in his arms, love for her burning more fiercely than he could have imagined, into the depths of his soul. "I survived."

"But your mother?" Her voice broke on the question.

Theo pressed his cheek to Pamela's, absorbing her warmth, her strength. "She was executed by my uncle while I was imprisoned."

A sob wracked her body.

She was trembling violently. He gathered her closer, holding her tightly.

"Wh-what happened then?" she asked.

"My brother Reinald became king when I refused to renounce my mother. He released me upon pain of death if I returned to Boritania. I was loaded onto a ship, bleeding and nearly dead, and I landed in England."

"Your own brother," she said. "How could he do that to you?"

Theo shook his head, for he had forgiven Reinald for the part he had played in what had happened to him, to their mother. "He was but thirteen, and he was beneath my uncle's influence. He hadn't a true choice. I don't blame him for what happened. The blame solely belongs upon Gustavson's shoulders. His hunger for power led to him betraying his brother's children and wife. In the end, Reinald's actions protected our sisters."

But with his disappearance, their sisters were no longer assured of their place in court. Theo had been poring over everything in his mind ever since Stasia had come to him with her plot. His sisters' only value to Gustavson was in marrying them off to foreign courts that would increase his influence. If they defied him, they would likely face the same fate as Theo had in the dungeon. Or worse.

And he couldn't bear that. Gustavson had to be stopped.

"You are far more forgiving than I would be, given your circumstances," Pamela said.

"I haven't forgiven my uncle. I *won't* forgive him. And no one in my family will be safe until he is dead." As the words left him, Theo acknowledged their rightness.

He had spent these last few days falling more deeply in love with Pamela, trying to find a means of avoiding the inevitable. But he understood with sudden and painful clarity that there was none. He would have to return to Boritania. And in so doing, he would leave her behind.

As always, Pamela sensed what he wasn't saying.

Rain began falling around them in truth, but he didn't feel the shock of the cold pelts permeating his coat. All he saw was her face.

Her expression was stricken. "What are you not telling me?"

Always so intelligent. She somehow knew him better than he knew himself.

He swallowed hard. "Reinald is gone now, and with Gustavson in power, my sisters are in danger. I'm in danger. Deus, you could be in danger, by mere virtue of knowing me. My uncle is aware that I'm in London; it was how my sister was able to find me here. She told me the state Boritania is in, told me of how Gustavson is pillaging the land and the people. If I don't return, my sisters may meet with the same fate as our mother and brother."

"Return?" she repeated, aghast. "But you've said that you will be killed if you do so."

He nodded, feeling as he had all those days he had spent in the dungeon, meeting his daily dose of torture. Mortal. So very mortal. The proud prince who had dedicated himself to hedonism at court brought low and made to face the undeniable fact that he was every bit as human, every bit as capable of facing death, as all his subjects.

"Stasia is willing to renounce my exile. In the old laws, anyone of royal blood can do so," he explained.

"But your uncle. Will he not kill you himself, or have you arrested and thrown into his dungeon again?"

He held her stare, willing her not to loathe him for what he had to do. "I haven't a choice, my love. I must return and face him, and hopefully vanquish him when I do. If not…" Theo paused, for they both knew what it would mean if he failed. It would mean certain death. "If not, I will have tried. I'm duty-bound to do so, for my kingdom and my sisters, and to avenge my mother."

Her cheeks were wet, but not from the rain. It was tears.

And how he hated being the source of her sadness. Loathed himself for being the reason for the sobs wracking her body.

"I'm going to miss you so very much," she said with gut-wrenching finality. "Every moment of every day."

There was nothing else to say, so Theo gathered her into his arms and held her tightly as the rain lashed them both.

CHAPTER 18

Pamela stared at the fan which had been left in her chamber on the table by her bed, opening it so that the scene which had been painted on it was visible.

It was the same fan she had been admiring earlier that day when she had taken Virtue shopping in a desperate bid to distract herself from the fact that she was in love with an exiled prince who was planning to return to his country and almost certain death.

She hadn't purchased the fan. But he had been watching, for he had accompanied them on their trip. And he had bought it for her. She knew it without question, just as she knew that he had stolen into her room to leave her the offering. Just as she knew he would soon be leaving her.

There wasn't much time, he had explained. His sister Stasia's betrothal would be announced, and they had to act before then. But his uncle's guards were watching Stasia and Theo both. When he chose to leave, it would be without warning. In the night. He refused to divulge any more of his plans to her, for fear that she would be used as a pawn by his uncle.

And so, they spent their days as strangers and their nights as lovers. By day, he was the stony-faced, cold-eyed guard who watched over Hunt House. By night, he was the tender lover who brought passion and love into her heart again. And one day soon, he would simply be a memory.

He would be gone.

And she would be alone again.

She closed the fan and replaced it on the table with a trembling hand. Was this his parting gift, then? Was the fan a sign that he was preparing to go? She had to know, though she was meant to be dressing for the Torrington ball. Pamela, Virtue, and Ridgely would be in attendance, and it would be the first time Virtue and her brother appeared together as husband and wife. They were hoping to blunt the sting of the gossip surrounding their hasty nuptials.

And the very last thing Pamela wanted to do was attend it.

But she loved her brother, and she loved Virtue, and she would do it for them. She would pin a smile to her lips and carry the fan Theo had given her, and she would pretend as if her world was not about to fall apart. Over the last four years, she had grown desperately good at pretending. And now, it was a skill she would require again.

Pamela ventured from her chamber in search of him.

It didn't take long. He was in the hall outside the library. Holding his gaze, she slipped inside the large, two-story chamber with its wall of books. Theo followed her inside, latching the door behind him.

She shot across the carpets as if she were a cannonball and launched herself at him. He caught her, arms banding around her waist, and buried his face in her throat.

Pamela felt the sting of tears in her eyes and she did her best to keep them at bay. He was all warm, solid strength, his familiar, beloved scent of citrus and clean soap teasing her senses. He felt so vital, so very alive.

Hers.

"Thank you for the fan," she murmured into his hair, so silken and dark and soft she couldn't help but to rub her cheek over it.

"A small gift." His lips moved against her throat as he spoke. "Hardly what I wish to give you."

How impossible it still was to believe that this proud, beautiful man was a prince who had been stripped of his title and home and everything that was rightfully his. That he had been forced to earn his bread in London as a mercenary. And yet, although she knew his means were modest, he had spent a small fortune on a gift for her.

"You needn't give me anything," she said. "You should save your funds. You'll need them soon."

Her voice broke on the last word, no matter how she tried to hide it.

"You were admiring it," he said softly. "I wanted you to have something beautiful. A trifle to remember me by if I'm not able to return."

If he wasn't able to return. She didn't want to think about the implications in his words. That she would never see him again and he would forever be lost to her.

"I'll not need a fan for that," she whispered, her voice thick with suppressed emotion. "I could never forget you, Theo."

"You should be dressing for your ball this evening."

But he didn't make any move to release her, and she didn't let go of him, either. They stood there in the hush of the library, holding each other as if it were their farewell. And perhaps, she thought grimly, it was.

"Is it tonight?" she asked, though she knew she shouldn't.

Knew he wouldn't tell her even if it was.

"The less you know, the better, love."

There was warning in his tone, but also an underlying tenderness. She liked to believe he would warn her in some way. That she would somehow know which of their secret meetings would also be the last. But she wouldn't push him. She understood the depths of the danger swirling around him. And she would not be the reason harm came to him if she could help it. He had already suffered unimaginably.

"I pray you will be safe, whenever the day comes," she told him. "I wish I had a gift for you. Something for you to remember me by, as well."

"I'll never forget you." He lifted his head, staring down at her with so much raw intensity and open love that it made her heart ache. "And as long as I am able, I swear to you that I'll come back for you."

His promise warmed her heart, even if she knew how impossible it would be. Even if he survived and defeated his uncle, he was a royal prince. She was a widowed marchioness with a widow's portion that wasn't even sufficient to support herself. They came from vastly different worlds. That they had come together at all was a miracle, and one she would treasure forever.

But when Theo left, she didn't fool herself that he would ever return.

"You needn't make me promises you won't be able to keep," she said softly. "You are a prince, and I'm a widow. If you defeat your uncle, you will likely have to marry for the sake of your kingdom."

"When I defeat him," he said firmly, "I will marry to please myself. I will marry the woman I love. *You.*"

Oh, her foolish, foolish heart. It wanted to believe such a future was possible, wanted it so ferociously. And yet her mind, in all its rationality, knew the hopelessness of their circumstances. She loved him anyway, so much that it was a physical ache.

Pamela blinked, her eyes stinging. "I'm no queen, Theo."

"You are *my* queen," he said, his voice bearing an urgency that was new. "You're the queen of my heart, and God willing, you will be the queen of my people. You are the only woman I would want at my side."

"Theo," she protested, for he spoke of a future that couldn't possibly happen.

But he stopped her with his lips. The kiss was slow and sweet, and she never wanted it to end. She kissed him back, trying not to give in to the tears that threatened to fall. To the fear that he would be captured and killed the moment he returned to his homeland.

Their mouths parted and he stared down at her, cupping her face in his hands. "Will you wait for me?"

He was so handsome, his expression so stern and serious. And she didn't hesitate to contemplate. Her promise came with ease.

"I'll wait for you forever." She turned her head and pressed her mouth to the sleek heat of his palm. "I love you."

"I would promise you more," he said, his voice hoarse with emotions of his own, "but I don't dare it. Not until I'm certain."

Something inside her broke. Pamela had not expected to feel again so deeply, so differently from what she had known with Bertie. It seemed to her suddenly that she had been so very young then, that she was no longer capable of being that same, frivolous girl. That time and loss and grief had fashioned her into the woman she was now, and that woman could live and love again. Theo had shown her that. Had shown her how to find her way back to herself.

A stubborn tear at last worked itself free, rolling down her cheek. "I seek no promises," she told him. "Only you."

"You have me," he said. "You have me always."

If only, she thought as he kissed her cheek where the wetness of her sorrow had slid. But she would take what she could. She would seize every moment that remained, tuck it into her heart so deep that the memories could never fade.

"Before you go, promise me that you will kiss me one last time," she pleaded, her pride crushed and ground into dust beneath the weight of her emotions.

"I promise, love." He kissed her temple, shifting his touch to her waist. "How much time have you before you need to dress for your ball?"

At his question, heat unfurled in her belly. Familiar longing.

"Time enough," she said, and took his hand in hers to lead him to a chaise longue.

Time enough, Pamela had said. But the words were all wrong. There would never be enough where she was concerned. And each tick of the mantel clock behind them reminded him that his time with her had dwindled.

He was leaving at dawn. Stasia had sent word that everything was in place. The day he had been dreading had almost arrived. But he wouldn't think about that now. Instead, he would make the most of their remaining time.

Theo covered Pamela's body with his on the chaise longue, reveling in the soft, pliant give of her womanly curves. Pamela had been made for him. Made for loving. How could he bear to leave her in the morning? With her beneath him, her lips clinging so deliciously to his, he was not sure he could.

He kissed her throat, her ear, across her jaw, and then leveraged himself on one arm so he could drink in the sight of her. There wasn't sufficient time to remove their garments, so he settled for pulling down the bodice of her afternoon gown, revealing a full, creamy breast and the tight pink bud of her nipple. He cupped her with a shaking hand, stroking the peak with his thumb until she sighed and arched into his touch.

He would kiss her a hundred times before he left. Theo vowed it to himself as he lowered his head and dragged his mouth over her nipple, delighting in the way she quivered beneath his lips, in her swift inhalation, the way one hand settled on his shoulder and the other found purchase in his hair. Her fingers threaded through the strands, urging him on.

As if he were caught in the helpless throes of a fever, he revealed more of her, the other breast popping free of polite constraints. He dipped his head, catching the stiff point of her nipple with his tongue. Lingering to lick hungry circles around it until it was pebbled and puckered.

"Please," she said.

He knew what she wanted. Theo dragged his mouth over the tip, sucking even as his free hand captured a fistful of petticoats and skirt, pulling it high to reveal her lovely legs. He thought he could happily feast upon every inch of her creamy, pink flesh, licking and kissing and tasting, and never have his fill.

"You're beautiful," he said. "Let me savor you while I still can."

Her fingers in his hair gentled, and he felt her stiffen beneath him at his reminder he would soon have no choice but to leave her. To chase the pain from them both, he kissed the hollow between her breasts, and then pulled her hems to her waist. She parted her thighs, revealing glistening pink flesh, sleek and hot and as made for him as the rest of her was.

How he wished he were on his knees, or that he had his leisure to devour her in bed. But the awkward fit of the chaise longue meant he could not fully pleasure her as he wanted. Later, he would make amends.

"I want to touch you," she murmured, her hand leaving his shoulder and gliding down his chest and stomach.

Her fingers grazed the hardness of his cock, before molding it in her hand, and he hissed out a breath as fire licked through him.

"Unbutton my falls," he commanded thickly, needing to feel her without the unwanted barrier of cloth.

She didn't hesitate, seemingly spurred to the same frantic, desperate edge of need as he was. Her fingers made short work of the buttons, and in a breath, her fingers were wrapped around him, stroking him in a firm grip.

"I want you inside me," Pamela said.

He *needed* to be inside her. To bury himself deep and forget everything and everyone else. But his legs were too long, and when he propped himself on one arm, it meant that he could not also hold her skirts and pleasure her at the same time.

The blasted chaise longue in the library was not nearly as obliging as the last one they had made use of. He couldn't seem to find a comfortable angle as he attempted to align his body with hers and give them both what they wanted.

"I'm too damned big for this furniture," he muttered, an idea occurring to him. "We'll have to try another way."

She gave his cock another tantalizing stroke, nearly making him spend in her hand. "But I ache for you, Theo. I need you now."

He gritted his teeth, willing a wave of desire to abate, every bit as eager as she was. "Let me show you."

Carefully, he arranged them so that he was seated on the chaise longue and she was draped over him, her knees bent alongside his so that she could straddle his lap. He held her waist, guiding her and keeping her from tumbling to the carpets.

With a low moan, she rubbed herself over him, coating him in her dew.

Heaven. That was what she felt like. No, better still, perfection. She was sunshine glinting off ocean waves, the life-affirming scent of salt air. She was as beautiful and powerful as the sea. And he was lost in her, pulled by her tide, away from the shore.

He tried to remember the man he'd been before, the skillful seducer who had won more women than he could recall into his bed. But with Pamela on her knees above him and the decadent swells of her breasts in his face, he couldn't remember a single way to woo or please or seduce. There was no courting, no slow, no gentle in him this evening. He was mindless in his need for her, and tomorrow he would lose her.

Possibly forever. These fleeting hours were all they had left.

"Put me inside you," he growled.

And once more, her hand was on his stiff cock, but this time instead of stroking him from base to tip, she was guiding him to the beckoning heat of her cunny. She pressed him to the heart of her, and she was hot and drenched, and he thought he might die before he ever returned to Boritania. Die from sheer pleasure. Save his uncle the effort of trying to kill him a second time.

She took him inside her, and she was as wet and wonderful as ever, and she clenched on him, drawing him deep, and he nearly unmanned himself. She moaned as she rocked on him, taking him to the hilt.

Oh, sweet Deus. He could not recall the English language for seconds, minutes, perhaps more. She was stretched around him, and nothing had ever felt more right. The pleasure of it nearly made him delirious. Her face was flushed a becoming shade of pink, the obsidian discs of her pupils wide and glazed. Her lips were parted.

"Theo," she whispered.

"Ride me," he murmured, touching her everywhere he could. Her breasts, her nipples, her creamy throat. Her hair, which was still bound in a chignon until his fingers undid the careful work of her lady's maid, and he plucked pins free to rain on the carpet.

He wanted her as undone as he was.

Had he latched the library door? He couldn't recall, but he was in no state to cross the room and do it now. Theo sucked a nipple into his mouth, reveling in her breathy sigh, the way she arched her back, and moved. Moved with punishing torpor, impaling herself on him, rising on her knees, then bringing him deep.

Her wetness sluiced down his cock, likely making an utter mess of his trousers. He would have to shed them and don a fresh pair when he could chance a return to his chamber. It didn't signify. There was nothing and no one in the world but this woman, who took his lips with hers as she found a rhythm that drove them both to distraction. He found her pearl and teased the swollen bud as she worked over him, and he swallowed her moan as they kissed.

There were so many words he wanted to say filling his head, his mind, his heart. Beautiful words, flowery words, promises he intended to keep. But in the end, he held her tight, meeting her thrust for thrust without ever tearing his mouth from hers. She came on him with a strangled cry, and he lost control, rocking into her, losing himself as she tightened upon him with such frenzied need that he could do nothing but give her everything. All of him. He surged inside her, filling her with his seed before he could withdraw as he should have done.

"I love you," he whispered in Boritanian, having lost his capacity for all other languages.

His heart was hers.

And one day, Deus willing, his throne.

CHAPTER 19

Pamela was dreaming of lips on hers. Masterful and knowing lips. Lips she knew too well, that belonged to the man she loved. He had come to her late, after she had returned from the Torrington ball where Virtue had made her debut as the Duchess of Ridgely with some small amount of tumultuousness, and they had made love once quickly and a second time slowly, savoring each other, steeped in sadness and tenderness.

The kiss lingered, found both corners of her mouth. Her jaw, the shell of her ear. And she realized it was real. She wasn't sleeping, and nor was she dreaming.

Her eyes fluttered open to a world of shadows, Theo stroking her hair as if she were as fragile as the finest crystal. She cupped his cheek and felt wetness kiss her palm along with the coarse bristles of his beard, and she knew.

He was leaving.

The day she had been dreading had arrived.

He was fully dressed, perched on the edge of her bed as he so often did before he left her chamber before the servants would be about. But his posture was different. His shoulders were stiff. He exhaled a gusty, heavy sigh.

"Today, then?" she whispered, voice breaking on the words, heart breaking at the knowledge.

"You have my solemn vow that I will do everything in my power to return to you," he murmured instead of answering her directly.

These were promises she knew he meant to keep, but also that were likely destined to be broken. His uncle was a vile, cruel, and powerful man. And he had assumed the throne of Boritania, with all its wealth and privilege. Theo was but one man, rightful king or no. He hadn't an army behind him. The danger he faced terrified her.

And it was that fear for him that thickened her throat, threatening to choke her.

"I worry for you," she said, stifling a sob that threatened to rise. "After all you endured before at that evil man's hands..."

"Hush." His lips feathered over hers. "I am older now. Wiser. Stronger. I've many others behind me. Together, we will triumph over evil. Good will win."

But good hadn't won, had it? Not before, nor since, and that was what had brought Theo here to England, to London. Evil had left him scarred and cold, embittered and angry. Evil had killed his mother and torn apart his family and stolen his birthright.

It amazed her that he could possess such tenderness where she was concerned. That he loved her so selflessly when the world had only shown him callous cruelty.

Tears overflowed, making hot paths down her cheeks. "Please be safe, my love."

"I will." He kissed her again slowly, lingeringly. "And I'll return to make you my queen."

She would have laughed at his words not long ago—how

impossible they sounded. And yet, she had come to know him well over their time together. Had come to know him outside and in. She knew he believed the words he spoke, the vows he made. She knew he loved her and that he intended to come back for her.

However, she also understood that if he were, by some stroke of fortune, able to regain his throne, his life would not be his. And marrying a childless widow who was possibly barren would not be the proper course for a ruler who intended to secure his kingdom. Understanding beat sure in her heart—if he miraculously survived whatever plot he had to regain power from his uncle, she would have to let him go.

"There is something I want you to have, to keep, until I return," he said suddenly, taking her hand, opening it.

The familiar cool metal of his ring, warmed by his skin, slid heavy and smooth against her palm.

"Your ring?" She tried to pull her hand away, for such a gift felt disturbingly like an admission he would not come back to her. "But you wear it always. You cannot give it to me."

"My mother gifted me this ring," he said quietly, pressing it into her palm, gently but forcefully holding her fingers, making her accept it as hers now. "It is all I have left of her. When I was being held in the dungeon, they took everything of value from me, but I had the forethought to bury this in the dirt. When I was freed, I dug it up and brought it with me. It's never left my finger until today."

She had wondered at the meaning, but she had never imagined it possessed such significance. "I can't accept it, Theo. It is yours."

"*You* are mine, and I want you to keep the ring for me. It is my promise I'll return. Wear it around your neck and think of me. Think of how I love you."

Her heart was breaking, but her fingers curled over the ring. "I'll keep it as you ask."

"Thank you." He kissed her again. "You are too good to me, Pamela."

But she wasn't good enough. He would see one day, God willing. And she would bear that day somehow, because she loved Theo. Loved the cool-eyed stranger with his scars and demons. Loved every part of him.

"I will always love you," she told him.

"And I will always, always love you. I leave you now for the sake of my people, but I'll return for you. This, I vow." In the darkness of the early morning's faint glow, he held two fingers to his lips and kissed them before lifting them into the air. "For Boritania."

How brave he was, how strong. He had suffered so that his siblings would live. Had refused to renounce his mother despite the vicious torture his uncle had inflicted upon him. And now, he was returning to the land that had so betrayed him.

She thought again of what he had told her, what now seemed a lifetime ago. *It's not a woman I mourn, but the man I once was.* But he had always been the man who was destined to rule a kingdom, and she understood it now in a way she hadn't before.

He had first come to her as a stranger in the night.

But he was leaving her as a king.

A chill traveled down her spine as she returned his gesture and repeated his words. "For Boritania. Long live the true king."

He kissed her one last time, and then, like a wraith in the night, he was gone.

As if he had never been.

There was nothing remaining but the scent of him on her bedclothes and the ache he'd left in her heart.

~

LEAVING Pamela had been more difficult than Theo had imagined it would be. He had left his homeland, bleeding and betrayed and nearly dead, and he had not once looked back to the shores as his ship had drifted away.

And yet, when he slipped from Hunt House just after dawn, he had looked back. He had looked to her window, to the lone candle burning there in vigil, so many times. More than he had counted. It had required all the determination in his soul—the need to help his people, to avenge his mother, to save his sisters—to keep his boots moving.

It was that determination which took him back to Archer Tierney, his unlikely friend and savior, one last time.

Tierney met with him in his study, and it didn't escape his notice that there was a Boritanian purple cloak draped over a chair in plain view. A garment which could only belong to one person.

"Stasia is here?" he asked Tierney, confused, for they had said their farewells already.

Indeed, they had agreed that the less they saw of each other, the better, now that their plan was underway. There was no need for her presence this morning. Nor for the danger slipping from their uncle's guards could bring down upon her head.

Tierney had extracted a cheroot and took a long puff. "Her Royal Highness? No. Why do you ask?"

"Her cloak is on your chair," Theo said, nodding in the direction of the garment.

"That cloak doesn't belong to her," Tierney said smoothly.

The devil it didn't.

"The color," he said. "It is Boritanian royal. Quite unique."

Tierney gave him a thin smile. "I'm afraid not. It belongs to a doxy I found at a house of ill repute."

"Tierney, if you are dallying with my sister, I'll carve your heart from your chest with my bare hands," he warned grimly.

Stasia was almost betrothed to King Maximilian. Theo thought again of her familiarity with Tierney. Of her use of his carriages. Her comfort at his town house. And Theo didn't damn well like it.

"I would never dally with your sister," Tierney responded, raising a brow. "I'm afraid that spoiled Boritanian princesses are not to my taste."

He didn't believe Tierney, but the plans had been set into motion, and he needed the man's help to secret him out of London so that he could board the ship bound for Boritania as arranged.

"She has suffered greatly beneath the dictates of my uncle," he warned his friend. "She is sacrificing herself for the good of Boritania. She is far from spoiled."

Tierney took another puff of his cheroot, seemingly unaffected. "The garment doesn't belong to her, St. George, and prince or no, you're overstepping your bounds. You've far more important matters to attend to, aside from a discarded cloak. The carriage has been prepared for you, and your time is limited."

His friend was not wrong about Theo having more important matters to fret over. His journey to Boritania loomed before him, lengthy and dangerous. He would not breathe easily until he had reached the delegation King Maximilian was sending to escort him to Boritania. But he was still leaving the woman he loved behind, and his sister as well, and that was not without its own upheaval.

"Tierney, promise me you'll look after Stasia whilst she is in London and Lady Deering as well," he said, voice rough and raw with emotion. "Are you any closer to learning who was responsible for the attacks on Ridgely?"

"We are," Tierney confirmed, not bothering to elaborate. "And you needn't worry. Your womenfolk will be well looked after."

He clenched his jaw so hard it ached, but he forced himself to nod. "Thank you."

Tierney inclined his head and tossed his cheroot into the fireplace. "God go with you, St. George."

Theo knew he would require all the assistance—heavenly or otherwise—he could get.

CHAPTER 20

FOUR MONTHS LATER

Pamela was on her knees in the Hunt House gardens, harvesting the first of the spring season's rosemary, heedless of the damp earth soaking her gown and petticoats. The sun had chosen that morning to pierce the fog which had been lingering over London with extraordinary persistence the last few days. And the sky was blessedly free of rain.

But more than that, she needed the distraction, even if ghosts lingered in these gardens.

For Theo was everywhere. In her heart, in her memories, in the sketches she kept in her folio. He was in the candlelight and in the darkness. In the rain and the sun, the day and the night. Everything she saw reminded her of him and the precious, stolen moments they'd had together.

She clipped a sprig of rosemary, the fragrance perfuming the air and chasing the scent of wet soil. It fell lightly upon its predecessors in the basket, and she moved on to the next, cutting away. She would hang the rosemary in tidy little bundles again this year, drying it. Next would come the sweet marjoram.

The cutting garden, like her drawings, kept her idle hands busy. Kept her mind from wandering too far. And with Virtue and Ridgely on a honeymoon at Greycote Abbey, which her smitten brother had purchased as a surprise for his duchess, Pamela needed all the diversion she could find. She hadn't been prepared for how empty and quiet Hunt House would be without them, but she well understood their desire to go.

It was a source of great solace that the woman who had been behind the attempts on Ridgely—a mad former mistress—was now imprisoned after she had intended to hurt Virtue as well. The woman was no longer capable of causing anyone harm. Gone were the bodyguards who had once prowled the halls.

Pamela was utterly alone.

Alone with nothing save the tiny fragments of news she read of Theo in *The Times* to placate her.

She snipped another herb and placed it in the basket, then plucked an errant weed from the soil. His uncle the king had been killed by revolutionaries, and Theo had come swiftly to power. And if the article she had read just that morning was any indication, the new king was in search of a bride.

The news stung, even if it was not surprising. She had known, from the moment he had left her, that his life would no longer be his own. She was merely grateful that he had lived. That his evil uncle had been removed from the throne and that he hadn't been able to inflict any further pain on Theo, his family, or Boritania. Her time with him seemed almost as if it had been naught but a fairytale, but it was one she would forever hold in her heart and treasure.

Completing her task, Pamela gathered up her basket and rose, brushing ineffectually at the muddied stains on her gardening gown. She wound her way through the maze of garden paths and was approaching the steps to the terrace when the sudden appearance of Ames, the butler, startled her.

"My lady, there is a caller," he said stiffly.

"I am not at home, Ames," she reminded him gently, since apparently he had forgotten.

She had no wish to endure yet another stilted visit from a polite acquaintance, wondering why she had not attended the latest ball, or offering the newest on-dits traveling through their set. It all seemed so very hollow to her. Instead, she preferred to devote herself to her drawing and, now that the weather had improved and spring had finally returned to London, her gardening as well.

"I advised such, however, the caller is insistent." He bore a card on a salver, which he offered her.

Pamela stared at the card, heart thudding hard, the words swimming before her on that small white rectangle. She blinked, half-expecting it to disappear. Or for the letters to take a different shape and prove her wrong. And yet there they were, crisp and undeniable.

Wonderful and terrifying.

For a moment, she wasn't able to force her mind to form any thought of coherent sense. She even forgot her own name.

After four months, here in London? But how could it be? The papers had said nothing of a royal visit.

What was he doing here? What did it mean?

Pamela wetted her lips. "Surely you are mistaken, Ames. Is this some manner of jest?"

"No jest, Lady Deering." The butler's countenance remained as somber and unreadable as ever.

She looked down at her ruined gown and muddied fingers, dismay sinking some of the tentative hope welling within her. Of all the days she had decided to eschew gloves, why this one?

"Where is he?" she asked past a tongue that had gone numb.

"In the drawing room, my lady," Ames intoned.

With her basket still on her arm, Pamela gathered her skirts and rushed past the butler, through the door leading into the main hall. She looked a fright. She was most certainly not in any state to greet a king.

A king.

Her feet tripped over themselves and she nearly fell in her haste and shock.

Theo had returned to her, just as he had promised. But she knew she didn't dare hope he would keep all his promises.

She reached the drawing room, its door open, and found what could have been a stranger, his back to her as he paced down the Axminster, were not his form and figure so very familiar and beloved.

Pamela stopped, clutching her basket, muddied and damp and uncertain.

So very uncertain.

She took a deep breath as Theo turned, the tense lines of his expression softening as his hazel stare bored into hers.

"Pamela," he said.

"Your Highness," she managed, dipping into the poorest curtsy she had ever fashioned, bogged down as she was by her sodden skirts and basket and heavy heart.

They stared at each other, the distance between them suddenly so small after these lonely months, and yet, it may as well have been a vast sea.

"You were tending your herbs?" he asked softly.

As if he had not left her bed at dawn four long, painful months ago and successfully reclaimed his throne. As if he were not a monarch, dressed in fine black trousers and matching waistcoat and cravat and coat, his crisp white shirt a remonstration to her sad, dirt-bedecked morning gown. As if time and distance and stations did not separate them at all.

"Yes." She swallowed hard against a rush of tears, summoning the courage to ask the question whose answer she feared most. "Why have you come?"

He was moving toward her now, taking long-limbed strides that brought him before her, near enough to touch. His hair had been trimmed, she noted, and his beard as well. He was as handsome and as beautiful as ever.

But he was no longer hers.

Difficult to remember, when all she longed to do was throw herself into his arms.

"Did I not promise you that I would?" he asked, his accent tingeing his query.

A reminder that he had spent many months in his homeland, speaking his native tongue instead of English. His skin was bronzed from time spent beneath the sun, and she suddenly ached to know everywhere he had been and everything he had done in their time apart.

"You did," she acknowledged.

But she hadn't expected him to keep it. Hadn't dared to hope.

"Will you set down your basket for a moment, Pamela?"

She clutched it in an iron grip, the sweetly familiar scent of rosemary drifting up to greet her like an old friend. "I am not sure if it's wise to do so."

If she didn't have the basket to cling to, very likely she would do something utterly foolish and reckless.

"Why should it be unwise?"

"Because if I'm not holding the basket, I shall throw myself into your arms."

He closed the last step separating them and gently took the basket from her, placing it on the floor before straightening and holding her gaze. "And what is the problem with that?"

She swayed toward him, as if her body had a will and mind of its own. "You are seeking a bride. The newspapers say it is so."

And he had not sent her a letter in all the months he had been gone, she reminded herself. Further proof that he had no intention of resuming where they had ended when he'd returned to Boritania.

"The newspapers are not wrong. I've already found the woman I want to make my queen."

Everything inside her withered. The tiny, faint lights of hope she'd kept burning inside her these four long months he had been gone faded and died. And although she had done her utmost to prepare herself for the eventuality that he would marry another, she couldn't deny that the blow was nonetheless so much harsher than she had anticipated.

She bit her lip, forcing all expression from her own countenance. "I wish you both every happiness."

A tear slid free of her attempts to keep it from falling and rolled down her cheek.

Theo caught it with his gloved thumb. He cupped her jaw, then paused, catching the fingers of his fine kid leather in his teeth and tugging so that his hand was bare and free. The first touch of his skin on hers had her closing her eyes, the force of it making her reel. Exquisite agony.

It had been so long.

So many lonely nights.

"Have I not been clear, my love?" he asked with such tenderness, that it was impossible to believe he did not care.

"You have been silent," she forced herself to say. "Four months without word of you, save what I have managed to find in the newspapers."

And she had read Ridgely's papers with intense devotion

to each detail, poring over every word, every day of those endless months. Desperate for any hint of him that she could find.

His brow furrowed. "Forgive me, my love. Boritania has been in upheaval. The royal mail was disbanded by my uncle in an effort to keep word of his crimes against the kingdom secret. When I first arrived, there were battles to be fought, revolutionaries to win over."

He looked wearier than she had ever seen him suddenly, as if his mask had dropped to reveal the true man hiding within. And she knew the sharp twinge of regret for thinking the worst of him. For wondering at his lack of correspondence when he was fighting for not just his own survival, but that of his homeland.

From what she had gleaned in the official accounts, the war had ended swiftly two months ago with the death of Gustavson. Supported by King Maximilian and revolutionaries alike, Theo had resumed his rightful throne.

"I know that you had far greater matters to concern you than me," she murmured, feeling suddenly selfish and foolish. "You are king, after all, and I am merely a widow in London who lives off the goodwill of her brother, dressed in a muddied gown and an old bonnet."

Belatedly, it occurred to her that she hadn't removed it when she had come inside, so desperate had she been for the sight of him.

His thumb traveled over her lower lip in a slow, maddening caress as he spoke. "You'll not speak of my queen so disparagingly. As King of Boritania, I forbid it."

She froze, her heart hammering hard. "Theo."

It was futile, any union between them. Surely he knew that. Surely it was why he had come to her. He would find someone else to wed. Someone young and innocent and royal. Someone who didn't have dirt beneath her nails from the cutting garden and stained skirts. Someone who deserved him, too, she hoped.

"My name at last." He smiled, and she felt the effects of it all the way to her toes. "I have dreamt of hearing it spoken in your voice at least a thousand times these months we have been apart."

"Theo," she repeated, a whisper, a plea. "Please don't. It's too painful."

His wandering thumb swept over her cheekbone now. A simple touch, and yet it filled her with so much yearning, such fire.

"What is?" he asked.

"Loving you, knowing you will wed another."

The confession was torn from her; her pride scarcely allowed her to make it, but she knew she had no choice. They had always spoken plainly, and although their circumstances had changed vastly, he had come to her today. That had to mean something.

"Is that what you think?" He gave an incredulous laugh, and she might have been distressed that it was over something she had said, had she not also been pleased to hear levity from him.

"What else am I to think? You must marry someone befitting your station."

"No, Marchioness. I must marry the woman I love. The woman who has been the inspiration urging me through every hour of each day until we could be together again." He kissed her softly, sweetly, fleetingly, and she thought she might melt. "You, my love, queen of my heart. Will you marry me and be the queen of my people as well?"

She swayed and caught the lapels of his coat for purchase. "Your people would never accept me."

"They accept me, and they will accept my choice of bride."

He spoke sternly, confidently, as if there were no question. But, oh, Pamela knew otherwise. For they had made love without him withdrawing from her, and she had not become with child. The discovery had been simultaneously the source of relief and tears, the first month of his absence.

"You need a queen who can give you an heir," she protested quietly, blinking furiously to keep the next rush of tears from falling.

"There is no reason to suppose you cannot," he countered.

But she would not allow either of them to cling to hopes that would almost surely be dashed. "I may not be capable of bearing a child after what happened before, the babe I lost."

"Then one of my sisters will inherit the kingdom, should that come to pass. Stasia, Emmaline, and Annalise would all make excellent queens."

"Your sisters," she said, thinking of the younger princesses who had been left in the dubious clutches of his evil uncle. "Are they well?"

"They are." His expression turned mournful. "We were able to give my brother Reinald the funeral he deserved. We are healing together, healing the kingdom and our family. But there has been someone missing these last four months, and I had to cross an ocean to find her and bring her home with me where she belongs."

He was being insistent. Of course, he was. Had she doubted that a man who would survive what he had would not also be firm in what he wanted for himself and his future? Even if that meant a queen who could not provide him heirs.

"I am glad they are well," she told him, "and I am glad your kingdom is healing."

He took her hands from his shoulders and brought them to his lips for a reverent kiss. "All we need now is you."

"I'm not fit to be queen, and you know it."

He released her hands and surprised her by reaching out,

his finger stroking her neck. She felt a tickle inside her bodice and realized he was pulling at the golden chain she wore every day, hidden within the modest decolletage of her gown.

"What is this?" he asked softly, thickly.

"Theo, don't."

The necklace tugged free, his ring hanging from it, landing directly over her heart.

"You wear my ring," he said, triumph in his voice.

Of course, she did. Because she loved him, and it was all she'd had left of him. More furious blinking occurred as she tried in vain to clear her eyes of the tears welling, fresh and hot and burning, within them.

"Look at me," he insisted.

She did. And the naked love reflected back at her stole her breath.

"The Boritanians believe in fate," he said. "We believe that there are certain parts of our life that are preordained, always meant to be. And from the moment I saw you that first day, with your bare feet and your folio, I knew you were my destiny. Nothing has changed that. Not war, not four months, not resuming the throne. I love you, Pamela, and I want to spend the rest of my life with you. I never want us to be apart again."

Her heart was simultaneously breaking and rejoicing. She was a calamitous mix of hope and despair, of love and joy and fear.

"I've missed you, Theo," she confessed. "Every moment of every day we've been apart. And I love you desperately. But so much has changed."

"I haven't changed," he said firmly. "And nor has my heart. Marry me, my love. Everything I've fought to reclaim is for naught if I can't have you at my side."

She was perilously near to accepting his proposal. To believing they could have a future despite everything.

"I don't know what to say," she said, overwhelmed.

He smiled. And it was a beautiful, slow, thorough smile. One that made her remember how very handsome and charming he could be and just how easily he could bend her to his will with his clever hands and lips.

"Say yes." His head dipped before she could answer, and his mouth angled over hers in a kiss that was voracious and intense, a kiss that made her knees threaten to buckle. "Please," he added when they were both out of breath and her heart was pounding so furiously that she swore he could hear it.

There was only one answer she could give, she realized as he held her in the circle of his arms. He had come back for her, he loved her, and she loved him.

"Yes," she told him.

He gathered her close, burying his face in her throat. "Thank you, my love. You won't regret it. This, I vow."

And she knew in that instant that she'd made the right decision. Because Theodoric Augustus St. George was more than just a king. He was also a man who kept and fulfilled his word. A man of unimaginable strength and perseverance. A man who had survived the unfathomable and who had triumphed over evil.

He was the man she loved, and her home was in his arms.

EPILOGUE

Through the crack in the partially ajar door, Theo saw his wife's toes.

Bare, without the veil of stockings or slippers, illuminated by the fading glow of afternoon light and an accompanying brace of candles in the solar. They were the toes of a queen who preferred to sketch in her bare feet, without hindrance of stays and petticoats. And he loved that rebelliousness in her, that hint of wildness beneath her calm demeanor of icy decorum, just the way he loved everything else about her.

He stood at the threshold, pleased with the changes she had wrought in the three months since they had wed. Together, they had stripped the palace of the ostentatious display of greed and wealth with which Gustavson had draped it, until every last hint of him was gone. Even his mother's garden had been restored.

Gold had been melted and repurposed. Paintings and furniture and instruments and jewels had been delivered to the best auction house in the capital and sold. The funds they had received in return had been used to lower taxes and rents, to repair roads which had badly needed paving, and to rebuild the once great Boritanian navy.

The people were happy. The kingdom, like Theo and his sisters, was slowly beginning to thrive again, beyond the pall of Gustavson's decade-long grip on the throne. They had formed a solid ally in King Maximilian of Varros, an island nation to their east. And Theo himself was well and truly content.

Content for the first time in as long as he could recall.

But there was one primary source for his contentment, above all others—though his love for his homeland and the Boritanian people was strong—and she was seated on a chaise longue, frowning down at the folio in her lap as she worked on her latest sketch. Theo lingered at the threshold for a moment, enjoying the rare opportunity to watch her as she worked. Between the immense fanfare of their traditional Boritanian wedding and settling in at the palace, along with the daily struggle of restoring the land to its former glory, their lives had been a whirlwind. He'd spent far too much time in parliamentary meetings and his privy council and not nearly enough time admiring his beautiful queen.

And what a queen she made. His mother, had she lived to see it, would have been proud. Pamela had adjusted to her role with ease and grace. She was beloved by the people, and he well understood why.

At last, he pushed away from the threshold and entered the chamber, closing the door at his back for privacy. Pamela looked up at his entrance, snapping her folio closed and placing it and her porte-crayon at her side before rising to her feet.

"My love," she said, speaking to him in Boritanian.

Her efforts to learn his native tongue pleased him, and he couldn't hide his grin. Deus, smiling was becoming quite commonplace to him these days. Happiness and joy, too.

"My queen," he returned in the same, reaching for her hand and bringing it to his lips for a kiss, chalk-smudged fingers and all.

"I didn't expect you so soon from the privy council," she said. "If I had known you would be joining me, I would have made a greater effort with my dress."

She was wearing a Boritanian gown of white linen that hugged her ample curves in all the right places, and he wholeheartedly approved.

"I like you this way," he said, reverting to English, for she had yet to master his complex mother language, and he wanted her to fully comprehend what he was saying. "It is how you looked the first day I met you in London. You were sketching in your bare feet then as well."

A soft look entered her eyes, curled the corners of her pretty pink lips. "How could I forget? You told me you were called Beast, but you were truly a prince destined to become king."

How different life had been then. He had lived his solitary existence, a nameless man without a past, for so long, that he had forgotten what it felt like to belong somewhere, to someone.

Best of all, to her.

"I could only truly be king when I had my queen at my side," he said, pulling her nearer, the slight swell of her belly brushing against him—the evidence of the child she had sworn she would never be able to give him, growing in her womb. "You made me the man I am."

And she had.

She had loved him when he had been nothing and no one. She had loved him despite his scars. Had taken great risks to be with him. When the time had come for him to serve Boritania, she had accepted it, and her loyalty to him had never faltered.

She had uprooted her life in London, left the only home she had ever known, and had begun a new chapter here in Boritania as his queen. She was learning the customs, the language, the tradition. And Theo could not be more humbled or grateful.

He may have been born a prince and crowned a king, but no title or honor in the land could compare to having this woman's love.

Her sultry scent enveloped him in a cloud of jasmine and hyacinth now. He couldn't resist lowering his mouth to hers for a kiss that quickly deepened, their tongues tangling. She tasted sweet, so sweet, like tea and honey with a hint of the Boritanian spices she'd grown to enjoy.

Her hand slipped between their bodies to cup the fall of his trousers. His cock leapt to attention for her seeking fingers, and she gave him a wicked stroke that had him groaning into her mouth and thinking about all the other things he loved about his queen.

Things that involved tongues and wet heat and curves and silken skin.

He raised his head and lost himself in her midnight-sea eyes. "Perhaps I should let you get back to your sketching. I had no intention of intruding."

Her kiss-swollen lips parted. "Theodoric Augustus St. George, don't you dare leave these apartments. My drawing can wait. It is a portrait of Virtue that I'm sending to her and Ridgely as a gift to commemorate her birthday, but I've plenty of time to complete it."

"It wouldn't be any trouble for me to return later," he teased, unable to keep the grin from his lips.

She caught his cravat and gave it a playful tug. "I love it when you do that."

He raised a brow, staring down into her lovely face, astounded anew that he had somehow found his way back to

Boritania with her at his side. It was a miracle he would never cease to be thankful for.

"When I do what, my love?" he asked.

Pamela cupped his cheek, looking up at him with so much love that his throat threatened to close.

"When you smile."

"You are the reason," he told her earnestly. "Only, always, forever you, my love."

And then, Theo took his queen in his arms and carried her to her bed and showed her just how appreciative he was of her, thoroughly and in every way.

THANK you for reading Pamela and Theo's happily ever after! I hope you loved their story as much as I do. The kingdoms of Boritania and Varros are the products of my imagination, but as always, I strove for historically accurate details in every other aspect of the book. If you're wondering what has been happening between Princess Anastasia and Archer Tierney, do read on for an excerpt of *Her Wicked Rogue*.

Please join my reader group for early excerpts, cover reveals, and more here. Stay in touch! The only way to be sure you'll know what's next from me is to sign up for my newsletter here: http://eepurl.com/dyJSar.

Her Wicked Rogue
Rogue's Guild
Book Three

ARCHER TIERNEY HAS DEVOTED his life to becoming one of the most powerful men in London. He's cutthroat and merciless to anyone who crosses him and ruthless in his determination to always maintain the upper hand over friends and foes alike. There's no situation he can't control, no battle he can't win. Until one fierce woman enters his carefully guarded world, leaving danger and desire in her wake, and bringing Archer to his knees.

Princess Anastasia St. George has lived beneath the tyrannical influence of her villainous uncle for ten long years. Her quest to find her exiled brother, the rightful heir to the throne, leads her directly to Archer Tierney. He's cold, he's calculated, he's handsome as the devil. And there's something about him she just can't resist.

When the desperate princess offers him priceless crown jewels in exchange for helping to find her long-lost brother, Archer accepts. It's her second, far-more-sinful proposition and its infinitely appealing reward, however, that tempts him most. But Anastasia is about to enter an arranged marriage, and a future between a wicked rogue and a royal princess is impossible. Even if Archer's foolishly stubborn heart tells him otherwise…

Chapter One

The first time he met Her Royal Highness, Princess Anastasia St. George, she offered him a king's ransom in jewels to help find her brother, an exiled Boritanian prince.

The second, she asked him to take her virginity.

It was a gray day laden with fog, fine mist falling beyond the windowpanes on the opposite end of the chamber. The princess had arrived at Archer's town house unannounced and uninvited, two facts which displeased him greatly. And despite all logic and common sense, he wanted to feel her lush, berry-pink lips beneath his with the fiery passion of a thousand burning suns.

Despite that aberrant desire, his answer was swift and curt. He didn't dabble in deflowering spoiled royalty.

"I'm afraid I cannot, Your Royal Highness."

Beneath the brilliant purple of the cape she hadn't removed for her unexpected call, she gave a delicate shrug, as if his response was of no concern. "I shall have to find another man willing to aid me, then."

He was beginning to think the woman was a Bedlamite.

"Another man?" he repeated in a growl.

Did she mean to imply that any chap with a ready cock would suffice for the task? Had she chosen him out of bloody *convenience*? And why did the notion rankle him so? It was hardly his concern who the stunning woman before him bedded or why.

The princess folded her hands demurely in her lap, looking effortlessly regal with her dark hair in a chignon and a myriad of perfect little curls at her temples. "If you don't wish to help me, then I must find someone else."

This, she said as if it were the most reasonable of utterances. As if she offered her maidenhead as a common occurrence. He shouldn't be curious. Nor should he be entertaining the twin sharp edges of jealousy and lust, but they were nonetheless a blade carving through him, preparing to lay him low.

Archer rested his elbows on the polished rosewood desk between them, leaning forward. "How do you propose to find someone else, Princess?"

"I don't desire to attend a house of ill repute for the obvious risks involved to my reputation," she said, frowning. "However, if I'm left with no suitable alternatives, I suppose I must consider it. Tell me, Mr. Tierney, are there discreet brothels for ladies in London, or do they only serve the appetites of gentlemen?"

Did madness run in the Boritanian royal line? It was the

only explanation, he was sure of it. And yet, she sat opposite him calmly—her English flawless as the rest of her—undeniably lucid. Holding his gaze without shame. Elaborating upon her utterly asinine plan to give her body to a stranger as if it were unexceptional.

"You cannot go to a brothel," he told her.

She arched a finely shaped brow. "Why can I not?"

Because the thought of her with some faceless man—of another man touching her at all—made him long to send his fist crashing into a skull. But there were other reasons, more important reasons, he would provide. Reasons that didn't make him sound so bloody mutton-headed.

"You are a princess," he said instead.

A small smile curved her lips, as if she were amused by his pronouncement. "I would take care to hide who I am, Mr. Tierney. Naturally, any establishment where I might obscure my face with a mask for the duration would be a necessity. I'm no fool. How do you suppose I have managed to escape my uncle's guards thus far?"

"I would imagine you've been slipping laudanum into their tea or something equally cunning," he drawled.

Her smile grew, and the full effect was like a blow to the gut—for a moment, he felt lightheaded. Until he firmly tamped down the sensation and reminded himself that desiring the woman before him was the height of foolishness. And he hadn't lifted himself from the bowels of London to his current height by doing stupid things.

"I do like the way you think, Mr. Tierney," she said smoothly. "However, my methods are far less diabolical, I'm afraid."

He waited for her to elaborate, but she didn't offer an explanation for the feat she had performed on two occasions thus far. He had eyes and ears everywhere, and his men had assured him she had arrived and departed alone. Just as he had been assured that the jewels she had offered him in payment were genuine.

Archer lost his patience. "You aren't inclined to tell me what your methods are?"

Dark lashes swept over brilliantly blue eyes, keeping her secrets. "Perhaps I prefer to make you wonder."

"Is it not dangerous to you, stealing away from the king's guards?" he pressed, for he did not doubt it was.

From the moment she had first come to him seeking his help in finding her exiled brother, Archer had turned his attention toward learning everything about her and the royal family of Boritania that he could. Her uncle, King Gustavson, was known for his iron rule.

Another shrug, her delicate shoulders rising and falling beneath the fine fabric of her cloak. "It is a danger I happily risk."

He didn't begin to understand her, and despite his best intentions, that intrigued him.

"Why do you want this?" he bit out, thinking again of her proposal, although he knew he should not. "Not the search for the exiled prince, but…the rest."

The loss of her virginity, he meant, but he couldn't speak those words aloud for fear of the effect they'd have upon him. Already, the notion of making her his, of having her beneath him in bed, was a sensual taunt he couldn't quite excise from his mind. Enough to make his blood simmer and his trousers far too snug.

"I prize my freedom," she said. "For ten long, merciless years, I have had to sacrifice it for the good of my people. And soon, I'll enter an arranged marriage for the same reason. I want something that is my choice alone. Something that is for me, before I must resume my duty. This time I spend in London may well be the only chance I have. If you're not amenable, I'll find someone else who is."

The devil she would. A strong, protective instinct rose, one that wouldn't be quelled. Because he understood, to his marrow, how it felt to sacrifice himself for others. He'd been doing it from the time he'd been born as the illegitimate son of a marquess and a London actress.

"You are intent upon this course, Your Highness?"

She held his gaze, unwavering. "I am."

Heat unfurled through Archer, the air in the room seeming suddenly heavy with possibility. "Then prove it."

Want more? Get *Her Wicked Rogue* here!

DON'T MISS SCARLETT'S OTHER ROMANCES!

Complete Book List

HISTORICAL ROMANCE

Heart's Temptation

A Mad Passion (Book One)

Rebel Love (Book Two)

Reckless Need (Book Three)

Sweet Scandal (Book Four)

Restless Rake (Book Five)

Darling Duke (Book Six)

The Night Before Scandal (Book Seven)

Wicked Husbands

Her Errant Earl (Book One)

Her Lovestruck Lord (Book Two)

Her Reformed Rake (Book Three)

Her Deceptive Duke (Book Four)

Her Missing Marquess (Book Five)

Her Virtuous Viscount (Book Six)

League of Dukes
Nobody's Duke (Book One)
Heartless Duke (Book Two)
Dangerous Duke (Book Three)
Shameless Duke (Book Four)
Scandalous Duke (Book Five)
Fearless Duke (Book Six)

Notorious Ladies of London
Lady Ruthless (Book One)
Lady Wallflower (Book Two)
Lady Reckless (Book Three)
Lady Wicked (Book Four)
Lady Lawless (Book Five)
Lady Brazen (Book 6)

Unexpected Lords
The Detective Duke (Book One)
The Playboy Peer (Book Two)
The Millionaire Marquess (Book Three)
The Goodbye Governess (Book Four)

The Wicked Winters
Wicked in Winter (Book One)
Wedded in Winter (Book Two)
Wanton in Winter (Book Three)
Wishes in Winter (Book 3.5)
Willful in Winter (Book Four)
Wagered in Winter (Book Five)
Wild in Winter (Book Six)
Wooed in Winter (Book Seven)
Winter's Wallflower (Book Eight)
Winter's Woman (Book Nine)
Winter's Whispers (Book Ten)

Winter's Waltz (Book Eleven)
Winter's Widow (Book Twelve)
Winter's Warrior (Book Thirteen)
A Merry Wicked Winter (Book Fourteen)

The Sinful Suttons
Sutton's Spinster (Book One)
Sutton's Sins (Book Two)
Sutton's Surrender (Book Three)
Sutton's Seduction (Book Four)
Sutton's Scoundrel (Book Five)
Sutton's Scandal (Book Six)
Sutton's Secrets (Book Seven)

Rogue's Guild
Her Ruthless Duke (Book One)
Her Dangerous Beast (Book Two)
Her Wicked Rogue (Book 3)

Sins and Scoundrels
Duke of Depravity
Prince of Persuasion
Marquess of Mayhem
Sarah
Earl of Every Sin
Duke of Debauchery
Viscount of Villainy

Sins and Scoundrels Box Set Collections
Volume 1
Volume 2

The Wicked Winters Box Set Collections
Collection 1

Collection 2
Collection 3
Collection 4

Stand-alone Novella
Lord of Pirates

CONTEMPORARY ROMANCE
Love's Second Chance
Reprieve (Book One)
Perfect Persuasion (Book Two)
Win My Love (Book Three)

Coastal Heat
Loved Up (Book One)

ABOUT THE AUTHOR

USA Today and Amazon bestselling author Scarlett Scott writes steamy Victorian and Regency romance with strong, intelligent heroines and sexy alpha heroes. She lives in Pennsylvania and Maryland with her Canadian husband, adorable identical twins, and two dogs.

A self-professed literary junkie and nerd, she loves reading anything, but especially romance novels, poetry, and Middle English verse. Catch up with her on her website https://scarlettscottauthor.com. Hearing from readers never fails to make her day.

Scarlett's complete book list and information about upcoming releases can be found at https://scarlettscottauthor.com.

Connect with Scarlett! You can find her here:

Join Scarlett Scott's reader group on Facebook for early excerpts, giveaways, and a whole lot of fun!

Sign up for her newsletter here

https://www.tiktok.com/@authorscarlettscott

facebook.com/AuthorScarlettScott
twitter.com/scarscoromance
instagram.com/scarlettscottauthor
bookbub.com/authors/scarlett-scott
amazon.com/Scarlett-Scott/e/B004NW8N2I
pinterest.com/scarlettscott

Made in the USA
Coppell, TX
15 June 2023